Anonymous

In Memory of Carlton Edwards

SALZWASSER
VERLAG

Anonymous

In Memory of Carlton Edwards

Reprint of the original, first published in 1863.

1st Edition 2022 | ISBN: 978-3-37500-087-5

Verlag (Publisher): Salzwasser Verlag GmbH, Zeilweg 44, 60439 Frankfurt, Deutschland
Vertretungsberechtigt (Authorized to represent): E. Roepke, Zeilweg 44, 60439 Frankfurt, Deutschland
Druck (Print): Books on Demand GmbH, In de Tarpen 42, 22848 Norderstedt, Deutschland

IN

MEMORY

OF

CARLTON EDWARDS

It is a heaven upon earth, to have the mind move in charity, rest in Providence, and turn upon the poles of truth.—*Bacon.*

ALBANY

1863.

CONTENTS.

LIFE AND CHARACTER.

When our friend dies, having finished the work given him to do among men, and we pause to consider our loss and dwell upon his character, we find all at once and with some surprise, how difficult it is to record his worth in human words. We feel that our language ought to be electric and subtle as the spirit of whom we speak, and it becomes to us suddenly clumsy, inapt and insufficient. To recount his labors and tell how many things he achieved in a short life is readily done, but it fails utterly to convey the thought we justly entertain respecting him. Like every other narrative of events and circumstances shaped and modified by human endeavor, the honest story inspires us with respect and kindles within us a certain interest, but it does not affect us like the presence of the living man. To our hearts it is a mere skeleton record of naked facts, and we make haste to speak of the qualities that belonged to him—of that certain something appertaining to his nature which attracted us towards him and justifies our regard. Incapable of speaking the vital word, we grow prodigal and lavish upon his memory all adjectives of love and affection, choosing them with care as one gathers a garland of flowers with which to adorn his tomb. It is the common resource of the simple and the wise—the last helpless effort of speech—grave and impressive just because it is the very voice of humanity.

Our language is rich, copious and capable of expressing the nicest shades of meaning, and yet it stands always a certain remove from our unspoken thought. A great multitude of our words are simply images and figures of speech, shadows and suggestions of the manner in which we think; and many of them are only tokens of the attitude in which we stand towards each other, or towards those who have departed from among us. This latent imagery of the language, the material element which runs through it, appears everywhere; and it explains how it comes to pass that whenever we would communicate a just estimate of our friend or speak adequately of his worth, we begin always by giving some account of him and of his relations with the outside world. Not because these relations are in themselves of any special value, but because they serve to reveal what we desire to make known.

Carlton Edwards — now a name of pleasant associations — was born in Albany on the 18th of July, 1829, and grew up here through all the years of boyhood, with its exuberant spirits, its activity, and its studies and trials. But we say nothing, for nothing can be said, of this long happy day when the bright boy danced through the house, touching all hearts and wounding none, filling home with the winning ways and unmatched gaiety of childhood. Like all the rest of the boys, he went to school in the Academy, and was trained there under the reign of the able and much loved Dr. Beck. At length, properly fitted, he entered Union College, where he graduated with credit in the summer of 1848, then twenty years of age. A friend of his speaks with great partiality of his oration on that occasion, as evincing remarkable vigor of thought, grace and culture. In the autumn of that year he became Professor of Languages in the Military Academy at Oxford, in Maryland, remaining there till the following summer. On his return, influenced doubtless by the example and implied advice of his father, James

Edwards, he entered upon the study of the law in the office of Stevens, Edwards and Meads, in Albany. In the winter of 1850, attracted by the influence of the Metropolitan city, he entered the office of Judge Davies, then counsel for the corporation of New York, where he remained a careful student of the law until he was admitted to the bar, a well-read and competent lawyer.

He had acquired the profession, without having acquired the tastes which fit a man for the active practice of the law. The bent of his mind drew him towards the republic of letters, and the press opened to him the most natural field of labor—a field more attractive than any other, perhaps, to men of sharp convictions and great activity and vigor of mind. The class of whom Carlton was a good representative, readily understand and relish the law as a system of principles, while they shrink with more or less aversion from the machinery and actual practice by which it is applied and vindicated in the relations of men. This aversion, which is generally found strongest in those men who have had least converse with the actual affairs of business, is a bias of mind in the opposite direction that evinces no lack of skill or natural tact. It is often the growth of long habit, much study and a wide range of reading, which in the end draws the active and fruitful mind into literary pursuits—pursuits which afford the supreme luxury of high intellectual activity, disburdened of the cares that belong to the minute details of professional and business life. It does not spring from a desire to escape labor, but from a strong choice of a special kind of labor.

These suggestions explain sufficiently the motives through which Carlton became associated with the press. The manner and the occasions were various and frequent. He wrote often for the newspapers, on many subjects, and in a style that drew upon him the regards and commendation of friends, whose judgment he valued. Step by step, as all such elections are made, he came to the choice of his vocation, largely endowed, and, in many respects, most happily equipped for its duties and its toils.

In the fall of 1853, he entered upon his work as the editor of the *Albany Morning Express;* an independent paper, which had no party patronage, and no temptation to subserve merely partizan purposes, and conducted the paper for some three years—as long as his connexion with it continued, without making any alliance whatever with either of the political organizations. He began by saying that, "in relation to politics and public measures, we shall claim and endeavor to speak with fairness and impartiality; and shall support such views as we deem just and conducive to the public welfare, without reference or respect to the party with which they originate." And the promise was faithfully kept.

It is not to be inferred that this attitude of independence was assumed from indifference to the action of public men or parties;—on the contrary, it was assumed becausé it gave greater freedom of speech on topics and measures of policy upon which his individual opinions did not happen to coincide with those of his political party. He had grown up in the midst of whig associations, adopting the sentiments and opinions of that great and patriotic organization. Having resided for some years in the city of New York, he was, at the time he became the editor of the Express, in sympathy with the conservative wing of that party; with those men who heartily adopted and upheld, through good and through evil report, the views and principles of such men as Henry Clay and Daniel Webster. But it is to be borne in mind that the period was one of transition; one that was likely to project itself far upon the distant future. The famous measures of compromise had been adopted by Congress in 1850, and formally ratified as a *finality* by both of the great political parties. They were not entirely acceptable, it is true; some of them impinged upon our ideas of what is right and fit. But on the whole, the compromise was deemed wise and necessary; and in that belief, it was acquiesced in by the country.

Not long after Carlton became the editor of the Express, Senator Douglas of Illinois, one of the great and influential men of the democratic party, introduced anew the exciting theme. He proposed, from his seat in the Senate of the United States, that the old compromise of 1820, by which slavery was forever prohibited in the territories north of thirty-six degrees and thirty minutes of north latitude, *should be repealed.* It was the most unwise and unfortunate proposition ever made in the Congress of the United States, and it was strenuously and ably resisted by the editor of the Express from the very outset. We record this fact as honorable testimony to his sagacity as a citizen of the Union. He foresaw, as did most men that were not too much immersed in schemes of partizan success, that the proposition, once matured into a law of the Union, would give rise to fierce discussions, that might end in disastrous consequences to the stability of the Union itself. It was not a party measure, though the author of it was able to carry with him a considerable portion of his party. Many democrats in the northern states, and among the rest the able and honest representative from the district of Albany,* opposed it resolutely as uncalled for, and fraught with danger. Every one knows the consequences that followed from that act. It opened a large and fruitful territory as an arena of contest. Emigrants from all sections flocked into it; those from the south on purpose to make it a slave state, and those from the north and west with the avowed design of making it a free state. It was a sharp and bitter struggle, that flowed back over the whole country. It dissolved first the whig party, and at length severed the old democratic organization. It did not create the rebellion; but it certainly was one among the hundred causes that led on to our present troubles.

We are bound, however, to say, that Carlton Edwards was not an abolitionist in any sense of that term, and did not oppose the repeal of the act referred to out of any special antagonism to the institution of slavery. He opposed it on grounds of sound public policy; and chiefly because it reopened a dangerous question, in a manner that appeared to invite the extension of a system of labor that had been repudiated in our own state. He knew that our people would uphold the constitution in

* Hon. Rufus W. Peckham.

its fair operation upon that subject, but would not take one step beyond it, which appeared to extend or affirm the institution on its own account. And as the act of repeal was unnecessarily obtruded upon the country, in a time of repose and political tranquility, he opposed the measure firmly and steadily; and we believe that, in the light of subsequent events, there are now but few men in the country that do not sincerely regret the failure to prevent the consummation of that rash and impolitic act.

Let no one suppose that, in this reference to the lamented Douglas, we intend any disparagement of his well-earned fame. Swerved occasionally, as all men are, by motives of ambition, and influenced from time to time by the stress of party ties and associations, he loved his country all the while, and served it with fidelity in eminent places, through a long period of years. A spot upon the sun does not obscure its light, and one mistake does not tarnish a patriot's fame.

We have spoken of the abrogation of the Missouri compromise as a political mistake, because it so appeared to us at the time; and the course of events that have followed it, seems to justify that opinion. We know, however, full well, that the life of a nation developes after a law of its own, which lies underneath the superficial transactions that usually form the topic of discourse. If the nation grow in a certain direction, the political measures that work on the surface cannot turn aside the current; and it may be that it was not in human skill to escape the civil war that has come upon us. For clearly there cannot be enduring peace and prosperity in the land, without integrity in the great body of the community, and justice to all in the organization and administration of the government.

We do not intend to dwell upon the general course of the Express under Carlton's editorial direction, but there is a single topic more of local concern upon which a word ought to be spoken. He had been familiar with the school system of the city of New York, and had seen how like a charm the spirit of emulation wrought upon the schools of that city, where the best scholars earned promotion to the Free Academy, as a soldier wins it upon the field; and he sought to introduce the same feature into the common schools of Albany. Calling attention to this subject through his paper, a general discussion arose in reference to our schools that grew animated and somewhat sharp; their defects were freely criticised, and their merits were as fully set forth by the Board of Education. In this discussion there may have been some heated and intemperate words used; but as the object sought on all sides was the same, and one of equal interest to the whole city, this free interchange of opinions served as we believe to make better schools that were already good. It deepened the general interest in the subject, and strengthened the hands of the Board. By-and-by we shall unquestionably engraft upon our schools the feature already mentioned, which has been found to work so well in other cities; and thus, by seizing upon the principle of ambition in the mind of the child, stimulate him to the highest activity along the right path in life.

Carlton's connexion with the Express ceased in March, 1856, when he parted with his interest in the paper. Some of his friends thought he made a mistake in leaving a paper which he had trebled in value in the short space of three years, and raised to a high rank among the newspapers of the city and state; but there were circumstances connected with the change that rendered the step advisable and necessary.

Early in the summer of 1856, Mr. Edwards returned to the city of New York, and became the Associate Editor of the *New York Evening Mirror*. This connexion continued for something over a year, when he returned to his home in Albany, and spent the following winter here, acting as the regular correspondent of the *New York Journal of Commerce*. His letters to that paper, condensing the current news, were highly valued by its proprietors, and he soon after accepted their proposition to become one of its editors—the Night Editor, whose duty it was to analyze the foreign and domestic news, and prepare and make up the paper. It was a post of great labor, and he continued in it until the early part of April, 1861, when the disease that terminated his life first manifested itself. He had been quite ill for a few days from a bronchial attack, to which he was occasionally subject. On this occasion it had been more severe than usual; checked rather suddenly, it re-appeared in the form of a severe nervous prostration that proved to be the commencement of a softening of the brain, which terminated fatally on the 20th of September, 1862.

Unacquainted with the business, it is difficult to appreciate the labors of an editor of a New York morning paper. Much of the news comes in late at night, and much relates to the transactions of the evening previous, and the right word must be said in reference to them at once and on the spot. It is a work that cannot be anticipated, and must be done at the very time it is called for. Every night the worker must come to his task on the alert, alive to the meaning and importance of each public event. Merely to understand them fully, his mind must be wakeful and active; but he must also comprehend them in their relations to the past and the future, giving to each the significancy that belongs to it. To a thoroughly competent man, it would not be counted hard work for a single night; but let him perform it for an entire year, through three hundred nights in steady succession, and it will *wear* upon a constitution of iron. Who has not felt the fatigue that results from giving long continued attention to a matter that taxes the full power of his mind? It is more exhausting than any physical labor performed by man. And then it is not an unimportant circumstance that this work is done in the night time, under the glare of a brilliant gas light. We do not explain the fact, but every one knows that a bright light acts upon him like a stimulant, raising his spirits and increasing his vigor, so that he works faster and becomes more quickly exhausted. Three years of such labor, with but few and brief intermissions, wrought sternly upon Carlton's nervous and delicate, though firm organization; and undoubtedly this long continued labor sowed the seed of the disease that carried him to his grave. His temperament made him a swift, willing and ambitious worker; and the place he occupied was such as to call forth all his activity, in season and out of season. His life was sacrificed? Yes, but it was he that made the sacrifice, like the miner of an English mine, serving a community that knows him not, and does not thank him for his toil. But there is something heroic in the worker that gives himself to his labor with every energy and faculty of his mind, looking for no gain on account of the perfection with which he executes his task; and though it makes us sad to say that he spent rapidly his capital of life, we feel just as strongly that such a life has in it an element of nobleness that belongs to the higher order of men. We that plod on steadily through our daily walks, may live longer, and see more revolutions of the earth and the sun, but we may not after all, live to any better purpose, or gain in our passage through a few more winters and summers any decided fortune on which to rest the weary head in the closing scene.

With a natural talent for the languages, Carlton early became a proficient in the Greek and Roman, and English classics, reading them alternately with the relish of one who appreciates equally well the thought and the manner in which it is uttered. He did not accomplish this by adopting and following out a prescribed course of reading, as if performing a self-imposed task, but he fell gradually into the habit drawn by his taste, and as if daily invited by some new enjoyment. As a result of this early and continued familiarity with the best writers, he grew into a genuine love of letters, that shaped his career, and made him rich in choice learning. We do not speak of this bent of mind as reflecting upon him either praise or blame, but simply as showing what style of man he was, and suggesting the process by which he grew until he became an attractive and beautiful character. No one can analyze himself, much less another, and tell what precise effect this author or that, this novelist, philosopher, poet or historian, has produced upon him, though he knows perfectly well that his reading and experience in life have raised and expanded him much above his former self. One author, or even one entire class of authors, may give him intelligence simply, without affecting him otherwise in the slightest degree; while another writer, or class of writers, interesting him more deeply, may leave a trace of their influence upon his mind while he lives. Doubtless a wide range of reading gives to the mind scope and breadth, retrenching its idiosyncracy and preventing it from falling into the rut of one dominant idea. To a casual and imperfect observation this equilibrium of mind appears to be gained through a loss of brilliancy and depth; for it is noticeable that men who give themselves wholly to one idea, acquire speedily a certain enthusiasm and intensity which secure to them a limited but very strong hold upon the community. They grow into splendid advocates, without becoming good judges, or safe and wise leaders; they are the radicals whose appointed service it is to keep the elements of society in motion, by pushing principles that are right in themselves, to the extreme point of rational action, troubling the state and the church as storms trouble the air, the earth and the ocean.

The conservatives, on the other hand, occupy the anchorage in the body politic, seeking and securing the rest and stability which are essential to its well being. The instinct of the class is to advance by slow steps, and in unison with the sentiments and opinions of the general community; and this advance is not made in company with, but at a measured distance in the rear of the eager band of sharp logicians. The conservative, such as was Carlton Edwards, feels the force of logic as keenly as the most adventurous reformer, but knows also that there is in man and in society much besides the mere faculty of reasoning. He sees that the great interests of men are blended into a complex organism that can not be reformed by statute, and made perfect all at once by an act of legislation. He has not much confidence in those happy enthusiasts that ride jauntily their special hobby, and foretell with easy faith the good time coming. A student of history, he has learned that events and reforms which affect the race or the nation deeply, ripen but slowly in the eyes of impatient men, so that the advance or growth of a people is to be measured by centuries rather than days. He believes in the future of man as he does in the forces of nature, but he expects that it will develop according to the law of history, slowly but steadily toward that civilization which is to be the ripened fruit of Christianity—a religion at once divine and intensely human.

We have said enough to show the conservative spirit in which Carlton wrought in his editorial labors. His style of writing was clear, direct and nervous; he made no effort at display and showed no weakness for what is called fine writing. Perceiving accurately the value and force of words, he was undoubtedly a careful writer, who shunned an incongruity of language, as a well-bred man does a vulgarity in manners. He did not imagine his reader less scholarly than himself, nor "cut under" to a supposed coarseness of taste; he did not use catch words or cant phrases, but wrote as he talked in private conversation, with self-possession and self-respect. One saw in his style a tendency to analysis and separation of thoughts; it was not a flowing and narrative style, but logical, piquant and often abrupt. Some of the fugitive pieces that follow were written while he was quite young, and are not the best specimens of his writing *; one does not find in them that severe beauty which characterized his later style. They are, however, good illustrations of his mode of thought, and they show to some degree the keen scrutiny with which he was accustomed to examine public measures and men.

The work of an editor is peculiar: he must write as swiftly as the man of business will read his editorial; he must strike right at the heart of his subject and say at once what the occasion demands. Writing under this pressure of time, Carlton's style, originally marked by idiomatic

* The sketches of lawyers were written in 1853 and published in a series in the *New York Evening Mirror*. The portraitures of John C. Spencer, William H. Seward, Ira Harris, Nicholas Hill, Samuel Stevens, Azor Taber, Marcus T. Reynolds and Daniel Cady were written by his friend and relative, Isaac Edwards of Albany.

strength and precision, soon became one of grace and flexibility. The brain was full and active and his perceptions rapid and accurate, and as he did not burden himself with mental reservations of any sort, he acquired the faculty of writing the language in its purity, and with a force and animation that seized the attention and satisfied one's critical taste. The style was a true reflex of the mind, as it always is, and there ran along the line of his clear sentences a fine edge of thought which made the reader feel the tone of his mind.

A comparison between his earlier and later writings is very interesting. He began with strength, using the ornaments of speech obviously and in a manner to attract attention, and grew by degrees into a style that is almost severe, though nimble and full of beauty. This we apprehend is the ordinary law of growth; while it is the exact reverse of what sometimes happens, as Macaulay has shown by a comparison of the earlier and later speeches and writings of two illustrious Englishmen, in whom the fancy and imagination grew rich and luxuriant with advancing years, who began writing with chaste severity and rose in their age into a redundant and gorgeous rhetoric.

Fidelity to the truth, requires us to say that Carlton Edwards possessed a good share of self-esteem, and placed a high value upon his family, his government and his country. His grandfather, Paul Todd, was long a major-general in the militia of the state; and his great-grandfather, Nathaniel Edwards, was a captain in the army of the revolution: and he did not forget the fact, that the blood of soldiers and brave men flowed in his veins. His good sense taught him that personal virtue and worth do not always come by descent; and he did not often allude to his family. On the other hand, his reason taught him that the nation of to-day is the heir, and ought to be the personal representative of whatever is noble and magnanimous in her past history. Acting upon this conviction, he proudly cherished the government and institutions founded by the fathers of the republic, counting it an honor to be ranked among the conservatives of that organized justice and freedom which are the soul of the state. This immediate relation of the present to the past, felt by him so strongly, furnishes us with the key-note to his political sentiments and opinions; and may serve also to explain the mingled pride and affection with which he spoke and wrote of the Union and the Constitution; those defences of the national life, and symbols of its honor.

Somewhat reserved in his manners towards

general acquaintances, there appeared in his address and conversation, and in his dealings and bearing in society, the unmistakable qualities and sensibilities of a gentleman. Though the term has been badly worn by men upon whom it rested with about the same propriety as that of knighthood upon Front de Bœuf or Bois Guilbert, it nevertheless conveys certain ideas of honor, truth, and nobleness, which always enter into our estimate of the man we trust, and willingly receive into our confidence. So expressive and full of meaning is it that the late emperor of Russia, it is said, did not hesitate to fortify his word by pledging with it the honor of a gentleman; it is safe, therefore, to infer that it has not yet wholly lost its original signification, and is not an unfit expression of those qualities of character which accredit the bearer, in cottage and palace alike, and which belonged to our friend, and gave to his social intercourse the unacquired and "unbought grace of life."

Nothing is small to which a man may worthily give his attention; and little things often serve to explain those that are important. In personal appearance Carlton was prepossessing—he dressed well, and did not find it burdensome to observe social usages; he was a lover of good books, works of art and beauty, and he sought and found relaxation from labor in the charms and graces of society. He possessed an easy independence of spirit, and there was in him a freshness and alacrity of mind, that attracted and secured to him the regards of men and women also. Of a nervous temperament, and considerable imagination, he entered quickly into the sentiments of others, adding force and volume to the feast of reason and flow of soul. His nature was finely strung; and he delighted in music and painting and statuary, and frequently sought among artists and men of genius that diversion which recreates, while it rests and refreshes the toil worn intellect.

Of a comprehensive and penetrating mind, he was capable of generalizing the facts of history; was a close observer of the springs of action in leading men and nations, in churches, states and corporate bodies, at home and abroad; was deeply imbued with the spirit of the age, and took a lively interest in every thing that, in his judgment, promoted or concerned the real progress and elevation of the race.

He was a man of principle, and not a man of much policy. He was too proud to assume a character and utter sentiments which he did not entertain, and he was too loyal and sincere to repress from politic motives his own well-formed and cherished opinions. He was brave and chivalric, "without fear and without reproach." He did not love money, and could not be easily influenced by selfish or pecuniary considerations. On more than one occasion, we saw him breast formidable flurries of public opinion that seemed to be the setting in of settled winters of discontent, and under circumstances well fitted to test a man's courage. It would be very inadequate to say he did not flinch, for he did not show the least sign of wavering. A firmness so complete, grounded on the consent and concurrence of every faculty, has no occasion to assert itself with an air of austerity. Undoubtedly austere men are often very firm, but the firmness of an even-tempered man, whose manners are mild and whose speech is without haste or harshness, is quite as sure to outlast opposition and win the victory of success in the end.

Educated in the Presbyterian church, he acquired early much of that intellectual force and firmness of opinion which have long distinguished this excellent school of religion. We do not know that he in form departed from its faith; but we do know that contracting pleasant and agreeable associations during his college life with the recognized teachers in the Episcopal church, he was ultimately drawn to that communion—that he approved of its government and polity, and loved the church and its service to the end. One's religion takes a deep hold upon his whole being; and it is on this account that a change from one church to another, made by a man of mature years, argues a certain lightness of disposition. But when the change is manifestly one of growth, as it was in this instance, it shows both sincerity of purpose and independence of mind. Moreover, this change was not in truth *from* his own church, because he had not by any act of his own adopted the church of his fathers; it was therefore strictly what we have termed it, a growth of religious opinion and sentiment—a deliberate adoption and choice of Christianity as taught by the Episcopal church. We do not doubt that his taste, reason and conscience concurred in this momentous election of the soul; for we know that he delighted in the reverent and beautiful service of that church, in the life-giving Christ, and in the sublime hope of immortality which is brought to light in him. And we know also that the prayer book was his companion and solace through the few and sorrowful months of his decline, shedding upon his gentle spirit the ministry of reconciliation to the last hour of conscious life. "Blessed are the dead that die in the Lord, yea saith the Spirit, for they rest from their labors, and their works do follow them."

His character developed manifestly from a central germ, and grew ever towards unity and proportion. The sentiments and opinions he entertained upon one subject bore always a natural and logical relation towards those which he entertained upon other and collateral subjects. The powers of his mind coalesced in action so entirely that the whole man seemed present and active in whatever labor he engaged. An individuality so marked can spring only from that constitutional integrity of soul, which won our regard and commanded the respect of the community among whom he lived.

Will his friends accept this imperfect estimate of Carlton? Certainly not they, who stood in the sunshine of his love, and knew how rich his nature was, how unselfish and faithful to every relation, how consistent and loyal to his higher life, and more personal than all, how gentle and kind he was in that home life of which we do not speak.

He died young; and nature herself confesses a regret for the early dead, as if in sympathy with the disappointment of broken hopes. We had trusted to see him accomplish the circle of life, and fill it up with continued fidelity and useful labor, winning the high honors that wait upon a character so finely tempered; and he fell suddenly, as the young soldier on the field of battle, under the proud eyes of kindred and friends that weep and look up, consoled by the clustering memories of a short but honorable life.

WRITINGS.

THOUGHTS AFTER A JAUNT TO NEW ENGLAND.

Travel is the universal panacea for local prejudices and traditions. A good and loyal citizen of the United States will look far beyond the horizon of his own town, city, or state; nor will his patriotism concentrate itself on the village pump, or the City Hall. The more he sees and knows of his own country, the deeper will be his respect and affection for it. A careful and thorough tour through the principal states, directed and controlled by a desire to ascertain the exact truth, will cure any man of extreme and ultra opinions, and he will return home convinced that, although the North, the South, the East, and the West differ greatly from each other in customs, modes of thought, and popular opinions, they are bound together, as with hooks of steel, by a common race and traditions, as well as by those great moral principles which give unity and strength to a nation.

The Northern man who visits Charleston, Mobile or New Orleans, in a fair and candid spirit, will find occasion to correct any exaggerated opinions of Southern institutions and life which have been instilled into his mind. The planter enjoys more good-fellowship and sympathy in the North, than he had a right to expect from the general tone of the Northern press. The New Englander learns to forgive the rough and wild recklessness through which the great West is moving forward to wealth and empire, while the Western settler sees in the East a culture and a growing civilization largely due to the maturing influences of time.

In fact, the more the people of the United States know of each other, the greater will be their mutual trust and forbearance. Enter the penetralia, or domestic recesses, in any distant sister state, and see how much you have in common with your fellow countrymen. We love the same principles, the same Constitution, the same freedom of the individual, properly and duly constrained by the hands of order and law. Through all the wild freaks of the politicians, the eager struggles of parties, and the fierce antagonism of opposing opinions, we can detect the strong and conservative basis upon which the Union stands as on a solid rock. The achievements of the early settlers, the glories of the Revolutionary strife, the calm courage and wisdom of the fathers of the republic, these are the joint property of citizens in all parts of the country. Their enthusiastic joy that they have such an inheritance, always felt more or less sincerely, once a year breaks forth into loud demonstrations. On the Fourth of July the hearts of the whole nation, inspired by these reminiscences, by the deeds of the past and the sanguine hopes of the future, beat as one.

We have cause to be dissatisfied with many things in New England. Along with much that is excellent and praiseworthy, Massachusetts seems to be beset with an under current of skepticism, and a saucy individualism which spurns all authority, unless accordant with its own notions of propriety. In politics, the fundamental principles upon which the Constitution and the Union are erected, are apparently forgotten or despised, and the state formerly the most true and loyal of all, is now the most trustless and disloyal. In this course she seems to be closely followed by many of the neighboring states, which appear to be more attracted by their own individual opinions and caprices, than by those duties which they owe to their nationalty and government.

But there is also a great backbone of conservatism throughout New England, and it will eventually assert itself. There is a large, prudent and loyal party there, which is disgusted with the general course of things, and despises the extreme and radical tendencies of the day. They may now, under the influence of disgust and indifference, stay away from the polls; they may appear just now overwhelmed by popular extravagance, the general impulse of an exciting contest and the unfortunate accidents of party; but at heart the great majority of the people are honest and patriotic. After the "fitful fever" is over, they will and must return to the line of duty imposed by common sense, prudence and loyal attachment to the whole country.

To drop politics—there is much in New England very worthy and admirable, and which appears more worthy and admirable as we make its better acquaintance. Passing up through the wild and sterile mountains of Western Maine, where the birch and maple two weeks since were fading into the autumnal colors, and the thin and dry soil shows itself in the stunted growth of grain and vegetables, one begins to realize the vigor, sturdiness and perseverence of New England enterprise. Here is moderate prosperity, personal independence, and general comfort; a cold climate and an illiberal soil, contrasting strongly with the rich savannahs of the South and the fertile prairies of the West. But the state of Maine is not dependent upon agriculture; she has an ocean of wealth in her heavy timber and fisheries. The harbor of the city of Portland is beautiful, as well as capacious and secure; the Casco bay, of which it is the arm, is without a rival in romantic beauty and the picturesqueness of its three hundred islands. In visiting the city, one is struck with the plain richness of the architecture, the profusion of forest trees, the attractions of gardens which surround nearly every residence, and a general appearance of decent order, sobriety, and cleanliness. Even the complexion is improved by the fresh and invigorating atmosphere; and as one looks upon the faces on the street, he can not help thinking that this is a happy, well behaved and good-looking people.

It is probable that several readable volumes could be compiled from White Mountain letters which have appeared from time to time in this journal, and the present writer distrusts his power to add anything to the many admirable descriptions which have thus been laid before the public. There is one thought which is perhaps worth recording. The traveler often meets persons who seem to have a monomonia for mountains, and whose summer months are passed in exploring their mysteries, and in lingering over the grand and magnificent scenery of the White Hills. There are gentlemen and ladies of education and refinement whose taste for these scenic effects is cultivated to a higher point than that of the amateurs in art, or the wanderers among the paintings and statues of Italy. The genuine lover of nature has here a series of studies which change daily in color and appearance, and even shape; and we do not wonder that there are scores of pedestrians who wend their way to the heart of the mountains every season, in search of new scenes of beauty and grandeur, or that in their eager pursuit they outwalk and astonish the guides. Indeed, to have stood but once on the pinnacle of Mount Washington, looking out upon an almost infinite horizon which embraces rivers, lakes, mountains and cities, is to have fixed upon the imagination a picture more gorgeous and permanent than the genius of art ever conceived.

Traveling down New Hampshire and up through Vermont, as well as in some of the counties of Maine, one meets a class of men, tall, vigorous, brave and energetic, who carry in their hands strength and prosperity.

In these Titans of the mountains, these giants of the forests, we find the representatives of that class which has gone forth and still goes forth to grapple with the wild stubbornness of nature, and by their strength and wisdom plant civilization in barren spots, and nurse the fertility of the soil on the banks of rivers. We see everywhere evidences of energy, will, progress, and good morals—cultivated farms, herds of sheep, cattle, and noble breeds of horses; school houses, churches, colleges and libraries, and the foundations of cities, like Portland, Me., or Burlington, Vt., which in substantial beauty and rich simplicity of architecture, are equal to anything in this country. Here every one seems to be "well to do" in the world, and without display, to have built himself a beautiful home. In fact, nothing charms a judicious and moderate man more than a New England village, or town, like those we have mentioned; nor can better or more intelligent society be found. Those mighty forests in Maine, the towering White Hills of New Hampshire, the sky soaring peaks of the Green Mountains in Vermont, seem to have impressed themselves upon the bold and aspiring New Englander; and we claim that the genuine, uncorrupted, and unabolitionized Yankee holds a very high place among his fellow-countrymen.

THE SPIRIT OF REBELLION.

The spirit which led to the recent acts of conspiracy and vandalism on Staten Island is not peculiar to that latitude; nor are the causes which impel men so to undermine the structure of civilized life and the foundations of law, local or superficial in their character. Rebellion to constituted authority is no longer sporadic and confined to localities, but epidemic, and spread over the whole body-politic; for, rebellion includes not merely overt acts of a treasonable nature, but that spirit of insubordination which is ready to oppose and beat down the law at every convenient, plausible or profitable opportunity. That spirit is the gist of the crime, whatever name or phase it may assume; Lynch-law, anti-rent, incendiary mobs, or vigilance committees.

The fault seems to be a national one, and its root strikes down to the principles upon which human governments are built. A portion of our people, especially that portion which plumes itself upon its radicalism in politics, has formed too low an estimate of the inherent sacredness of our government, and is disposed to allow it no binding force, except that which is derived from expediency. Such regard it, not as a moral power, carrying with it a certain and well defined moral obligation, but as a mere brute or physical force. Rulers, in their view, are merely agents, intrusted with certain powers over life, liberty and property; and society is debased into a mere contract for mutual peace, security and protection.

From this barter and sale theory, it results that a man has an implied right to repudiate the law and resist its execution the moment it becomes profitable for him to repudiate or resist; having no high sense of duty to consult, it is merely a question of policy whether he shall break or fulfil the loose and intangible contract he has made with his fellow citizens. From his point of view, the whole system of government is a political agency for the protection of life and property, and he estimates its right to command by its power to punish. If he can be disobedient with impunity—if he can escape the fines and penalties, pack a jury, corrupt a judge, or commit certain acts of arson in a county where grand juries are likely to connive at and applaud them—he feels himself at perfect liberty to outrage the law. If a contest, on this basis, ensues between the executors of the law and the violators of the law, the only questions to be decided are, which has the most cunning and skill, or which can bring to bear the greater amount of physical force.

Under such a false and degrading theory, government loses its noblest attribute, the right to command. It no longer appeals to the conscience and religious sentiments of men; is no longer invested with the rights and attributes of command; is no longer a Heaven-commissioned, God-ordained institution, constraining cordial and universal obedience; is no longer clothed with the privileges and majesty of the authority it represents; but, degenerated and robbed of all that would give it efficacy and power, of all element and shadow of divine right, there is no form of folly or wickedness to which it may not be made subservient.

It cannot be denied that very many of our people fall far short of the virtues which go to make up a good citizen, of the principles which underlie the whole structure of the government, and of the examples of obedience and self-restraint presented in the lives of the founders of the republic. There is such a thing as loyalty in friendship, in love, in religion; and it is that which vivifies those relations which we ought to cultivate in those equally important relations which we sustain to the fundamental law of the land. Without this loyalty, gracefully yielding to light and temporary annoyance, manfully bearing up even under severe grievances, but courageously doing them battle in all legal and constitutional methods, sacrificing much of personal comfort and convenience for the public good, and ever mindful of the primary duty of allegiance, which is the highest expression of patriotism, there is no such thing as government, in the genuine sense of the word; the majestic shelter of the law becomes a mere shadow, and all that is wholesome, restraining and conservative in the republic is swept away by the swift surges of license, discord and wild anarchy.

LOCALISM AND PATRIOTISM.

Written in December, 1860.

This is a good time to remember that "we are all Americans." That noble sentiment should override private opinions, state prejudices, local ideas; always and without wavering, it should stand the highest and the best among the merits of the true patriot, submerging and *drowning* every disloyalty. "It is," said Webster, "as Americans that we are known, the world over. Who asks you what state you are from, in Europe, in Africa, or in Asia? Is he an American? Does he belong to the United States? Does that flag protect him? Does he rest under the eagle and the stars and stripes? If he does, all else is subordinate and of little concern."

We want a renovation of public sentiment on this subject, a revival of a more patriotic spirit, a deeper devotion for the common cause and our common country. State prejudices, local ideas, sectional opinions and geographical prejudices, have brought this country very near the point of severance and destruction. The elements leading to these results were early at work, and the fathers of the republic saw through the horoscope of this free and hopeful land, one baneful shadow portending and threatening the future. As they looked forward to the golden-tinted perspective of that future, their hearts beat with apprehension. In that shadow they foresaw the ill-starred policy of localism. While they lived they labored to link the confederacy together, their last words before their death were praises for the Union, and prayers for its preservation. The baneful influence of our own perversity grows apace; the dusky shadow rises up from the past, lowering, fierce, and threatening, spreading itself over the thirty-three states, a fearful menace now almost fulfilled.

Whence comes the insidious attack which threatens to overwhelm the nation? Local agitation has gained too much power. A mammoth party has gathered its cohorts at the North, whose leaders are led by ambition and an insolent spirit of persecution, — men who have condemned themselves by their own words. That party does not claim to have any connection with the South. There is a class of men in the South, not truly representing the Southern people, who are ready to ruin, if they can not rule. Whether the malign influence comes from the North or the South, we care not; those who strike the insidious blow, are parricides, not patriots. They should be denounced and crushed out as the seed of discord and destruction. How insignificant are all localisms and sectional spites compared with the safety and perpetuity of the Union! The wicked enterprise has been especially fostered by politicians, who make it a special business to legislate for a part of, not the whole country — men who neither honor the Union, nor respect the fundamental law They live by localisms, make it their speciality to think and speak and decree localisms, and are so forgetful of their loyalty that they seem ready to gratify their selfish ambition among the very ruins of the republic. Unless there is a stronger nationalty to bind us together with "hooks of steel," until we begin to appreciate and live up to the principle that we are all Americans at heart, the Union can not be safe. We must reject the low and groveling theory that society is a mere contract, and that its security depends only on the whims, prejudices and conflicting passions of the governed. How much higher and nobler than this is the sentiment of loyalty which controls the conduct of the good citizen, and makes him recognize and apply the higher and more responsible relations which he holds towards the republic. Without such a sentiment as this, the structure of civilized life has no secure foundation.

LOYALTY TO THE REPUBLIC.

The citizen who can not realize the true significance of Law, Authority, Loyalty, as affecting his relations as a citizen, is not worthy of the protection of government. His reason and his judgment are in an infanttile or chaotic condition, which disables him from the discharge of the duties that belong to organized and civilized society. He is fit only for the solitudes of some Juan Fernandez, where separated from the counsels and restraints of his fellow men, he may give full vent to his idiosyncracies, and wander a free vagrant in the wilderness of his own caprices.

Such a mode of life seems to be appropriate for a class of modern philosophers and politicians, which grows each year larger and more influential. A portion of our northern metaphysicians for a long period have been teaching the public that there is something higher and better in every man than either divine or human authority, and have set up for the admiration of their followers a kind of refined individuality, which exalts itself above all the lessons of human experience and the wisdom of the ages which have gone. The man, they say, is better than the state, the common law or the constituted authorities of the nation; let him accept or reject what he chooses, and worship his intellect above the powers of heaven and earth. Emerson and his cohorts of small followers delight in painting the isolated grandeur of the individual, and would have men sit apart, like gods, on the peaks of Olympus, and issue their self-sufficient decrees from the pinnacles of their self-conceit. After these misty doubters of everything but their own infallibility, come a crowd of so-called clergymen, somewhat behind the metaphysicians in the march of religious heterodoxy, but far more influential over the people, preaching up disrespect for the law whenever the law happens to contradict their political prejudices, sending out rifles to settle a political campaign, declaring from the pulpit their determination to disobey such and such laws, excusing treason and lionizing the traitor. To make this motely procession of rebels complete, we have only to add the ultra politicians of all classes and sections who teach an habitual disregard of certain laws, and who, while living under a republican government, virtually assume the responsibility of rejecting any system of legislation which does not square with their individual opinions.

These extreme and unbalanced modes of thought find

expression from time to time in various forms of lawlessness more or less dangerous to the nation, but generally originating in contempt for constituted authority, and in the reckless passions excited by the sectional controversies. We have seen them developed in open resistance to particular laws, in cowardly acts of nullification attempted by dead letter statutes, in rebellion to acts of congress provided for the territories, and in treasonable conspiracies against sister states. The seed of the evil is sown by the new fashioned leaders of popular thought, who have no respect, and pretend to none, for the fundamental law of the land when it conflicts with their cheap philanthropy, their one-sided sentimentality, or their quack remedies for the betterment of mankind. Like the ferocious and bloody Clootz in the French Revolution, they go about bellowing that they are "the friends and representatives of human nature," and are no doubt ready, like him, to crown their wild theories by a feast of revenge and murder. They give us to understand, also, that the American government was framed for the benefit of human nature, and a certain vague and dreamy humanitarianism. Now we surmise that the founders and builders of this republic did not labor for universal human nature, in the spirit of Garrison, Gerrit Smith, Wendell Phillips, and the other Clootzes, and that they did not include the people of Congo in their theory of freedom at all. Doubtless they had a brilliant and glorious ideal of a single and great republican nation, bound and riveted together in a noble confederacy of states, powerful abroad and respected at home, and above all, loyal to the government of its own choice and creation.

That word *loyal*, implying faithfulness to the law, is a good, old fashioned word, though somewhat out of use, owing to the low and lax views which prevail on the subject, and to that spirit of insubordination which stands ready to beat down the law at every convenient or plausible opportunity. The journalists, humanitarians, metaphysicians and clergymen of the radical or destructive school, have no conception of loyalty as a sentiment, nor any comprehension of its power as a moral force, in giving unity and strength to a great nation. To the followers of Clootz and "human nature," the word is almost entirely unknown; for in their devotion to general but indiscreet philanthropy, and the development of "human nature" on a large scale, they forget their fealty to their own government and country. They can not be "representatives of human nature" and loyal citizens at the same time. The most moderate of them attach but little importance to the inherent sacredness of government, and allow it no binding force, except that which is derived from expediency. Rulers are only agents entrusted with certain powers, and society is degraded into a mere contract for mutual preservation. Under such a low and groveling theory, government loses its authority over the hearts and consciences of men; its security depends only upon the prejudices and conflicting passions of the governed. The true and loyal citizen takes a more elevated view of the relations which exist between him and the government, which he regards as a divinely ordained institution, clothed with the privileges and majesty of the authority it represents. He is slow to set himself up against the powers that be, or to array his private opinions in hostile conflict against the supreme decrees of the nation. That sentiment of loyalty which controls him in friendship, in love, in religion, which keeps him always faithful to his plighted faith, and the honest instincts of his nature, he recognizes and applies in the higher and more responsible relations which he holds to the republic. Without such a sentiment in the hearts of the people, the structure of civilized life has no secure foundation, and the majestic shelter of the law becomes a mere shadow.

UNITY AND THE UNION.

We can not believe that the earnest devotion to and love of country which once animated our fathers, has yet entirely died away. We can see no coherent and logical reason why our people should fall away in a mass, from the patriotic influences of their youth and the cherished principles on which they owe allegiance to the general government and to the Union of the confederated states. France has waded through the blood of many revolutions; Saxons, Normans, the Scotch, and some of the other Celtic races, have had fierce internal conflicts in the North of Europe; but the unity of great nationalities has never been substantially impaired, nor have the brave and sympathetic bonds which have bound Frenchman to France and the Anglo-Saxon-Celtic Englishman to the United Kingdom of Great Britain, ever been seriously and permanently broken. Their discords, family quarrels and intestine wars left deep wounds to heal; but no absolute and eternal severance of nationality was ever effected, because the people always came back to the organized and fundamental principles without which no great nation can live. Is it possible that the great American nation can be broken like a wisp of straw, or that it can be shattered by a single blow into ruin and petty but perhaps belligerent republics?

Can these things happen to us in this epoch of an advancing civilization, and when the world seems to be growing better in knowledge, charity, and Christian benevolence, advancing not so much in the spirit which once wrought with the sword for whatever was considered virtue and truth, but in chaster and more peaceful culture which inculcates those elevated and refined principles of justice, truth, mercy and love, which dignify and ennoble human nature? What will become of our proper and just national pride, if the link of the chain of mutual forbearance and self-restraint should be severed, and a great gulf separate states and brothers? Will the American feel better pleased with himself in the European capitals, the centres of consolidated empires; will not the blush of shame rise on his cheek when he visits Italy and beholds her reunited in those natural ties of race and affection which can only bind together a civilized and independent nation?

If the real sentiments of the voters in the United States could be proclaimed this day, and all selfishness, prejudice, obstinate and impractical theories, be moderated — could every man be free to act with unperverted common sense and manly independence, unrestrained by the exactions of violent partisans, peace and union would assert themselves with enthusiasm.

But there is an influence abroad that is at work bringing forth discord, confusion, and perhaps ultimate ruin. There is a spirit which strikes down everything that is good, noble and generous; which prefers selfishness and personal advancement to every other consideration; which to advance ambition would destroy the Union — would seize upon every noble impulse and even the instinctive love of liberty itself, as a means of making discord, and gaining power; which would prevent reconciliation and fair compromises, through the lust of self-aggrandisement. It is the teaching of fanatics who would destroy what they cannot control. It is the false hue and cry of the so-called, but pretended friends of freedom, who have insidiously and persistently trampled upon the constitution and corrupted public sentiment.

But we have a horror of believing that the Abolitionists, or their sly, intriguing cousins, the extreme anti-compromise Republicans, will finally and forever prevail against the bonds of civil strength and the defense of constitutional rights. This is a truth which can never diminish, it should gather force day by day; for it quickens the duty of all honest and single-hearted citizens to renew their pledges of fidelity and loyalty to their common country. What true man can look at the excitement, confusion and fanaticism, which now prevail in congress, as the representative of the sectionalism which extends throughout the country at large, without feeling prompted to new exertions for the maintenance of that land in which he rejoices and glories with a faith *once* unfaltering? The spasmodic struggle of those intriguers whose patriotism is bounded by degrees of latitude, and who do not pretend to conceal their hatred and contempt towards other sections of the country, should prompt every good citizen to enter into a new and stern crusade against sectional opinions, geographical prejudices, and local ideas.

THE SPHERE OF LEGISLATORS.

We have always thought that a legislator should address himself chiefly to the practical duties of his office. It is his business to make the laws and mould the policy of the nation, as much as it is the business of the baker to make bread, or of the builder to erect houses. Not that we measure him by the quantity so much as by the quality of his work; but work he must with the energy, assiduity and skill which are required of any mechanic or professional man. When the English parliament assembles, its members go to work like men: they grapple with the difficulties before them in a manly and business like fashion; ministers and members of the opposition alike meet the issues presented, in a short but fair fight. If the issue be vital, one party or the other goes down, and there is a fresh appeal to the wishes of the people. If the battle be one of details rather than of outlines, of policy rather than principle, the members don't stop to fight about abstractions, or side issues; but each, and each in his place and in accordance with his ability to grapple with the theme, bends to the work before him with the determination of doing, if not the best thing, the next best thing which the exigency of the case demands. There are not many harangues; but those that are made are delivered by those who speak to the point, and have studied, and in many cases exhausted the subject. In a word, the houses of parliament, like the halls of the corps legislatif of France, and like the legislative councils of other European states, are the places for the transaction of business, and not the theatres of a vain and personal display.

It is a humiliating confession that the legislature of this state, those of many of our sister states, and even the congress of the United States, do not compare favorably, in the points we have mentioned, with the legislative bodies of the leading nations of Europe. The most active and energetic people in the world is certainly entitled to be represented by active and energetic men. But in taking up the reported proceedings of our national legislature, one can not fail to be struck, not only with their lack of dignity and decorum, but likewise with the slipshod and immature manner in which their business is transacted. We are everywhere met with a superfluity of words which weakens the force of ideas and wearies the patience of people of sense. Whole days of the precious time of the present congress are given up to the delivery of speeches which could profitably be condensed to the limit of a single hour. There is a wonderful preponderance of words over ideas; of speech over action; of things said over things done. Even the strongest men in congress seem to think that their connection with an important piece of legislation is completed when they have delivered a long speech on the subject. The labor of systematizing the vast business before them, of harmonising conflicting opinions, of marshaling discordant theories up to a point where they can meet and coalesce in some practical act, of reducing chaos to some kind of order and law — all this seems to form no part of the duty of American legislators. To make a speech which will read well in some remote locality in the interior; to deliver an essay more appropriate to a quarterly review than to the halls of congress; to talk Buncombe by the hour, or to reel off platitudes by the square yard in the Washington *Globe*, seems to be the ambition of too many of our representatives in congress.

Add the time that is consumed in personal explanations, or on questions of privilege, in bandying epithets and settling disputes — add occasional scenes of discord and confusion worthy of a bear garden or a kennel of fighting dogs — and we have a specimen of actualities not at all creditable to the assembled wisdom of the nation.

BRIEF NOTES IN CANADA.

Have you ever heard of the Wild Dog of Niagara? Just below the suspension bridge on the Canada side, and hanging over the river to a height of some two hundred feet, runs for some distance a huge, broken and over-reaching precipice, which no human being could climb or descend without assistance. Near the surface of the water and on the broken rocks, a large, noble looking and peculiarly marked New Foundland dog has been seen and heard, at various times during the past two years, and lately within a few weeks. This fact is authenticated by the testimony of many respectable and veracious eye witnesses, and as there is no way for the poor animal to return to civilized life and the amenities of human intercourse, he is a subject of much curious speculation. He is a kind of Robinson Crusoe among dogs, and it is supposed, picks up his precarious living from the fish and small animals on his *beat* which is only half a mile in length. His howling lamentations from the rocky recesses of his retreat are often heard at midnight, and a daring attempt to approach and save him was rendered fruitless by his ferocity. An additional air of romance has been thrown around his fate by the story that he is bemoaning his master whom he *lost* at the Clifton House some two years since. It is probable that he (the dog, and not the man), was washed ashore by the rapids, which sweep along here with terrific velocity. But whether an exile or a disheartened misanthrope, the poor cast away has the hearty sympathy of every one who approaches the spot and conjectures his probable fate.

St. Catharine's, now quite a famous resort for tourists and invalids, strikes the visitor as rather a dull and uninviting spot. There is nothing in the adjacent scenery to charm the eye; nor are there any local attractions, save St. Catharine's Well, worth visiting. The town, which covers a good deal of ground and contains 7,000 or 8,000 inhabitants, is the first of any size and importance on the line of the Great Western Rail Road; the well and the leading hotels lie about a mile from the station house. Altogether the visitor with a sound body and a mind desirous of entertainment, would find it a difficult task to kill a week there.

The well, which is attached to the grounds of the Stephenson House, the leading hotel, is now sunk to a depth of nearly 600 feet. The water is forced up by a small steam engine, and is supplied in great abundance to the bathing establishment, which lies almost directly on the great Welland canal. Received into a cup directly from the well, the water effervesces very much like a seidlitz powder, but instantly subsides into a clear and transparent fluid indescribably nauseating to the taste. The "concentrated water" as it is called, from which the grosser salts are evaporated, is less unsavory, but it requires considerable practice to enable a patient to go through his doses without a grimace. I found the cold baths very invigorating, and causing an almost painful excitement of the nervous system. These baths should be used with great caution, and never by invalids without medical advice and superintendence. The hotels during my visit, early in August, were crowded, and invalids desiring permanent accommodations should apply early.

One hears and sees much in Canada of runaway negroes. The taverns and hotels in Upper Canada are abundantly supplied with black servants, a large portion of whom have been transplanted from the South.

Their settlements, also, are chiefly in the region of the lakes, comparatively few venturing towards the St. Lawrence. Their condition is described by all impartial observers as pitable in the extreme. Unsuited by nature to the rigors of a northern climate, they soon "dwindle, peak and pine," amid all the pangs of starvation by cold and hunger. Intelligent Englishmen say that if the Southern states would pass laws prohibiting the division of slave families, nine out of ten of the runaways would return to their homes. The colonial system of attempting to raise the black man to a level of the white man is pronounced an entire failure. The encouragement of black emigration has loaded the poor houses and the jails, while the loathsome intermarriages which are allowed, and even encouraged, have caused in some localities a terrible demoralization.

Stories abound of the dissatisfaction expressed by the expatriated blacks. A short time since an extensive planter from Kentucky visiting the Clifton House, received many voluntary attentions from a poorly dressed young black, who finally said, "Massa Col'nel, don't you know me?" "No," said the Colonel, "I never saw you before." The young fellow then declared himself a runaway from the Colonel's plantation near Louisville, and demanded alms. His old master gave him a sufficient sum of money to replace his rags with a decent suit of clothes, when the following conversation is described as having taken place:

"Massa, should like to go back to Kentuck." "Well, Jack, I shall not give a cent to help you back. You have run away from a good home, and you can run back again, where, if you behave yourself, you will be taken care of."

What became of Jack is more than is known; but if there be any return tickets by the underground rail road, Jack will avail himself of the first passage.

The total negro population of Upper Canada is set down at 4,669 (about the same as the Indians) out of a total of about a million. In Lower Canada, there are some 800 blacks in a census of some 900,000. So they form a very small fraction of the community, after all.

The towns on the Canadian side of the St. Lawrence present a thriving appearance. Toronto is a beautiful city, with a handsome university and a college, under the patronage of the English church. The city is said to resemble English towns more closely than anything on this continent. You notice on the Canada side evidences of individual wealth, and a desire of the government to make a handsome show in the shape of substantial public edifices. But prosperity seems to be less generally diffused than on the American side. The English are far better agriculturists than the French; indeed, in driving about Montreal one can tell almost instantly the nationality of the owner of nearly every farm by the roadside. The French farm-houses are quaint, old fashioned, and too frequently out of repair; in many of them the front door opens directly into the sitting-room; an arrangement which occasionally gives one a glimpse of curious family pictures. The gardens are over-run with weeds, and the fields with thistles. The English dwellings are more neat and substantial, and the grounds as well as the grain fields generally in prime order.

After the Thousand Islands are passed, the great remaining attraction on the route to Montreal is the passage of the Grand Rapids on the St. Lawrence. The old Indian pilot so long known to the traveling public no longer presides at the helm; intemperance has robbed his eye of its keenness and his arm of muscular strength. The boats at this season are frequently so heavily laden that they are obliged for the sake of safety to pass the rapids by the parallel canals. Our party was more fortunate; or rather so clamorous to be "put through" that the captain ordered the boat, although largely freighted, to make all the rapids except a dangerous one called the Long Sault, which we evaded by the southern passage. The most thrilling scene, of course, was at La Chine; the current here runs at the rate of twenty-five miles an hour; and for several miles, the waters boiling furiously among the rocks seemed likely to dash us to pieces at every moment. The bow of the boat was loaded with passengers all standing in eager attitudes, and all more or less excited; the sun had set, and a blood-red, nearly full moon alone lit up the darkened and seething waves. A glorious picture, such as one sees only once or twice in a life-time; and none the less pleasant on account of the confidence every one on board felt in the pilot, a Canuck, whose keen eye fairly glowed with excitement and intelligence. A moment's dimness in that eye, or a tremor in the hands that held the wheel, would have dashed us all into the jaws of death; but so great was the faith that not even a scared face or a woman's scream marred the "fun" of passing La Chine.

Next to the massive stone buildings and wharves in

Montreal, and which the neighboring quarries supply so profusely, nothing strikes the visitor more pleasantly than the union and good feeling which seem to exist between the French and English—races which do not often coalesce. Anglican enterprise and solidity married to French taste and politeness have made Montreal one of the best and most attractive cities on the continent. One sees all around him the evidences of a good government, and of a substantial, honest and straightforward way of doing business, public and private. The police is a handsome and efficient body of men; their clean appearance and neat uniform would make some of our dirty-looking patrolmen blush for shame. A new and convenient style of cab has been introduced; and as fares are cheap and the drivers under good disipline, nearly every one rides instead of walking. The proud parish church of Notre Dame, the many hospitals, nunneries (and especially the Angelus service of the Grey Nuns at the chapel) the piers, Exchange, city buildings and the Mountain, are all worthy of notice, but have been often described. One of the engineers of the great tubular bridge remarked in my presence that the work would not be completed under a year. The foundations of the last pier have been laid, and the structure, which will be the longest, most elaborate and thoroughly built of the kind in the world, has an imposing appearance from the river. The subject of the change of the capital still causes much discussion; it is now being removed from Toronto to Quebec, whence after two years it will be permanently transferred to Ottawa in accordance with the queen's decision.

These brief notes may be summed up by saying that Canada is a great and growing country, that the people are full of pluck and enterprise, and are fond of Americans, who indeed spend a great deal of money among them at this season of the year. One does not notice many symptoms of the Americanization of the colonists; the most noticeable is the decimal currency now established. We recommend the railroads and steamboats to introduce the wholesome American custom of checking luggage through; for the present necessity of turning baggage-smasher every few miles, is enough to upset the equanimity and destroy the good nature of the most amiable traveling Yankee in the universe.

THE NEGRO RACE.

There are certain great facts in reference to the negro race, from which there is no rational or logical escape. A morbid philanthropy may attempt to pervert them; but they stand out so clearly and distinctly on the records of science and history, that a sensible and unprejudiced man can not deny them.

He who has studied the difference between the natural races and families of men, knows that a superior and an inferior race can not continue to occupy the same territory on terms of equality. Either the inferior race will be enslaved, and in that condition increase and multiply, if treated with reasonable kindness, or, in the attempt to compete with the superior race, be ultimately wiped out of existence by their greater skill and strength. We use the words *races of men* in a strictly ethnographical sense; and mean that kind of superiority of race which the Circassians and Anglo-Saxons manifest over the Indian, African, Malay and Mongolian races. We do not recognize in the Norman and the Saxon, the Gaul and the Oriental, the Celt and the Russian, any positive or absolute superiority of race, as compared with each other; for nature has marked no great or controlling differences in their physical and mental structure. But we can define, by means of physiological and anatomical science, the difference between the white man and the negro, or the Indian; and we know, also, that neither the Indian nor the free negro can contend successfully against the white man, when they occupy the same soil and compete with each other. All history proves that the inferior race, in order to survive the aggressions and greater activity and energy of the superior race, must be brought to a condition of servitude, serfdom, or slavery.

These principles may not be in accordance with the belief of many who think they are guided by the purest spirit of philanthropy; and yet they are founded upon facts which are indisputable. And there is another natural law which applies to these races, particularly to the negro, and which is equally unsatisfactory to some who fear to meet the truth face to face. Negroes and whites can not perpetuate a new race; the divine laws are indestructible barriers against such unnatural experiments; and we have the direct testimony of acute and honest travelers in Central America and the West Indies, that the mongrel or hybrid races are incapable of perpetuating themselves, and have greatly deteriorated in mind and body. Anything, then, like equal social relations between the two races, is physically impossible.

We do not make these incontestable statements from any dislike to the negro, or from any partialities for the institution of slavery. But in these days, when distinguished statesmen, and public journals representing a powerful and vigorous party, are constantly teaching the people theories which inculcate violent and hostile opposition to an institution recognized by the constitution and by the framers and fathers of this republic, and promise, in substance, that an "irrepressible conflict" is to result in overwhelming humiliation and decadence of the south, it is time to grapple the question boldly, and not to dodge the pending issues, or to mince matters too much, or to confess that there is but one side to this irritating and dangerous slavery controversy. There are four million reasons in the south, clad in flesh and blood, against the wild political crusade now going forward, and which becomes more obstinate and reckless as it advances. If history and science tell the truth, the immediate or unprepared, or hasty freedom of these slaves, will produce their extermination, accompanied by a train of events most horrible to contemplate.

And we advise, also, the professed philanthropist whose sympathies have got the better of his judgment, to reflect upon the great barriers which have been placed by nature between the whites and blacks, and that whatever may be the ultimate destiny of the latter, they are infinitely better off than if they had been born and bred in their native land. The records of travelers in Africa tell a sad but true tale of the negro race as it appears at home, and especially in Eastern Africa. The native African is an habitual drunkard, a thief, a liar, revengeful, licentious, groveling in his habits, almost destitute of natural affection, unprogressive in character, and in religion a devotee of the obscene mysteries of Fetichism. Moreover, the great bulk of the population is made up of masters and slaves. Indeed, slavery is almost universal. The principal occupation of the Africans, and the real object of almost all their wars, is the kidnapping of slaves; while the treatment and condition of negroes in our South is benevolence itself compared with the cruel system which prevails in Africa. This is the picture drawn of the native African by disinterested and reliable travelers; and a more disagreeable one is not to be found in the history of barbarians. In truth, the negroes, held in slavery in the United States, are much better off, physically and morally, than their ignorant and degraded brothers in Africa. Everybody knows this; and believes in his heart that the condition, prospects and character of the negro improve under the refining influences of civilized life. We may safely say, also, that scarcely a fraction of the people of the United States are in favor of now freeing the slave. Why then, in the face of the well authenticated facts we have stated, do the abolitionists, fanatics, and many leaders of the Republican party, persist in their wild and reckless theories, whose development is dragging the Union to the verge of the precipice? To raise up the great African race from serfdom to a condition of advancement and civilization, or to place them in a position where every favor and liberty and right, social and political, shall be allowed them, just as it is allowed to the whites, is a possibility of which we may dream for coming ages. But in the present posture of affairs, and with our present knowledge of the insurmountable difficulties in the way of such an event, we know, first of all, that only those who own slaves can abolish slavery; and then, that every imprudent, or concealed, or violent opposition on the part of northern men, does more injury than good, and impedes the advancement of genuine humanity.

THE EXECUTION OF BROWN.

The reader will learn from the despatches published elsewhere, that John Brown suffered the extreme penalty of the law yesterday, in accordance with the sentence of the courts of Virginia. Deplorable as are the causes which have led to the necessity of thus consigning to the scaffold one whose energy of character and high impulses might, if properly directed, have led to a career of usefulness, rather than of crime, all fair men must concede the exact justice of the fate which has overtaken him. The law must be vindicated, offended justice satisfied, and the majesty of government sustained. Brown has rendered himself amenable to the statutes of Virginia, by committing the highest crime known to her laws, and neither he nor his friends have a right to complain of his fate.

We regret the demonstrations on the part of the abolitionists in the Northern States on this occasion. At Concord, N. H., and other places, bells were yesterday tolled in honor of Brown; in Boston, citizens wearing crape paraded the streets, while in both houses of the legislature of Massachusetts strenuous efforts were made to adjourn for the day. This is natural conduct to expect from men who have derided the decisions of the supreme court, and attempted to nullify laws of the national legislature. But the consequences of the course of these men who, however, do not represent the feeling of the nation, may one day be apparent in the trampling down of law in their own communities, when those barriers erected by society for its own protection are overthrown, and men who have labored to bring law into contempt, find that there is no security for their own lives and property. Furthermore they may anticipate retaliatory acts from those parts of the country, against which their spite is directed — these again may be followed by acts still more vindictive from the opposite section — each in turn adding fuel to the fire. But after all, this is what many of them most desire. They do not appreciate the value of the institutions which they enjoy, and so would ruthlessly destroy them.

There is one other aspect of the case which deserves a remark. The extreme writers of the North have done their best to convert the wretched Brown into a hero, and to-day we shall hear a fresh wail over the pseudo-martyr and patriot. The calmness and courage with which he met his fate will give his eulogists fresh arguments, and we may expect whole pages of praise and lamentation. The clamor of the weak-minded and the unbalanced will not, however, affect the judgment of the country, nor the innate convictions of our people that the punishment was legal, and that he who has allied himself with murder and treason, those "two yoke-devils," dies justly. Nor can all the cheap sympathy of the Republican newspapers cover the criminal with the halo of moral heroism, or make anything of him except a foolish and one-sided fanatic, who fell a victim to his mental caprices and to a weakly indulged monomania. The morbid excitement which the press manufactures to order, will be short lived; the sympathy for those whom folly or crime has led to ignominious punishment is superficial and transitory. The law sometimes demands painful, almost cruel, sacrifices, but the American people will acquiesce in them rather than run the risk of destroying civil order and overthrowing the foundations of government. In the great calm which comes after the fitful fever of excitement and passion, they will recall to mind the duties which they owe to the state, and remember that there can be no rational compromise between public authority and individual license. As for Brown, we do not believe that he will occupy so large a space in the records of his country as his friends and admirers claim; those who put him to the greatest political use will be the first to forget him, and when the history of his times comes to be written, he will be merely the hero of a little, ill-advised, ill-matured and ludicrously hopeless conspiracy, which caused the nation some little trouble and a great deal of unnecessary excitement.

RADICALS, HOLD ON!

The untrained and awkward foot of radicalism has led so often into the paths of destruction, that it must be set down as a fragile and unreliable support for governments and nations. To be a thorough radical, as he usually develops himself, is to set up the individual will against the decrees of Providence as written in nature and life; to deny the accredited and well-authenticated traditions of history; to wage a fierce warfare against the settled foundations and principles upon which the wholesome structures of society are founded; and habitually to violate in spirit or action, the LAW, of which "no less can be acknowledged than that her seat is the bosom of God, and her voice the harmony of the world."

To stand up for those divine laws which govern the universe; for the orderly system which binds nations into brotherhood; and for those wholesome truths which all civilized races acknowledge in heart — these are the marks of a loyal man and the man of the right stamp. Let such a man have such a faith, and he will not wander far from the path of duty, or set himself up like Lucifer, against all the powers of the air. But, if he doubts everything but the immaculate accuracy of his own opinions, and selfishly sets up his own individuality, however refined and delicately cultivated, against all the powers and authorities of the law; if he finds nothing in history better than his own crude theories, and nothing in all the universes and all the systems of civilized nations which suits his arrogant fancy, — then he is a radical in heart, a thorough-paced, reckless radical, who would build up vain and unreliable theories upon the wrecks of all that is substantial and well established.

The present political crisis in the United States, which fills every true-hearted man with sorrow and apprehension, illustrates the preceding remarks. If the Union is to be trampled down, it will be the work of radical and destructive opinions, waging war against all the well settled principles upon which this republic was founded. Large portions of the people, North and South, have lifted up the standards of rebellion against the constitution of the United States, and destroyed, more or less completely, the fibre of union which unites different soils, climates and systems of labor. For the first time since the war upon moderate and conservative influences was commenced by the cohorts of radicalism, we notice that recent startling events have begun to reach the prevailing prejudices of many who presumed to set themselves up against the constitution. If the Union is to be saved, we must all come back to the broad, conserving and law-abiding platform on which our fathers established the republic.

SECESSION AND REVOLUTION.

At this crisis in the history of the republic, which, in the words of the weird sisters in Macbeth is "not lost but tempest-toss'd," certain questions in regard to the reciprocal duties of states to the federal government are worthy of being considered. The president says in his message, that "secession is neither more nor less than revolution;" and certainly there is no secession clause in the fundamental law of the United States, for such a contingency was not contemplated. Webster elaborated a most logical argument on this subject, contending that the Union is not a compact between the states, or their mere accession to the Union, which would imply, perhaps, the right of secession;—but that it is a confederation, founded upon the constitution, and duly ratified by all the states. He summed up the whole legal principle involved, when he declared that a seceding state "must show that she has a right to *reverse* what has been ordained, to *unsettle* and *overthrow* what has been *established*, to *reject* what has been *adopted*, and to *break up* what she has *ratified*." The constitution, thus ratified, had a voice and spoke authentically; created direct relations between the government and individuals, is not a contract, or compact, but a government proper, "a relation which no state can dissolve but by revolution." These opinions, sustained as they have been by all conservative statesmen, are fully confirmed by the president in the declaration that secession is revolution.

The corollary which follows this proposition of the president, namely, that secession "may or may not be a justifiable revolution, but still it is a revolution," is equally demonstrable. Our own government was founded on a revolution, which, had it failed, would have been judged and pronounced to be a rebellion.

According to public law and the agreement of nations, a country, or a province, which can permanently protect and defend itself against oppression, or the interference of enemies from within or without, is recognized as an independent power.

As members of the common republic, we must admit that any state has an abstract and natural right to attempt revolution under certain provocations and oppressions. If she succeeds, she becomes sovereign over herself, and receives back those rights which she had surrendered; but if she fails to conquer by military prowess, she is, according to the law of nations, a rebel and a traitor. But between attempted secession (which the president truly confesses the machinery of the federal government can not overcome without further legislation) and open revolution leading on to bloodshed and civil war, there runs a wide and broad path, through which South Carolina and her seceding sisters may pass out of the Union in order and peace. The Union can not be made a unit, or the constitution made inviolate, by force; the whole naval and military power of the federal government could not preserve permanent peace in a State revolting with the intelligent consent and spirited support of a genuine majority. She can depart, however, with calmness and dignity, by going back to the fundamental law, and having its decrees, once deemed irrevocable, so modified by some judicious amendments as to recover her original sovereignty without staining her fame, or reflecting dishonor upon the mother of the states. Should the great crash come, this is the only wise and prudent path to pursue.

We have thus briefly expressed our views on this subject, but not without a thrill at the heart, and sad forebodings for the future. What a painful thought it is, that the Union may be broken and dissolved even by a peaceful and constitutional process! But still greater trials and sharper calamity may come upon this confederacy like a thunderbolt. To borrow and adapt Macaulay's figure of national destruction, we may live long enough to stand musing and philosophizing over the disintegrated republic and the broken columns of the Capitol; wondering, above all, how such a gallant and loyal nation, impelled during a few years towards more than the highest glories ever attained by political organizations, should thus be struck to the heart before youth has passed to maturity.

SNEAKING NULLIFICATION.

Some of the *progressive* republicans of the legislature are endeavoring to put the state of New York in the precise condition of a man tugging at the waistband of his breeches for the purpose of lifting himself into the air. They are making themselves very busy in passing acts which can have no validity; which on their face are in direct conflict with the constitution and laws of the United States, and which, even if promulgated under the broad seal of the state, and vouched for by the signatures of the governor and the secretary of state, will have no more authority or weight with the magistrates, courts or people than so much white paper fresh from the mill.

There is something so puerile and absurd in the enacting of dead letter laws, not worth the paper on which they are written, something so ludicrous in the attempt to do what is legally and logically impossible, that it requires an effort to treat the subject seriously. Every one knows that the personal liberty act, pending in the state senate, requiring in substance, an arrested fugitive slave to be liberated, when it appears he is held to servitude in another state, will have no influence upon a conscientious and upright officer or judge; that no decent advocate would dare to rely upon such a transparently void enactment; and that it would be kicked out of any decent federal or state court as a piece of impertinence. Every one knows that if the legislature should pass, as is proposed, an act granting fugitives from labor in sister states a jury trial, when the laws of the United States require such cases to be exclusively determined by United States officers, no honest judge could be found to empanel such a jury, or no honest jury to sit in a case over which they would have no jurisdiction; or that if treasonable judges and juries could be found, their action in the premises would be absolutely illegal and void. Every one knows that the correct principles which govern these cases have been settled by the national legislature, assented to by the North and the South, ratified by an immense majority of the people, and affirmed and definitely settled by the authoritative voice of the supreme court of the United States. In the face of these conspicuous facts, the sham lawmakers and political dodgers at Albany, attempt to enact a nullity, to pass a void law, to override an act of congress by a state statute, and to put the state of New York in a hostile attitude towards the federal government. It is barely possible that legislators enough will be found to place the state in this surly, unmanly and undignified position — the position of a barking dog who can't bite — but we are inclined to believe that the attempt, like the bills themselves, is a miserable sham, got up for the purpose of tickling the radical abolitionists, and gaining a little favor with the Garrisonians, Gerrit Smiths and Fred Douglasses, who openly oppose the laws of the Union and the Union itself. When the matter comes to a test vote we shall see if these fast republicans are really willing to humiliate and belittle the empire state by the passage of nullification laws as sneaking in spirit as they are practically impotent of accomplishing mischief.

DEATH OF LEIGH HUNT.

The steamer Anglo Saxon brings out intelligence of the death of James Henry Leigh Hunt, who died at London on the 20th of August. He was born in Middlesex, in October, 1784, and was partly American in descent, Stephen Shewell, of Philadelphia, being his maternal grandfather. His mother's aunt was the wife of Benjamin West, the celebrated American painter; his father was a West Indian, and the son passed his early youth in the West Indies, and at one time, we believe, resided in Philadelphia.

Young Hunt commenced his literary career at a very early age, being only eighteen when, in connection with his brother John, he issued the first number of *The Examiner* which soon acquired great popularity. It was in this newspaper that he applied to the prince regent the witty epithet of "Adonis of fifty," for which offence the two brothers paid a fine of some $4,000, and were imprisoned for two years. His experiences in Horsemonger jail are related with much humor and pathos in his autobiography, published in 1850; and on the occasion of his imprisonment he certainly showed a great deal of pluck, as the government offered to remit the penalties if he would promise to make no similar attacks in future. He founded and edited at various times *The Reflector*, *The Tattler*, and *The London Journal*, and contributed also to the *Edinburgh* and *Westminster Reviews*. The *Story of Rimini*, his *Autobiography*, *Men, Women and Books*, *Stories from the Italian Poets*, and his shorter poems, including his famous *Abou Ben Adhem*, are the best known of his works in this country; but he was a very voluminous writer, and his contributions to the press during the past fifty years would fill a good sized library.

Hunt was a contemporary of the great modern *litterateurs* of Great Britain, and formed one of the few surviving links which connect us with the literary world of Scott, Byron, Wordsworth, Shelley, Rogers, Coleridge, Keats, and Southey; for, although in genius he equaled none of these, he yet belonged to their epoch and was to a certain extent associated with them. With De Quincey, now almost the sole survivor, he formed one of that illustrious galaxy of bright names which made the early part of this century so illustrious in literature. He was at one time an intimate friend of Byron, Shelley and Hazlitt, with whom, as coadjutors, he established *The Liberal* in 1822, a short-lived periodical, of which only a few numbers were published. During the same year, he visited Italy with Lord Byron, and occupied the same house with him; but the friendship soon cooled from incompatibility of temper, and Hunt took revenge of his noble friend in a mean and malicious book called *Byron and his Contemporaries*, but which is now almost entirely out of print.

Leigh Hunt, although he can not be classed in the very highest rank of modern literature, leaves behind a name which will always be dear to the hearts of lovers of "books which are books." The expression of Charles Lamb reminds us of a kind of inexpressible resemblance between the prose writings of the two men; both possessed a lively fancy, an easy, almost colloquial style, and a wonderful power of word-painting; their essays are among the most genial and graceful contributions to modern literature; although Hunt's coldness of temperament and occasional exhibitions of selfishness are in strong contrast with Lamb's tenderness of heart and infinite sympathies with humanity. The best poems of Hunt, like Rimini, are graceful and highly finished, reminding one of Keats in their general style and rhythmical flow; but he lacked the genuineness of feeling and the poetic inspiration which made his younger contemporary so dear to the popular heart.

Mr. Hunt has been described as a delightful companion, retaining to old age all the vigor and vivacity of youth; no one could listen to his conversation without delight. His religious belief was somewhat peculiar, and he might safely be classed among the leaders of the *broad church.* For many years he has enjoyed a pension from the government, and his son is now the editor of one of the leading literary periodicals in London.

DEATH OF DE QUINCEY.

On the eighth of December, Thomas De Quincey died at Edinburgh, near which city he has resided for the past sixteen years. For nearly fifty years he has been more or less of an invalid, and when lately his health was seriously affected, no especial alarm was excited, and his death was in a manner unexpected. That with his frail and delicate constitution, racked and torn by the most acute mental sufferings and agitations which the human mind ever underwent without losing its sanity, he should have lived to the ripe old age of seventy-three years, is a remarkable fact; but it is stranger still that his intellect retained to the last its vigor and acuteness, and that the spirit which animated his diminutive and shriveled body, shone on his dying bed with the lustre and brilliancy of youth.

In the twenty or more volumes which De Quincey has left behind him, ample materials are furnished for an accurate picture of his strange and interesting life. Able to read Greek at the age of six, and to harangue an Athenian mob at fourteen, we find him at the latter age in an open quarrel with his guardian, a runaway from school, a proud but poverty-stricken wanderer in the streets of London, receiving his crusts from protectors almost as wretched as himself. This exposure and starvation laid the foundation of acute diseases, for the relief of which he resorted to opium. He acquired this habit when he was about eighteen, and it was continued with greater or less excess until 1820, when he was about thirty-four, at which time his celebrated *Confessions* appeared. In the meantime, he had been reconciled to his friends, taken his degree at Oxford, and acquired a thorough and massive education. In 1819, by way of amusing his tortured brain, he took up the study of political economy, and three years after published an essay on the system of Ricardo, which is regarded as the greatest and most profound treatise on *value* which was ever published. Since this time he has been an incessant writer for the British periodicals, his essays embracing every variety of subject in philosophical criticism, history, biography and metaphysics. He wrote only at certain intervals, and with the utmost rapidity, throwing the blurred manuscripts hastily over his shoulder upon the floor, whence they were picked up by his daughters and sold to the periodicals. Of late years handsome editions of his works have appeared both in Great Britain and in the United States, and have been extensively sold and read.

The striking feature of De Quincey's mind was its logical force and subtle power of analysis. Upon this basis was a superstructure of solid, accurate and comprehensive learning; while above all, rose his brilliant and impassioned imagination, stretching upwards towards immeasurable space. In his splendid dreams he never forgot his logic; and his most profound essays are lightened by a playful and discursive fancy, and warmed by a gentle and delicate humor. His style was rich, vivid, elastic, and a model of pure and undefiled English. In such sketches as *The Vision of Sudden Death*, he shows a dramatic power of the highest order; his *Knocking in Macbeth* is an analytical criticism which proves how thoroughly he understood the great dramas of the human soul. His sensibilities were exquisite and impressible; and his inner life embraced the wildest and most wonderful experiences. Many like him in opium dreams, have soared among the stars and had celestial visions; but no one else has had the art to describe and paint, in immortal colors, these gorgeous flights of the imagination, and that awful after plunge into the lowest abyss of misery and despair. So far as we can judge from his works, De Quincey's moral nature was not perverted by the evil habit which sapped so much of his happiness; he wrote like a christian as well as a scholar, and was loyal to the faith which is the ground and pillar of the truth. He was the first man in Europe to appreciate Wordsworth, a fact which speaks volumes for the purity and moral elevation of his tastes.

DEATH OF JAMES MONTGOMERY, 1854.

One by one the grave is closing over the poets and men of letters of the last generation. But a few months have elapsed since we recorded the deaths of

William Wordsworth, Thomas Moore and Thomas Campbell, and to-day we have to announce the death of James Montgomery, their contemporary, and the competitor of Crabbe, Byron, Southey, Coleridge, and of Rogers. Of all those celebrated men, the last named is the only survivor.

Montgomery, as we gather from the notes and preface of the last edition of his works, was born in Irvine, Scotland, on the fourth of November, 1771. His father was a Moravian minister, who, leaving his son in Yorkshire, went to the West Indies, where he and the poet's mother died. At the request of his parents, who desired to educate him for the ministry, he remained for ten years in one of the seminaries of their church. At the end of that time, he became dissatisfied with the ministerial profession, and was placed with a shop keeper in Yorkshire. One day, however, he set off for London with a dollar in his pocket, and a manuscript volume of his poems, which he vainly endeavored to sell to the publishers.

For five years, this young poet struggled on, without friends, an orphan, and penniless, until 1792 he was engaged as an assistant editor of the *Sheffield Register*, a weekly gazette, published by a Mr. Galles; and two years afterwards, his employer having fled from England to avoid a prosecution threatened by the government, he became editor in chief, as well as proprietor, and changed the name of his journal to *The Iris*, which he conducted with much literary taste and ability. He advocated the claims of religious and political freedom so boldly as to secure the attention of the attorney

8

general, by whom he was prosecuted, fined twenty pounds and imprisoned for three months in York Castle. This seems to have had no effect upon the ardor of the young poet, for almost immediately on his release, he was again imprisoned for an offensive passage in an account which he gave of a riot in Sheffield.

He continued *The Iris* until 1825, a period of thirty-two years, having in the mean time published many of his most celebrated poems, and established his rank as a poet. Among these poems are his *Prison Amusements*, written during his second confinement in York Castle, *The Ocean* in 1805, *The Wanderer in Switzerland* in 1806, *The West Indies* in 1809, and the *World before the Flood* in 1812; *Greenland* appeared in 1819, and the *Pelican Island* in 1828.

On his retirement from the editorial profession in 1825, his friends gave him a public dinner in Sheffield, at which Lord Milton presided. In reply to a sentiment complimentary to the integrity and ability with which he had conducted *The Iris*, the poet made a brief speech, in which he reviewed his literary career. "Success upon success," he said, "crowned my labors—not indeed with fame and fortune, as these were lavished on my greater contemporaries, in comparison with whose magnificent possessions on the British Parnassus, my small plot of ground is no more than Naboth's vineyard to Ahab's kingdom; but it is my own, it is no copyhold; I borrowed it, I leased it, from none. I attribute this to no extraordinary power of genius, or felicity of talent in the application of such power as I may possess. The secret of my moderate success I consider to have been the right direction of my abilities to right objects." * * * "I appealed to universal principles, to imperishable affections, to primary elements of our common nature, found wherever man is found in civilized society; wherever his mind has been raised above barbarian ignorance, or his passions purified from brutal selfishness. I sang, likewise, the love of home; its charities, endearments and relationship; all that makes 'home *sweet* home.' I sang the love which man ought to bear towards his brother, of every kindred, and country and clime upon earth. I sang the love of virtue, which elevates man to his true standard under heaven; I sang, too, the love of God, who *is* love. Nor did I sing in vain."

During the latter part of his life, Montgomery lived at The Mount, Sheffield, where he died on the 30th of April, 1854, in the 84th year of his age. He enjoyed a well deserved pension of £200 a year.

In estimating, critically, the poetical powers of Mr. Montgomery we can give him credit neither for dramatic power nor for those electric inspirations of genius which glowed in the pages of Keats and Shelley, and Byron and Scott, his great contemporaries. His longer pieces are full of grace, but devoid of plot and meager in incident. It is in his little songs and ballads and religious hymns, so full of simplicity, earnestness and unaffected piety, that he rises to the dignity of a lyric poet, and becomes a compeer with Wordsworth and Cowper. In the language of the *Westminster Review*, we can say with truth that "there is something in all his poetry which makes fiction the most impressive teacher of truth and wisdom, and by which while the intellect is gratified, and the imagination roused, the heart, if it retains any sensibility to tender or elevating emotions, can not fail to be made better. Montgomery was a religious enthusiast, a pious, unaffected gentleman, in the best sense of the term, and a poet of the heart.

Among his miscellaneous poems, none is more admired, nor better known to the public, than the little lyric called *The Grave*, and the closing verses may be appropriately quoted as his own requiem:

> There is a calm for those who weep,
> A rest for weary pilgrims found;
> And while the mouldering ashes sleep,
> Low in the ground,
>
> The Soul of origin divine,
> God's glorious image, freed from clay,
> In Heaven's eternal sphere shall shine,
> A Star of day.
>
> The SUN is but a spark of fire,
> A transient meteor in the sky,
> The SOUL immortal as its sire,
> SHALL NEVER DIE.

WAIFS AND STRAYS.

Who thinks of Curran but as the pet of the populace and the favorite barrister of Ireland. We imagine a very little man with a comical face and a more comical coat; a homely little Bacchus, full of good humored wit and innocent satire, the glory of the dinner table and the pride of good livers. No brilliant man was ever so loved; whoever stepped within the magical circle of his influence was irresistibly attracted to him. He touched the chords of the heart as magically as he did his violin; you wondered, you admired, you were charmed; his wit delighted, his eloquence fascinated you. Yet the most envious felt no envy, and the self-love of the proudest was not offended. He was so simple and unaffected that his best efforts excited no ill will, and, it is said, that in conversation the quiet grace of his manner was so sympathetic, that though you felt your inferiority, it was quite a contented one.

A good for nothing schoolboy,—the glory and shame of his college,—an occasional scribbler in the magazines of the day,—Curran's progress in early life was slow, and gave little promise of eminence. But the first great effort he made gave him both confidence and reputation. He rose rapidly in his profession and was soon at the head of the Irish bar and a member of parliament. No man could be better adapted to become a successful advocate than Curran. His eloquence was electric and carried the jury by storm—he was fluent, polished, acute and persuasive, and there was a charm in his manner, and a sympathetic cadence in his voice, which no one could withstand. At a cross-examination he was unrivaled; no falsehood was so ingeniously fabricated that he did not find it out and expose it; there was no web which he could not unravel, no subtlety or stratagem, which could escape him.

Curran's speeches were seldom reported, and his best efforts are preserved by tradition, not by books. His *bon mots* have passed down to us by "word of mouth;"

and these repartees have done more to make him generally popular than his most elaborate professional exertions. He was a bold, independent fellow, and when unjustly attacked, his invective was severe, and his ridicule irresistible.

When a young man, he was engaged in an argument before a Judge Robinson, a dignitary who had risen to position by no very honorable means. In controverting some position of his legal opponent in an argument before this fellow, Curran remarked that he had searched all his law books, but could find no such principle laid down as the one contended for by the opposing counsel, when Robinson suggested that "perhaps his law library was rather contracted." Such a speech from the court would have crushed almost any young man, but Curran's spirit rather rose than fell under the brutal assault, and he turned upon the judge with a stinging rejoinder.

"It is very true, my lord," said he, after a moment of contemptuous silence, "that I am poor, and the circumstance has certainly rather curtailed my library; my books are not numerous, but they are select, and I hope have been perused with proper dispositions. I have prepared myself for this high profession rather by the perusal of a few good books, than *by the composition of a great many bad ones.* I am not ashamed of my poverty, but I should be of my wealth, could I stoop to acquire it by servility and corruption. If I rise not to rank, I shall at least be honest; and should I ever cease to be so, many an example teaches me that an ill-acquired elevation, by making me the more conspicuous, would only make me the more notoriously and the more universally contemptible."

The memory of Curran lives in a few anecdotes like this, the only records we have of his eloquence, his wit, and his readiness at repartee.

"My lard—my lard,"—vociferated a peasant witness, writhing under the mental excruciation of one of Curran's cross-examinations—"My lard—my lard—I can't answer yon little gentleman, he is putting me in such a *doldrum!*"

"A doldrum! Mr. Curran, what does he mean by a doldrum?" exclaimed Lord Avonmore, the presiding judge.

"Oh, my lord," said Curran, "it's a very common complaint with persons of this description — it's merely a confusion of the head arising from a corruption of the heart!"

One day, when it was known that Curran was to make an elaborate argument in chancery, Lord Clare brought a large Newfoundland dog upon the bench with him, and during the progress of the argument he lent his ear much more to the dog than to the barrister. This was observed by every one in court, and the chancellor so far lost all regard to decency, as to turn himself quite aside in the most material part of the argument and to fondle the animal. Curran stopped at once.

"Go on, go on, Mr. Curran," said Clare, in his most coxcombish manner.

"Oh! I beg a thousand pardons, my lord — I really took it for granted that your lordship was engaged in consultation."

Lord Avonmore, chief baron of the exchequer, was

an old and intimate friend of Curran and a brother member with him of a convivial society, called the Monks of the Screw. Flood, Grattan, Lord Charlemont, and a whole host of the distinguished men of the bench and bar of Great Britain were members of this club of which Curran was grand prior. We will not fatigue our readers with an account of the many good things said and done by these holy monks, for they are immaterial to the story. Some unfortunate difference of opinion had interrupted the frendship of Lord Avonmore and Mr. Curran — a friendship which had commenced with their infancy and which had grown with their growth. The cause of their reconciliation was honorable to both, and grew out of a reference made by Curran in the argument of the great case of The King versus Mr. Justice Johnson, before Avonmore, to the memorable meetings of these Monks of the Screw. After alluding to a previous decision in the king's bench against his client, he turned to Lord Avonmore, with whom he was not then on speaking terms, and pathetically said:

"I am not ignorant, my lords, that this extraordinary construction has received the sanction of another court, nor of the surprise and dismay with which it smote upon the general heart of the bar. I am aware that I may have the mortification of being told in another country of that unhappy decision, and I foresee in what confusion I shall hang down my head when I am told of it. But I cherish too, the consolatory hope that I shall be able to tell them that I had an old and learned friend, whom I would put above the sweepings of their hall, who was of a different opinion; who had derived his ideas of civil liberty from the purest fountains of Athens and of Rome — who had fed the youthful vigor of his studious mind with the theoretic knowledge of their wisest philosophers and statesmen; and who had refined that theory into the quick and exquisite sensibility of moral instinct, by contemplating the practice of their most illustrious examples — by dwelling on the sweet-souled piety of Cimon, on the anticipated Christianity of Socrates, on the gallant and pathetic patriotism of Epaminondas, on that pure austerity of Fabricius, whom to have moved from his integrity would have been more difficult than to have pushed the sun from his course. I would add, that if he had seemed to hesitate, it was but for a moment; that his hesitation was like the passing cloud that floats across the morning sun, and hides it from the view, and does so for a moment hide it by involving the spectator without ever approaching the face of the luminary; and this soothing hope I draw from the dearest and tenderest recollections of my life, from the remembrance of those attic nights and those refections of the gods which we have spent with admired and respected and beloved companions — over whose ashes the most precious tears of Ireland have been shed. Yes, my good lord, I see you do not forget them — (Lord Avonmore was in tears.) I see their sacred forms passing in sad review before your memory. I see your pained and softened fancy, recalling those happy meetings when the innocent enjoyment of social mirth expanded into the noble warmth of social virtue, and the horizon of the board became enlarged into the horizon of man; when the swelling heart conceived and communicated the pure and generous purpose—when my slender and younger taper imbibed its borrowed light from the more matured and redundant fountain of yours. Yes, my lord, we can remember those nights with no other regret than that they can return no more, for

"We spent them not in toys, or lust, or wine,
But search of deep philosophy,
Wit, eloquence and poesy—
Arts which I loved; for they, my friend, were thine."

But, my lords, to return to a subject, from which thus far to have departed, I think may not be wholly without excuse."

"He then"—Mr. Phillips, the eloquent narrator says—"proceeded to reconsider the legal argument, in the midst of which this most beautiful episode bloomed like a green spot in the desert."

Of course this was an end of the difference between Curran and Lord Avonmore, who sent for him immediately after the adjournment of the court, and clasped him to his bosom, his eyes still wet with the tears extorted by the pathetic appeal of his friend and brother monk.

Curran died in the autumn of 1818, a wreck only of his former greatness. His mind was manifestly gone sometime previous to his death, which was mourned by Ireland as a public loss, and by his friends as a personal calamity. His country's history will ever have a page for the services of her favorite orator, and his epitaph will be found in the hearts of all true Irishmen.

SHYLOCK VS. ANTONIO—OPINION OF THE VICAR.*

The vicar desires briefly, modestly, and by way of suggestion, rather as amicus curiæ than as an advocate, to lay before his learned brethren of the law a legal point or two, for their consideration.

The case to which I refer is well known to all the members of the bar as that of Shylock vs. Antonio, reported in full in 2 Shakspeare, 299. The decision which I am desirous of having reviewed is that of the chief justice, or ducal magistrate, who heard that curious case, and who yielded to the extraordinary arguments of the young woman, Portia. The judgment rendered and the argument or decision of the lady advocate, on that occasion, have been regarded as models of judicial acumen, have received the approbation of many worthy and enlightened students, and, when theatrically represented, have been greeted with the plaudits of nearly every theater. It may be arrogant to impugn a judicial decision of such antiquity and acknowledged authority; but, as a member in full standing of the worshipful P. B., I have the right to be slightly arrogant; for I am well aware that this is a

*The article which we publish from the *Continental* for May, was one of the last productions of the late CARLTON EDWARDS of this city. It should be stated by way of explanation of some personal allusions, that it was written and read before a literary club, of which Judge Whiting of New York was president.

tribunal the circumference of whose jurisdiction is infinite, or rather, is a circle whose center is a little village on the Hudson river, where I reside.

No false modesty shall restrain me, therefore, from discussing this case upon its merits. Before entering upon it, however, I desire to call your attention to a few preliminary points. In the first place, I ask you — who are all familiar with the record — if an undue sympathy for the defendant, Antonio, was not felt on the trial? The favor and good wishes of the court, the spectators, and of the reporter, were evidently enlisted for him as against his opponent. This Antonio, perhaps, was a very worthy fellow in his way; and in a criminal action — as on an indictment for murdering a family or two, or slaughtering a policeman — might have been able to prove previous good character. But such a plea, in a civil action for *debt*, is entitled to no weight; while the fact that he was a good fellow in a series of scrapes, not the least of which was matrimony, does not entitle him to our sympathy. The prejudices of the court ought to have been against instead of for him. He had failed in business, could not pay his outstanding liabilities, and thus stood before the commercial world in the position of bankruptcy. The fact that he had made a foolish contract, which imperiled his life, does not improve his moral condition, or entitle him to any just sympathy, unless it could be shown that there was insanity in his family. No such plea was entered. His counsel did not attempt to prove that his great-grandfather owned a mad dog; a plea from which the court, fortified by many modern criminal decisions, might have inferred his moral insanity. No such attempt to relieve Antonio from the consequences of his criminal folly was made, and I can see nothing in the case to entitle him to the sympathy which was and had been always entertained for him.

Again: The lengthy and much admired plea of the defendant's counsel on the subject of mercy was clearly out of place, especially if, as I have endeavored to show, the defendant was not entitled to any particular clemency or sympathy. The remarks of Portia, commencing,

The quality of mercy is not strained,

(and by the way, who but a woman would talk of straining an emotion as one strains milk) are wholly irrelevant to the issue, and ought not to have been allowed. They were eloquent, indeed, but had nothing whatever to do with the trial, which arose, on a very plain case at law: A owed B three thousand ducats, due and not paid on an ascertained day. Whereupon B moves the court for the penalty, and demands judgment. If the defendant had no answer at law, there is an end to the case; and it was very irregular, impertinent, and contrary to well-settled practice, for the defendant's counsel to endeavor to lead off the mind of the court from the true issue of the case. Portia, in what she says of mercy being "twice blessed" and "dropping like the gentle rain from heaven," &c., &c., was, I fear, "talking Buncombe," and all that part of her speech should be stricken from the record, especially as it was addressed to the plaintiff instead of the court, a highly indecorous proceeding. Instead of indulging in all this sentimentality, her true course would have been to have filed a bill in equity against Shylock, and have obtained an injunction on an *ex parte* affidavit, which only requires a little strong swearing; or to have patched up a suit against him for obtaining his knife under false pretences; than which (under the New York *Code of Procedure*) nothing can be easier. But what better conduct of a suit can you expect from a she-advocate — an attorney-in-petticoats?

And this brings me to another point of some delicacy, and which nothing but a very conscientious devotion to abstract justice would induce me to touch upon. What law, or what precedent, can be cited to authorize a woman to appear as an advocate in a court of justice and usurp the offices and prerogatives of a man? I will not dwell upon the impropriety of such conduct; but on my honor, as a member of the bar, the behavior of Portia was outrageous. This young female, not content with *cavorting* around the country in a loose and perspicuous style, actually practices a gross swindle on the court. She assumes to be a man when she is only a woman, dons the breeches when she is only entitled to the skirts, and imposes herself upon the Duke of Venice as a learned young advocate from Rome, when in fact she is only a young damsel of Belmont, with half a dozen lovers on her hand, on her own showing. And yet this young baggage, whose own father would not trust her to choose a husband, whose brains are addled by her own love affairs, and who had no more business in court than the deacon would have in Chancellor Whiting's suit in the Lowber claim, not only came into court under a fraudulent disguise, argued the case under false pretences, but actually took the words from the judge's own mouth, and decided her case on her own responsibility. I venture to say that such unparalleled impudence was never witnessed out of the court of a justice of the peace, and that even judge —— (unless the editor of the —— had interfered) would have marched this false pretender out of court, or have deposited her in the Tombs on an attachment of contempt.

But these preliminary points appear of small amount when we come to consider the plea, if it be worthy of that name, which the counsel for the defendant opposed to the suit of the plaintiff. The bond is admitted, the penalty is confessed, the pound of flesh is forfeited, the bosom of Antonio is bared to the knife — when this brief but briefless barrister, this skylarking young judge of Belmont, steps jauntily forward with a most preposterous quibble on her lips, and manages by an adroit subtlety to defeat the judgment to which the plaintiff is legally entitled. She awards the flesh, fibers, nerves, adipose matter, in controversy, to Shylock; but declares his life and fortune confiscated if he sheds a drop of blood, or takes more or less than the exact pound.

Now if there be one principle of law better settled than another (and probably it was as clearly set forth in the *Revised Statutes* of Venice as it is set forth in our own common law) it is that a party entitled to the possession of a commodity, whether grain, guano, dead or live men's flesh, bones and sinews, is entitled, also, to pursue the usual necessary and appropriate means of obtaining the possession of the same. I appeal to Colonel W——— if this be not good law, and asking whether, if he be entitled to a dinner, he has not a right to seize upon it, whenever or however he can find it; whether, if a man owes him a bottle of champagne, he has not the right to break the neck of the bottle if a corkscrew is not convenient? So, to use a drier example, the sale of standing timber entitles the purchaser to enter the land upon which it is situated, and to cut down and carry off his own property. On the same principle if A sells B a house and lot, entirely surrounded by other land owned by A, B has clearly a right of way to his own wife and fireside over A's land. (2 *Blackstone*, 1149.) A hundred examples might be given in point, but it would be insulting the dignity of this court to argue at length a theory so transparently clear. If the shedding of a few drops of blood, more or less, was incidental and necessary to the rights of the plaintiff, if the article of personal property, forfeited to him on the bond, could be obtained in no other way, then according to all the principles of law and common sense, he had a right to spill those drops more or less; and that, too, without legal risk.

If the penalty was legal and that were admitted, the method of exacting it was legal also. Portia's quibble was so transparent and barefaced that the decision of the court can only be explained on the theory that the court was drunk, or in love, which seems to have been the condition of several of the prominent parties in this proceeding, excepting always the plaintiff. As to the other part of Portia's plea, it is doubtless true that the plaintiff would take more of the commodity involved in the suit than the court awarded him at the peril; but as half a pound, or a quarter of a pound, cut off from the right spot would have answered his purpose, I do not see under what principle of law he was defrauded of that satisfaction. There was nothing to have prevented him from cutting less than a pound from Antonio's body, and of so releasing him, the defendant, from a portion of the penalty; and the court should have instructed the plaintiff as to his rights in this particular, instead of adopting a quibble worthy of only a Tombs lawyer or a third rate pettifogger

I can not then believe that Mr. Reporter Shakespeare, in handing down to posterity the record of this remarkable case, meant to express an approval of Portia's subterfuge. My inference rather is that he was aiming a covert sarcasm at those women who thrust themselves conspicuously upon the notice of the public, and that he meant to hint that those who unsex themselves, often make a showy appearance without displaying much solid merit. If this subtle, sharp, and strong-minded female, did not turn out to be something of a shrew, before her husband was done with her, I am much mistaken. Possibly, however, Shakespeare's sarcasm might bear a more general interpretation, and implies that women in an argument seldom meet the true issue presented to them, but are prone to go off at a tangent on some side quibble, and to repel the arguments of their antagonists by the subtlety of their inventions rather than by the cogency of their logic. I appeal to my friend, the sage of Cattaraugus, who has a large knowledge of the customs of the sex, if this be not the usual result.

Not to cut the reply of the deacon too short, I go on to remark that whether he agrees with me or not, neither he nor any other well-balanced man would have descended, on the trial of so important a case as the one we are discussing, to a trivial playing upon words. Even my friend, the district attorney, than whom no man is more remorselessly given — in private life — to the depraved habit of quibbling, and who never hesitates to impale truth upon the point of a verbal criticism, would by the temptation of a fee commensurate with the vigor of the moral effort required, have discussed the question on broader and truer principles. Had he been retained on the part of Antonio, he would have proved himself equal to the occasion, and have unfolded a logical and consistent answer to the claim of the plaintiff.

He would have boldly attacked the bond itself as absolutely void in its conception, because it was aimed at the life of a citizen of Venice, and would have called upon the court to abrogate a contract which violated the very laws that the court was bound to administer. With his usual eloquence, he would have urged that a penalty so illegal, immoral, and monstrous, and which involved the commission of the highest crime, except treason, known to the laws of the state, could never be enforced in a civilized country. He would have offered to the court no woman's quibble like that of Portia, based upon the assumption that the penalty of a bond which sanctioned a high and capital crime could be enforced in a court of law; and in fine, would have addressed an argument to the reason and understanding of the court which might render a consideration of this case by the tribunal unnecessary.

But no good plea to the plaintiff's cause of action was made on the trial, and the court was, and I fear that the whole world has been deceived by Portia's subterfuge. We must, therefore, regard Shylock as a badly used man. After all, he was no worse than many creditors and note shavers of this day, who only demand the life blood of their victims; and if on the pleas before the court he was entitled to judgment, like them he should have had it. Doubtless in private life Shylock was a very honest and well-behaved gentleman, not a mere mountebank as he is sometimes represented on the stage, but a vigorous and energetic man of the world, shrewd, sagacious, and long-sighted in business, honored on 'change, respected by his friends, and a pattern of prudence and morality. And then, perhaps, he was only carrying on a joke, a kind of *Jew d'esprit*, conceived in a moment of amiable eccentricity, and never to be executed. If not a joke, however, the judgment of Judge Portia should be set aside, and a new trial with costs, should, in my opinion, have been ordered.

HAMLET A FAT MAN.

I have seen on the stage several Hamlets, more or less successful in that sublime dramatic creation of Shakespeare, to say nothing of small-calfed personifications at private fancy balls. Young Booth, in these days, is doubtless the most ideal and accurate interpreter of the great Dane; although Mrs. Kemble's rendition is certainly beyond the reach of hostile criticism.

In this paper I propose to consider Hamlet not as he is represented on the stage, but as he is described in the original text. At the theater, he usually appears as a dark-complexioned, black-haired, beetle-browed, and slender young man, wearing an intensely gloomy wig, eyebrows corked into the blackness of preternatural bitterness, while on thin and romantic legs, imprisoned in black silk tights, he struts across the stage, the counterfeit presentment of the veritable prince.

I once read a brief line or two in a work by Goethe, alleging that Hamlet was a fat man. At first I was inclined to regard this as a joke of the majestic German. Later reflection induced me to examine this surmise in detail, and to conclude finally that the theory is true, and that the enigma of Hamlet's character can be solved through calculations of pinguitude.

Εὕρηκα. Perfect tense, indicative mood, I have found it. In fact, the whole Hamlet problem must be regarded in an obese, or adipose point of view. The Prince of Denmark is not the conventional Hamlet of the theater, nor the Hamlet of Shakespeare. He was a Northman, and like the greater number of the inhabitants of Northern Europe, was, doubtless, a blue-eyed and flaxen-haired blonde. My lord was far from appearing thin or delicate; on the contrary, he carried on his belly a large portmanteau well-rounded by the swell of the digesting nutriment.

That our honored prince was a fat man, is proved by his own confession, as well as by the evidence of the queen. Tossed about in a hot desert of doubt and despair, he exclaims in one of his incomparable soliloquies:

> "*Oh! that this too, too solid flesh* WOULD MELT."

What thin man would melt away even in the hot solstice of June? In the fencing scene (Act iv), his flabby muscles are soon fatigued, and the queen exclaims:

> "*He's fat, and scant of breath:*
> *Here, Hamlet, take my napkin, rub thy brows.*"

However, to be serious, it must be confessed that there are splendid traits in the character of the prince; every grandeur or folly can be found in him. From the lowest pit of despair, his soul debates the question of suicide as a logical proposition, forgetting the divine prohibition against self-slaughter. Eloquence, genius, and brilliant fancies, are constantly manifested, and also a gorgeous imagination.

It may be mentioned, incidentally, that Hamlet's character has been contrasted with that of Orestes, the Greek, who, when he arrived at years of manhood, avenged his father's death by assassinating his mother, Clytemnestra, and her adulterer, Œgisthus. In other words, he avenged a crime by a crime.

And now let us drop these serious comments, and return to the more humorous side of our theory — the plumpness of the prince, overlooked as a mere accident, by critics and actors. It is a physiological propriety that he should be of a phlegmatic temperament — a temperament often united to an acute intellect, but also, to a sluggish and heavy person. A weak, wavering inactivity, fickleness of purpose, a keen sensibility, or sensitiveness, are also noticeable; while the subtlety of his theories is sharply penetrating, and forms the keystone to the arch of his character.

Truly, Hamlet's intellect is that of a giant; his strength of will, that of a child. He has, so to speak, no executive talent. He is the doubting philosopher, the subtle metaphysician, the self-analyzer, always 'thinking too precisely upon the event.' He sees so far into the consequences of human action that he is fearful of taking decided steps. He has the nerve to kill neither his uncle nor himself, although he debates the latter question with great dexterity. He never *effected* any one of the plans upon which he had deliberated. Any one who reads *Hamlet*, under the influence of this theory, will see that it is confirmed by every incident in the tragedy.

A series of accidents hurried the prince to the final catastrophe. His was a lovely, great and noble nature; but it lacked one element of heroism — strength of will. It was an exquisite touch in the mighty poet to make Hamlet gross in figure, as he was phlegmatic, inactive, and irresolute in temperament. Had he been a thin, brown, choleric, and nervous man, the tragedy would have ended in the first act. Had he been a fiery Italian, instead of a doubting, deliberating Dane; had he been of a passionate, or yellow complexion, instead of a calm blonde; had he possessed a wiry, high-strung, and nervous constitution; had he, in a word, proved himself a man of action, and not a man of metaphysical tendencies, his sword would have soon cut the perplexing meshes which surrounded him, and he would have executed instant vengeance upon the authors of his misfortune and disgrace. Else he would have put an end to a life too wretched to be endured.

The conventional critic may smile at the conceit of a *fat* Hamlet, but I am satisfied that my theory is amply sustained by the text, as well as by the true solution of the alleged knotty points of Shakespeare's mental character, over which the ponderous but inflated brain of Dr. Johnson stultified itself. He accuses the Avon bard of introducing spirits, ghosts, myths, and fairies; of being guilty of exaggerations, absurdities, vulgar expressions, and other naughtiness. (*Boswell's Johnson*, vol. IV, pp. 258, etc.) All of which proves that the doctor was sometimes prejudiced, ill-natured, jealous, and ponderously silly on certain points.

But they who have cracked the kernel of this grand tragedy, and formed a just conception of the real disposition and peculiarities of the true hero, must admire and appreciate the marvelous skill of the great bard who understands the relations between physiology and the passions, and can analyze the temperament physical, as well as dissect the soul immortal.

THE CHEAP LITERATURE OF THE DAY.

It is more than one hundred years since good and brilliant Lady Montague wrote—"no entertainment is cheaper than reading, nor any pleasure so lasting." Her ladyship was an immense devourer of books, especially of new publications; nothing came amiss to her, from the heroic verse of Pope, to the grandiloquent mock-heroics of Richardson, and the ephemeral trash of the fashionable scribblers. It is difficult to ascertain the price of books from 1700 to 1760; but we conjecture that her ladyship's reading would not be called *cheap* at this day; nor should we have been anxious to settle her account with her bookseller.

The *Spectator*, after the stamp duty was imposed, was sold at four cents a copy, now equal, on account of the depreciation of the currency, to about eight cents. The papers of Addison and Steele do not average in length more than a single column of this sheet; so—to measure such things by the quantity,—had the *Spectator* been of the same size of the *Journal of Commerce*, it would have sold at $3.20 a copy, and the subscription price would have been upwards of one thousand dollars a year. From 1700 to 1756, about 5,280 new works were published in England, or about 93 per annum; from 1816 to 1851 the average was 1,252 for each year; while in 1853 there were 2,530 new works published; and since then the average has steadily increased. Including pamphlets and ephemeral issues, some 10,000 new publications appear annually in

Germany; some 2,300 volumes in the United States; and the total number of volumes annually put into circulation throughout France is estimated at 10,000,000 copies, at prices ranging from a franc down to a sou.* Mr. S. G. Goodrich, the author of *Recollections of a Life-Time*, estimates the amount of the production of the American book trade for 1850 at $12,500,000; and for 1856 at $16,000,000; $6,000,000 whereof he allots to the city of New York.

One or two other facts may be mentioned in reference to the high price of books in old times. St. Jerome (A. D. 380), it is said, impoverished his estate to procure the works of Origen; King Alfred gave an immense tract of land for one book; in 1274 a copy of the Bible sold for £34, when labor was 1d. a day; in 1466 at from £60 to £20, and about the same time the *Romance of the Rose* for $150. Compare these prices with the cheapness of modern works, and especially with the enormous sale of some of our late publications. It is said that 35,000,000 of Webster's *Elementary Spelling Book* have been sold; that its annual issue is over 1,000,000; while some 3,000,000 of his Dictionaries are annually circulated. Of Mitchell's geographical books there is a probable issue of 1,000 per day, and of Prof. Davies's mathematical series 300,000 were sold in 1857. There were sold of Livingstone's *Travels in South Africa* 10,000 copies; of Kane's *Arctic Explorations* 65,000; while dropping down to fiction, we find that the serials of Dickens have a sale of 35,000;

* *New American Cyclopedia.*

that 310,000 copies of *Uncle Tom's Cabin* were sold; 70,000 *Fern Leaves*, and 45,000 of the *Life of Barnum.**

Here now is a fine opportunity to compassionate the mental poverty of our great-grandfathers, to expatiate on the intellectual progress of this generation, and to tweak the tail-feathers of the American eagle, preparatory to a triumphant scream over the enlightenment of our people.

Much of this kind might be truthfully said; but as there are two sides to every question, so the enormous circulation of modern books doubtless has its drawbacks as well as its advantages. Of the thousands of new publications annually cast broadcast over the land, how many will bear Charles Lamb's description of "books which are books?" How few princes in this kingdom of literature; how many plebeians and grovelers; once or twice only in a generation, do we uncover and bend low before the throne of genius! True poetry blooms into full flower as rarely as the century plant; once only in an age do mortals kindle their little torches with Promethean fire, or from the heights of Olympus speak with the "larger utterance of the early gods." But the little song-singers twitter each around his little Parnassus, and the small thinkers and the small writers swarm around their small circles as thickly as insects in the summer air. The best thoughts of to-day have been better thought; the best things of to-day have been better said; and the best poem and novel of to-day are but a repetition of the passions, thoughts and senti-

* *New American Cyclopedia.*

ments of the life drama which is as old as the world itself.

We frankly admit that this is an extreme view; we mean it to be such. The truth is sometimes exhibited in exaggerations; and, after all, we have only repeated Solomon's proverb, that "there is nothing new under the sun." But to speak more guardedly, and of modern books; how many of the great mass put forth during the last year or so, are really of a superior order, or likely to survive the present generation? We can almost count on our fingers the live books of this period.

But over and above the inferiority and ephemeral character of the great mass of the publications of the day, and the number of stupid and sham books annually inflicted upon the public, there is a positive evil in modern literature which demands a passing allusion. The evil is sown broadcast with the good; and a million teeming presses scatter tares among the wheat. The sensation stories which are cried in the street, and the yellow covered publications under which the shelves of the book shops fairly groan, implant in the bosom of the young and the immature in heart, false ideas of honor, of principle, of life, of morality and of religion There is nothing which so inflames the passions and imagination of the young as these pictures of *life*, dressed up in gaudy colors and disguised with the thin covering of manly and generous impulses. A slimier and more venomous reptile still, lurks under the counter of the bookseller, and in the bosom of the boy-peddler. Should the statistics on this subject ever be published, the good citizen would lose hope for the morals and principles of the rising generation. An investigation, made by a committee of the house of commons in 1851, showed that the sale of immoral and infidel publications amounted to 29,000,000 annually. And we have reason to believe that an *expose* in this country would be scarcely less appalling.

We admit again that we have presented only one side of this subject; and that there is a better and more hopeful one. The true hope, however, is in the latent but vigorous virtue of the great bulk of our people, the good and humanizing influences of the day, and the growing intellectual and moral culture of all classes. Were it not for such influences as these, we should mourn rather than rejoice over the cheapness of modern literature, and pray for a mighty censor of the press to separate the good from the bad, and winnow the wheat from the chaff.

FREIDRICH THE SECOND.*

The modern public demands, over and above all other excellencies, that the historical work submitted to its judgment, shall be readable; and spurns with impatience the routine of dry facts and figures which satisfied the old fashioned chroniclers of the past. Whatever other fault may be laid at the door of Carlyle, he is eminently free from that of dullness. No one can read these

* History of Freidrich the Second, called Frederick the Great, by Thomas Carlyle, in 4 volumes, vols. I and II, New York, Harper & Brothers.

volumes without admiring the freshness and vigor of his style, and being more or less carried beyond himself by the graphic, and at times dramatic force of the narrative. With all his oddities, eccentricities and love of exaggeration and paradox, the historian has in his heart some living truths struggling for utterance, and the most casual reader can not fail not only to be impressed with Mr. Carlyle's mental idiosyncracies, but to bear off with him a distinct picture of the times and men who for the first time have been worthily presented to the public.

Of these men, the most notable, are Frederick, the grand-father, in whose reign Prussia became a kingdom, remarkable chiefly for his broken back and his expensive habits; Frederick William, the father, serious, solid, soldier-like and penurious; and Frederick, the son, afterwards surnamed the Great, whose life from the swaddling clothes to the death of his father, Mr. Carlyle minutely lays bare in the present volumes, leaving his interesting but not altogether lovely character to be developed in the remaining half of the work.

The leading fact in the history of this family, which is the history of modern Prussia, is the education and training of the young prince who became Frederick the Great, and for forty years was the most conspicuous man in Europe. The father was a tyrant, but a judicious monarch; despotic, but generally right; penurious, but the careful husbandman of the resources of his kingdom; somewhat mad, but in the eyes of Mr. Carlyle, a true hero and an "unspoken poem." Unto this royal oddity the young prince was bound in a slavish apprenticeship, from which he constantly rebelled, and was as constantly brought back to his obedience; the volumes closing with the imprisonment of the son, his reconciliation with his father, and his marriage with the wife his father had chosen for him.

This apprenticeship was cruel, but it was wholesome. There were, occasionally, scenes of brutal violence in the palace; the old king not always, or even habitually sober, beat his son and his daughter, Wilhelmina; he was rugged, coarse and despotic, but the moral and intellectual culture of the young crown prince was not altogether lacking in good sense. He was taught to fear God, abjure popery and Latin, and stick to German, French, mathematics, artillery, geography and orthodoxy. At the age of ten, he was at the head of a miniature regiment, and taught to mount batteries and fire minute brass ordnance; he already knew how to ride, fence, swim and dance. His father's instructions in reference to his daily life are exceedingly minute, but the following abstract, which we find in an English periodical, is sufficiently explicit:

"Up at seven; stand by, somebody, and see that he does not turn in the bed after he is called, but rise up at once; up at seven, slippers on, kneel, pray, so that all in the room may hear, a given prayer, then rapidly and vigorously wash, dress, powder and comb, breakfasting meanwhile. Prayer, with washing, breakfast, and the rest, to be done pointedly within fifteen minutes. Then it being quarter past seven, Duhan and the domestics enter, there is family prayer, Duhan reads a chapter, and all sing some proper psalm or hymn. At a quarter to eight all the domestics withdraw, and for the next hour and a quarter Duhan is to read with Fritz the gospel of the day; expounding it a little, adducing the main points of Christianity, questioning from Noltenius's *Catechism.* At nine he brings my son down to me; who goes to church, and dines along with me (at noon), the rest of the day is then his own. At half-past nine in the evening he shall come and bid me good night. Shall then go directly to his room; very rapidly get off his clothes (it is again and again urged that he learn to dress and undress with the utmost human speed), wash his hands, and so soon as that is done, Duhan makes a prayer on his knees, and sings a hymn, all the servants being again there. Instantly after which my son shall get into bed; shall be *in* bed at half-past ten."

"On Monday, as on all the week days, he shall be called at six; rise briskly, pray as on Sunday, as rapidly as possible get on his shoes and spatterdashes; also wash his face and hands, but not with soap. Have his hair combed out and queued, but not powdered; breakfasting meanwhile on tea. All to be ended before half-past six. Then family prayers until seven. From seven till nine history with Duhan. Christian religion with Noltenius till a quarter to eleven. Then Fritz rapidly washes his face with water—hands with soap and water; clean shirt, powders, and puts on his coat; about eleven comes to the king and stays with him till two — dining meanwhile. The king at Wusterhausen dines under one of the four lime-trees set at the four corners under the terraces, and falling asleep afterwards bakes in the sun. At two Fritz is in his own room, where Duhan takes him upon the maps and geography till three o'clock. From three to four Duhan treats of morality. From four to five Duhan shall write German letters with him, and see that he gets a good style (which he never in the least did.) About five, Fritz shall wash his hands and go to the king; ride out; divert himself in the air and not in his room; and do what he likes, if it is not against God. Subjects of study varied with the days, but the days were alike, except nearly a whole holiday on Wednesday and a half-holiday on Saturday, if the morning's repetition then showed that the lessons of the week were properly remembered."

Altogether, we have perhaps as clear and minute a history of a Prince as was ever written; and as we have no intention of going further into it, we cannot do less than commend Mr. Carlyle for the thoroughness with which he has delved into this branch of the subject. Two radical errors, however, will strike every reader. The first is, Mr. Carlyle's obstinate determination to make heroes out of only half men, and to mistake force for virtue; and the other is, the theory that society can be governed and reformed only through the efforts of a single man, or two, ignoring entirely the forces of social progress and the vigorous outgrowth of the people. The world, in his opinion, can only grow through a tyrant, like Frederick William, or a catastrophe, like the French Revolution. He has no faith in his age or the people of modern times, but bows humbly before some rough-hewn idol of the past generation, in whom he sees the prototype of "the coming man" who is to reform the world by the sheer vigor and obstinancy of his will. If the world can only be kicked and beaten into decency, Frederick William was a true reformer; but if it is to be regenerated by inward and spiritual graces, he is the last man to be set up for a Christian hero. Mr. Carlyle's estimate of the son of this vigorous but somewhat savage sire, we shall learn in the sequel.

MR. HOSMER'S LECTURE.

Those familiar with the lyrics of Mr. Hosmer did not require the evidence, afforded by his lecture on Thursday evening [Dec., 1849], to convince them that he possesses many of the elements of a true poet; nor did many, we venture to say, who listened to his essay —for so he modestly termed it—on *Scottish Song*, hesitate to form the same opinion. Nor is this assertion at all extravagant. Many a good poem is written in prose, without the mysteries of trochees and iambi. Poetry is something that exists *per se*, in thoughts, not in words; in the idea conveyed, not entirely in the manner of conveying it. The jingling of rhymes, and the harmonious collocation of words, are by no means indispensable. The poet is not to be measured by the length and shortness of his syllables, nor by the precision with which he places the cæsural pause. He may be ignorant of the rules of prosody, and unable to distinguish an iambus from an alexandrine. But if he be imbued with the true spirit; if he be pure in heart and noble in nature; if he love the beautiful, and cherish kindly feelings for his fellows; and if, in addition, his fancy be glowing, and his imagination cultivated, then he possesses many of the elements of a true poet, though he may never have written a line, or cherished an ambitious longing—though his effusions be neither quoted in literary circles, nor set to music by fashionable composers. It is, then, no equivocal compliment to Mr. Hosmer to say, that his lecture afforded many evidences to those whose acquaintance with him commenced on Thursday evening, of his more than ordinary powers as a poet. It would, perhaps, be nearer the truth to say that it needed only versification to have made it a poem. It will, of course, be impossible to analyse it; and if we succeed in preserving a few of its fragments, we shall be more than satisfied.

He regarded a rude and uncultivated age as especially favorable to the poetry of the passions. Sterility of language begets a luxuriant imagination. An intimate communion with nature and the elements, a habit of personifying natural phenomena, of assigning to the spring, the mountain, and the forest, its peculiar genus loci, of regarding the "blue drapery of the hills" as the garments of a superior race, who mingled and took part in the affairs of men; these circumstances all combined to quicken the imagination, and to give rise to the rude poetry which has come down to us from the early races of men. These traditionary legends are not only worthy of admiration in themselves, but they are of great service to the historian and the antiquarian;

and the *Old Mortalities of literature* learn that the past is not all a shadow. . History survives in tradition and song, as well as in huge rolls of parchment, in the simple ballads of shepherds, as well as in densely packed libraries. To these fountains, many great poets have resorted to draw an inspiration from the past; and Scott not only strengthened his powers by a communion with nature, but by drinking deep draughts of truth from the simple ballads of peasants.

In selecting Scottish Song for his subject, it was not his purpose, he said, to speak particularly of those great poets of Scotland whose fame is placed beyond the attacks of criticism, and of time itself. He intended to speak only of a few who had been neglected — to brush away the dust that had gathered on a few of the gems of Scottish song — to mention those whose names are almost unknown beyond the Highlands; but whose ballads and songs are perpetuated among the peasantry, and handed down, like heir-looms, from father to son. The Scottish muse is honest, chaste and truthful. Has no painted face, nor any of the meretricious charms of more elegant and cultivated poetry. The ancient minstrels were men of action, as well as men of song — they marched to battle with their clans, and cheered them on to victory; and in doubtful conflicts they hesitated not to grapple with their foes. They were naturally imbued with the war spirit, and it is not to be expected that their rhymes should be governed by the rules of prosody, or be as smooth and polished as those of drawing-room poets. He alluded to the rude ballad of *Chevy Chase*, and the effect which it had upon the polished and courtly Sir Philip Sydney. To Campbell's *Hohenlinden*, written from personal recollection of that awful scene—to Sheppard, Motherwell, Ramsay, Tannahill and Hogg, whose ballads and songs, clothed though they be in a quaint garb, shine like stars in the dusky twilight—or which, like magic mirrors, give a faithful reflection of the past. He repeated, with great effect, selections from the ballads of Tannahill, to which he added a sketch of his unhappy life and unfortunate death; adding another to the list of "great poets in misery dead."

The lecture concluded with a vindication of the poet from the charge of living an idle and aimless life. He claimed for him a high mission, and a vocation not to be despised. He is a watchman in the night, as well as a workman in the tower. He is the sympathetic chain that binds head to heart, and generation to generation. Let not his faults be scrutinized too closely; they can generally be traced to constitutional organization and the excitability of a highly sensitive nature. Let the sledge hammer strike upon the anvil, but not upon the sensitive strings of the harpischord.

Mr. Hosmer's remarks on poets can, with equal truth, be extended to men of letters generally. It is to be feared that they do not occupy the position nor receive the consideration that they deserve. Unacquainted with their peculiar trials, and with the difficulties with which they must contend, we are not apt to sympathise with what we call their imaginary sufferings. Nor is sympathy always due to them. It is squandered upon the misanthropic gloom of Shelley and the wild wailings of Byron. But the memory of the crushed hopes of Henry Kirke White and the broken heart of Keats should inspire us with pity for unfortunate genius. Poverty is frequently added to misfortune, and a famished body to a racked and tortured mind. They struggle, suffer and die for the want of only a portion of that which men of wealth and *taste* squander upon a favorite *danseuse* or a *protège* from the opera. Too late they offer the assistance which can not save them. They perish of hunger, and we erect a monument to their memory — they ask for bread, and we give them a *stone.*

This perhaps is overdrawn: but if it contain the shadow of truth, we have reason to blush for ourselves. The sufferings of Edgar A. Poe, in the bitterness of poverty, and the names of a host of others, who, with equal ability, have perished by the wayside, are a testimony against us. Mr Hosmer informed us that the minstrels of a rude and barbarous age "feasted with barons and princes, and enjoyed the friendship of kings." We, with all our boasted civilization, too often leave our poets and men of letters to struggle on in solitude and misery. We are becoming slaves to utilitarianism, and drudges to accumulation. We seem to be born for no other object than to buy and sell, to speculate and make money. In such a desert, moral and intellectual, a lecture like that of Mr. Hosmer, is a refreshing oasis.

REV. THEODORE PARKER.

Whatever may be the general opinion as to the soundness or fallacy of Mr. Parker's tenets, philosophical or religious, it is allowed by all that he is a man of more than ordinary ability. His fitness to teach may be questioned, but no one can doubt his ability to interest and charm. His lecture on Thursday evening [Dec., 1849], evinced a well developed mind, reasoning powers of no low order, and an extraordinary power of generalization. Its deductions, if not sound, were plausible. Its style was forcible and luminous.

His subject was by no means a novel one. The Progress of Mankind has been, latterly, a fruitful theme for orators, poets and philosophers, and is an especial favorite with a class of persons who idolize the present, and regard the nineteenth century as the point to which has concentrated all the wisdom of the past. But the subject, though a trite one, was treated with great originality. Indeed, parts of the lecture were of so novel a character, that we venture so say that to many of his audience they had never been previously advanced, except perhaps in the pages of Voltaire, or in a clever little work called the *Vestiges of Creation*. But of this presently.

In the consideration of the impediments to human progress, there were many practical remarks which were valuable and worthy of remembrance. The first impediment he mentioned was the *misapplication of productive industry*. By an ingenious calculation he showed, that the amount annually expended in the manufacture of the single article of *rum*, would be sufficient to comfortably house 200,000 people. The annual labor and expense of cultivating tobacco — calculating also the pecuniary loss resulting from its use — would produce, if applied to the culture of Indian corn, a crop of 40,000,000 bushels. He presented the subject of slavery in a very strong light.

There is a striking difference between the increase of wealth and population in our own state, and in Virginia. In New York, the population has more than quadrupled during the last fifty years, in Virginia it has not doubled. Nearly all the improvements in the manufactures and in the arts originate in the non-slaveholding states. But two per cent of all the moneys contributed for benevolent purposes and foreign missions comes from the South. The largest proportion of poets, historians, men of science, and men of letters comes from the North. Slavery, like a mass of ice in a garden, chills and destroys everything around it. He mentioned war, as the third and last object to progress. The amount expended in the Mexican war would construct two rail roads, one of which would unite the Mississippi and the Pacific — form together an aggregate length of 2000 miles. The earnings of those engaged in that war would have produced, if they had been employed in industrial pursuits, a sum large enough to build a magnificent college in every state of the Union, and to educate annually fifty young men in every state. So that this one item would annually afford a superior education to fourteen thousand young men.

But this was rather an episode than a constituent part of the lecture. The general design of Mr. Parker was to present a sketch of the progress of mankind. He argued from historical data that there has ever been a gradual advancement and improvement in the human race. He went back to remote times, and presented man as he first appeared on earth, without mind, without speech, a cannibal. He possessed no laws, no government, he was guided only by his instincts. When hungry, that instinct teaches him to seek bread, he seeks for it and receives not only bread, but a thought. Presently he demands more bread and of a better quality, and he obtains it, and acquires thereby a little more wisdom. In this way, and by a slow process, he learns to put facts in a row; he finds a fact common to a number of facts, and thus he deduces a general law. To illustrate: He has been accustomed to pluck and eat grain without caring to know how it came there, or how it was germinated. By and by he examines it more attentively; he observes the grain, the blade, and then the root, near which he finds the decayed *germ* from which it sprang. He straightway concludes that by planting the seed, the fruit can be produced. He tries the experiment, and finds that the seed thus planted produces sixty or a hundred fold. Thus, said the lecturer, thought began! But this is not all. He finds himself a prey to the wild beasts by whom he is surrounded. They are stronger than he, they are fleeter of foot. He has, therefore, no other method but outwit them. And thus he takes his second degree. But, continues the lecturer, the early monuments show that men were once cannibals; not a tribe or a nation or two — like the Feegee Islanders — but the whole human race were Feegees. Their principal article of food was human flesh. But as natural instinct, their only guide, taught them to save their own lives, they soon learned to be wary and careful, and to use every device to avoid falling a prey to their fellows. Thus man takes his third lesson in the acquisition of knowledge, and so he learns to think. But he must learn to work also. He is naturally lazy. But as some work must be performed, he first conquers the woman; he has a bigger head, a brawnier arm, and a harder heart, and he succeeds in making her a slave. One wife does not content him, and so he marries two, three, and perhaps more. So that man, in his laziness, learns that another can do his work. He thus concludes that it would be more profitable to enslave than to eat his captives, and hence the origin of slavery. Thus began productive industry among the Hebrews, in Egypt, Greece, and Rome. But as arts and manufactures advance, he finds that he also is capable of labor, and gradually, free industry is introduced by the side of slave labor. And now that man has learned to *think* and *labor*, society and government must be formed, and laws enacted.

Primitive instinct organized man into families, in which the whole was subordinate to one — the head. But as war was then the constant state, and peace only the exception, the family organization was found to be too limited, and men were gradually formed into tribes and nations. The stronger were chosen to be chiefs or king. Here was the first form of government—the elective monarchy—in which was complete unity of purpose, but little or no personal freedom. This form was succeeded by the hereditary monarchy, the oligarchy, and the democracy. That government would come up to the standard of ideal perfection, in which complete unity of purpose is united to the greatest amount of personal freedom. But none of these forms have reached this standard; they have only approximated to it.

Such is a rude but correct outline of Mr. Parker's theory of civilization. It was delineated with great ability, force and perspicuity. Many of the minor considerations were truthful and well presented. But to minds well poised, and accustomed to take sensible views of things, it must appear utterly false. The remark of the *Quarterly Review* in reference to a book of essays from the pen of another eminent but erratic Bostonian, is equally applicable to it:—that it contains more of paradox than of truth, and more of evil than of paradox. Mr. Parker presents—as a type and original of early civilization—a man, or something that he calls a man—idiotic, speechless, feeding on human flesh, and governed only by the instincts of the brute. He can neither perceive, nor reason, nor imagine. He dwells in the open air, wears no clothing, and feeds on bitter roots and raw flesh. He has no natural affections; knows no laws; and is governed only by his appetites. He can have no moral sense—no conscience, and is ignorant of the distinction between right and wrong.

Mr. Parker's lecture was very cautiously worded: it left much to be inferred. But from his *expressed* opinions, we judge that he believes, with a certain French school, that the lowest type of human organization was developed and elaborated from the highest type of animal existence. His theory is certainly not far removed from that of Le Marc, and is equally degrading to human nature. How degrading to trace the descent of Shakespeare, of Bacon, and of Franklin, to a set of chattering idiots! How degrading the belief, that *our* ancestors learned to think and to reason from the lessons of the brute, and the instincts of a cannibal nature!

A book, called Genesis, is, or was once, universally credited and reverenced, and was highly prized and cherished by the inhabitants of New England. This book narrates that a man and woman were created in the image of their Maker and placed in a beautiful garden; that from them sprang the human family. The book also narrates the subsequent increase and advancement of the race, and what befel the early generations of men. But this account is a very different one from that given by Mr. Parker. *So* conflicting are they, that if Mr. Parker be believed, the book must be a fable.

THE LECTURE SEASON.

The season of musquitos has nearly passed, and the season of lectures has fairly commenced. It is possible that there is something satirically suggestive in this conjunction of events; at least, it seems a merciful provision that we are not simultaneously afflicted with the tormenting buzz of the aggravating insect, and the hum drum of the stipendiary bore of the lecture room. A double assault upon the tender epidermis and the equally sensitive tympanum of the ear, would prove too much for human nature, even amid the comforts of this most glorious season of the year.

To speak more seriously and in moderation — it is a question whether or not the mental aliment provided at these fashionable entertainments be suitable for the intellectual wants of a young and vigorous people. That the most famous of these Peripatetics (though no Aristotles) give the public the worth of their money in pleasure, is proved by the crowded houses they draw. Something of this is due to curiosity; half a dollar is a small sum for a good stare at a notable face, especially if the owner thereof be an infidel philosopher, an eccentric or a conspicuously heterodox clergyman, an author who has quarreled with his wife, or been guilty of a notorious *scan. mag.*; an adventurer, like the heroes of a French novel, with tight gloves and loose principles; or a foreign intriguante, with no principles at all.

That there is another class of lecturers who know how to tickle the dainty palate of the public with what, for the lack of a better name, we may call the whip-syllabub of literature. They do not pretend to set out a substantial repast, but they manage to serve up a delectable dessert. They add nothing to our stock of knowledge; but they spin off admirable rhetoric. They do not feed us with wholesome and practical truths; but they create a morbid appetite for those savory and highly seasoned tit bits which the uncultivated sometimes mistake for eloquence. They do not lead us hand in hand along the rugged paths of physical or political science, but they entice us with syren voices into the flowery and shaded lanes of literature, soothe the brain with the pretty conceits of fancy, or conduct us to their little Parnassus, and introduce us to the rosy bower of their diminutive muse.

Over and above three honied mouthers of commonplaces, with their stilted language and limping thoughts, with their cyclopædia lore and sentimental platitudes, there is a class which affects novelty of doctrine, and delights in assaulting all which is substantial and conservative in morals and religion. There is one school or clique of these instructors of the public, who flit every winter between Boston and Chicago, the schedule of whose principles may be thus stated: politics, abolitionism, and woman's rights; religion, materialistic or transcendental; philosophy, Emersonian or Parkerian; and who perhaps have no more distinctive point in common, than a mutual strife to ascertain which one can be more radical, heterodox and startling, than the other. This school of thinkers and talkers originated in orthodox New England, and have so far succeeded in infecting their young countrymen with their new notions, that in many of the villages and cities of tho middle and western states the stock of winter-lectures is, to a great extent, made up of this material.

Of course, we do not mean to intimate that all our popular lecturers come under any of the classes we have enumerated; on the contrary, there are many sound and really learned and good men who appear creditably before the public in the capacity of lecturers. We merely mean to say that the American lecture room is too often disgraced by pretenders and charlatans; and that pleasant and entertaining, but uninstructive lectures, are not the food which young people who frequent lyceums and institutes really need. Properly speaking, the lecture-room is a place for instruction, for mental and moral improvement. And what a field of subjects from which to choose! What great topics are suggested by the rapid advancement of physical science, the gigantic strides of geology and chemistry, and the glorious revelations chronicled from year to year by the astronomer. Even a well-read man finds it difficult to keep up with the new and important discoveries of physical science. How many there are who would be glad to attend a course of lectures on such subjects, for they are beyond the reach of a single isolated lecture. When we think also of the collateral branches of knowledge, such as natural history, political economy, history and belles lettres, it is plain that lecturers have texts enough for popular and instructive lectures on the different branches of useful knowledge. Systematic courses of lectures on such subjects would soon elevate the public taste to a point far beyond the reach of the "birds of passage" who now make the lecture room and the lyceum the theatre of vain display, and who rather stimulate a false and morbid appetite than satisfy the yearnings of those who hunger and thirst after knowledge and mental advancement.

RUSSIAN DIPLOMACY—1854.

Having pointed out, rather than discussed, in an article in yesterday's *Express* why American sympathy can not, and should not be found on the side of Russia, in her recent aggressive acts towards Turkey, and why, judging from her past domestic and foreign policy, republicanism has nothing to gain, and probably much to lose, from her success in the encounter which now promises to involve the great powers of Europe in a protracted and bloody warfare—we propose to-day to review in a general manner, and without unnecessary details, the immediate causes of the present threatening aspect of Eastern affairs.

We believe that when the facts are properly presented, and we hope to do so without "special pleading," that no one will be misled by a recent remark of a contemporary that Russia "stands upon the record in a most plausible position."

The controversy is not a new one. It has formed the basis of oriental diplomacy for three hundred years. The possession and peaceable occupation of the holy places, as certain sanctuaries in and near Jerusalem are called, were the immediate cause of the Crusades. France has always asserted her right to these holy places with more spirit than discretion. In both the years 1535 and 1740, she succeded in obtaining a recognition of these claims from the Porte, which however did not prevent the subjects of the Latin and Greek churches from engaging in continual disputes and occasionally in disgraceful and bloody combats on the high festival days — such as Easter and Christmas, which are observed simultaneously by the two churches.

Seven years ago she considered herself much insulted by an act of sacrilege supposed to have been committed by the Greeks. A silver star was stolen from the tomb of the Saviour, and M. Lavalette, her ambassador at the Porte, demanded satisfaction. A commission was appointed to amicably decide and settle the matter, and to guaranty the members of the Franco-Latin church the privileges secured by the treaties of 1535 and 1740.

All would have been well if Russia had not been true to her instincts, and had not interfered in her usual arrogant and audacious spirit. She demanded that the commission should be instantly dissolved. The Porte felt compelled to assent, and it was almost as instantly dissolved. Nicholas demanded a new commission, and a new commission was awarded by the Sultan. A compromise was patched up, the stolen silver star was replaced, and the Porte trembling between its fear of France and its dread of Russia, commenced its usual game of diplomacy, and trusted much to time and Providence for a settlement of the difficulty.

There would, however, have been no open rupture if Russia had not been spurred on by her ulterior designs. M. Lavelette had been recalled, and M. Lacour his successor, aided by the British embassador, used every exertion to settle the dispute. The French claims were modified, many of them withdrawn, everything in fact might have been amicably settled, when Russia was compelled to play her trump card.

Really, she had neither begun nor continued the negotiation thus far with a wish or real effort for a settlement. Her policy was to keep the dispute open, and when a fair opportunity offered, to seize upon it and the principalities at the same time. She had foreseen that she could never capture Constantinople without the principalities — the distance from St. Petersburgh to Constantinople being too great to allow the passage of an immense army, without arousing all Europe. She had then two objects to obtain:

1st. To squat in the principalities.

2d. To do so without driving the allies to an open rupture.

But now that France, and England, and Turkey professed their readiness to bury the past troubles, and had even excited the indignation of their own people by a peaceful and compromising policy, Russia drew Prince Menschikoff, her trump card, from her pack, and played him with her usual diplomatic success.

The prince was of high rank, thoroughly in the confidence of the czar, and he went to the porte, attended by some of the highest officers of the Russian government. Huge military and naval arrangements were made in the south of Russia, ready to follow up the *peaceable* mission of the prince. His very first act, after his arrival in Constantinople, was an endeavor to stir up the Greek subjects of the porte. His next was to insult the grand vizier, and the minister of foreign affairs, who was compelled to resign. His next was to send special missions to Egypt and Athens to excite a revolt; and he completed the first act in his little drama, by threatening the sultan with the direst consequences if he dared to communicate to the English and French ambassadors any *treaties which he, the sultan, might make with Russia.*

But the plot had already so far ripened that the porte was compelled to communicate with his allies. The English fleet was called into the Dardanelles, and the prince sent in a preliminary note, which the porte began to consider, aided unofficially by the British embassy, when the *ultimatum* of the prince was issued, *which changed the whole ground of the controversy*, The former claims of the prince were of trivial importance compared with the contents of this note.

It had the effect of immediately opening the eyes of the British embassy, who, it must be confessed, had hitherto been thoroughly blinded by the skillful diplomacy of the prince. The news was received by them at a ball given by a distinguished Greek merchant. They of course immediately retired, and the war steamers of the allies departed from Constantinople on the same night.

The porte weakly consented to another conference, and the injury sought to be consummated was accompanied by a gross insult. The time for a conference was appointed, and the ministers of the sultan anxiously awaited the approach of Menschikoff. He passed them by in utter contempt, and proceeding to the palace of the sultan, demanded an audience. In vain he was informed that *it was Friday*, a day upon which no business could be transacted, and that the *recent death of the mother of the sultan* would render it indecent for him, according to the usages of his country, to receive a foreign embassy. In vain was he referred to the ministers who were waiting for him; the prince obstinately and insultingly persisted, and the disgraceful transaction was only terminated by the drawing of a curtain before the sultan. This, of course, settled the business of the czar for the present; the *ultimatum* was rejected, and although the negotiations were resumed by the new ministers of the sultan, for the others had indignantly resigned, no new step of importance was taken until the previously prepared armies of the czar invaded the principalities. Then, of course, one great object of Russia was obtained, and it only remained for her to prevent the allies from acting in concert against her. Recent events have proved that although her skillful diplomacy for a long time gave her success in this branch of the scheme, she was finally thwarted by the tardy but powerful and concerted action of France and England. The *ultima ratio regum* is now the only resort of the czar.

It only remains to allude to the *ultimatum;* its contents are well known. It introduced in the controversy a new and entirely unexpected feature; and the sultan ought not in decency to have ever entertained it. The disposition of the holy places, so long considered the basis of the diplomatic conferences and negotiations, was left out of view. Menschikoff demanded for the czar *political privileges over the Greek subjects of the sultan*, which must soon have dismembered the Ottoman empire. The Greek clergy, a most rapacious and degraded priesthood, were to be restored to political rights long obsolete, and which Turkey for centuries had been modifying. The Latin church would have fallen; and the advancing and liberal policy towards foreigners and the different sects of protestants, so long an eye-sore to the contracted vision of the czar, would have been succeeded by a state of things most apparent to those who best know the settled policy of Russia. Turkey, in a word, would have become a part of Russia.*

We have always sided with the Turks against the Russians in this eastern business, and we have endeavored to state our reasons pretty fully in this and a preceding article.

NOW AND THEN.

As the infinite combination of forms in the kaleidoscope sometimes assume a familiar appearance, and the eye is caught by occasional resemblances in the shifting phantasmagoria of colors, although the reflecting surfaces are never twice in the same relative position; or as the old player of the game of chess sometimes sees on the board the same plots, combinations and marshaling of pieces which taxed his ingenuity years ago, although no game ever repeats itself in all its details; so the events of history sometimes reproduce themselves in their general outlines, if not in their lesser

* Those who desire to see the foreign relations of England in reference to the eastern affair thoroughly discussed, are referred to an article in the January number of the *Wesminster Review.* Also to the *London Quarterly* of the same date.

shades; and the exciting occurrences of the present are foreshadowed and typified by the memorable transactions of the past.

The mind of the intelligent reader of the stirring events now occurring on the continent of Europe, reverts naturally to the grand turmoil of states and nationalities at the commencement of the present century, and especially to the opening scenes in the dramatic campaigns which ended in the ruin of the first empire and the remodeling of the map of Europe. Then, as now, the civilized world was conscious that it was on the eve of great events. Every one felt the premonitory thrill of the coming earthquake which threatened a grand upheaval of the political forces of Europe. Then, as now, parties and governments anticipated that the national disputes which had been gathering force for a dozen years, would be brought to a final and decisive issue. Then, as now, the eyes of Europe were turned upon one man who had risen from obscurity to empire, and had so impressed himself upon the destinies of the leading powers, that no important movement could be made without reference to his attitude and designs. Both the Bonapartes were carried into power on the waves of a popular outbreak, dignifying itself by the name of republicanism; a revolution placed both at the head of the republic, and their individual finesse and popularity afterwards established them as the emperors of the French. As the first emperor was the dread and bugbear of Europe, so the present emperor has been constantly held up as an innovator and a dangerous man; an adventurer, seated by accident upon a throne; a bombshell, with the fusee lighted, ready at any moment to explode among the old dynasties.

The general attitude and designs of the great powers half a century since, were not entirely dissimilar to their present attitude and designs. Austria wished to be supreme in Italy, and to extend her restrictive and arrogant policy on adjacent territory; Russia had no objection to push down her bulky frame towards the Adriatic and Bosphorus; England desired peace, colonies and commercial prosperity, but above all, would submit to any sacrifice rather than to the undue preponderance of France; Prussia and the German states also desired peace, but sympathized with England against the aggressions of French ambition; Italy was full of hot blood, but had the will rather than the strength to be free; while in France the army really ruled, and the army was all for glory and empire. The reader, fresh from the pages of Alison, is struck with these resemblances, and especially with the anxiety which attends every movement of Louis Napoleon; the adventurer has more power than any other man in Europe, after all: and if he is agitated, the whole hive seems ready to swarm. One can scarcely avoid a smile as he takes up the recent address of Napoleon on his departure to join his army in Italy. It reads like an old song, for the first emperor was also ambitious to be called the liberator of Italy, and laid there the foundation of his fortunes and military success.

How far the present emperor really sympathizes with the people of Italy, how far he designs to carry out the aggressive policy of his uncle, or how many crimes he intends to commit in the name of liberty, will be written by some future Alison. It must be confessed, however, that he has hitherto moved with more prudence and circumspection than his supposed ideal, that he has shown much respect for the public sentiment of Europe, and that he has especially desired to secure and retain the good will of the people of England. It is true that he now represents the revolutionary idea; but it is equally true that the fortunes of his family are bound up in the other idea of legitimate and hereditary succession, and this must cause him always to reflect the conservative ideas of Europe. It is true that he may dream of uniting the states of Italy under his sceptre; but it is by no means certain that the change would weaken the force of the progressive and liberal party, or that any state beside Austria would suffer loss by French influence in Italy. If he intends to pursue the arrogant and unscrupulous policy of Napoleon I, he must take the consequences, and will probably find also his Waterloo and his St. Helena.

Looking at the relative position of the two men, in reference to their prospects of retaining power, either within or out of France, it must be confessed that Napoleon III has better chances and greater advantages. It is now generally conceded that Napoleon I gained nothing by his long coveted alliance with Austria; and that the calamities which overwhelmed him dated from his forced marriage with Maria Louisa. The plots and intrigues of Austria, at any rate, figure largely in the closing scenes of his eventful career. Napoleon III, on the other hand, can never forget that the house of Hapsburgh thoroughly hates and despises him, as it hated and despised Napoleon I. He has accordingly acted upon the fact, that she is not only his dangerous neighbor and rival, the least frank and magnanimous nation in Europe, but that she is his natural enemy by race and by instinct. Russia, on the other hand, whom Napoleon I never took sufficient pains to conciliate, and against whom he directed the famous Moscow campaign, next to Waterloo the most disastrous event in his life, is the natural friend and ally of France. Russia will probably never materially interfere with the projects of France, as she would probably never have interfered with the projects of Napoleon I, had he let her alone. The present friendly relations between the nephew of Alexander I and the nephew of Napoleon I is an additional point therefore, in favor of the success of the policy of the latter, whatever that may be. Lastly, the first Napoleon entertained the most hostile feelings and destructive designs against England. It was the consciousness of this enmity and the memory of the contemplated invasion of English soil, which caused the general apprehension in England that her prosperity would never be secure so long as he sat on the throne; an apprehension which rendered the English government inexorable when he sincerely desired and prayed for peace. This error his successor has also avoided; for his alliance with England has been the great moral force of his throne. It is true, that to effect that alliance he had to encounter a temporary quarrel with Russia; but the war in the Crimea was brought to such a conclusion that he secured the secret good will of the czar; and it is generally believed that the relations more or less close now existing between the two grew out of Louis Napoleon's participation in the sudden and unexpected termination of the war. In view, then, of his double friendship with England and Russia, and his open and frank hostility towards Austria, his natural foe, we may infer that the attitude of Louis Napoleon is not without its advantages over that of Napoleon Bonaparte. To what use or misuse he may put these advantages, it is impossible to foretell; especially under the shadows of the storm which now threatens the south of Europe. Certainly his responsibilities to the world and to God are fearful to contemplate!

AUSTRIAN ITALY.

The success of the Italian patriot Garibaldi in Lombardy, is not more due to his own skill and the bravery of his volunteers, than to the hatred existing among the people of that country towards their Austrian oppressors. Some of the grounds of this hatred, over and above the national sentiment which more or less pervades all Italy, may be gathered from the following facts.

A writer in a recent number of the *London Quarterly*, after a consultation of a number of volumes on the economical condition of Lombardy, printed and sold in Austrian Italy and some of them with the direct countenance of the viceroy, states that the taxes in the

Italian territory of Austria are twice as large as those she imposes on her German territory. Upon the authority of Pasini, a writer of Venice, the existing tax on landed property in Austrian Italy is stated at 27 per cent. of the estimated income. In the German districts it ranges from 16 to 18 per cent. In 1851, an impost extraordinary was added to the previous burdensome taxes of the Italian provinces, which swelled the gross amount to 40 per cent of the income, not including the taxes upon transfer and succession. In Venetian Lombardy, the real amount of direct tax on the net receipt is 43 per cent; and taking into account and making the estimate on the wealth of the provinces and the value of the crops, Lombardy pays about a seventh, instead of about a thirteenth (which would be her fair proportion) of the landed taxes of the Austrian government.

The amount of these mammoth burdens may well astound even a New Yorker. Allowing that the latter pays two per cent on the estimated value of his real estate (which is on an average one third below the real value), the taxes of the Lombardo-Venetian land owner exceeded his eight times. In fact, nearly one half of his annual income is swept into the coffers of Austria; for he actually pays in the form of direct taxation two dollars out of every five he receives.

It is also a mistake to suppose that the soil of Lombardy is in the hands of the nobles. Out of a population of 2,723,000 in 1850, the signori numbered less than 3,000; and of 437,000 landed properties, there were 350,000 landed proprietors. This proportion, seven times greater than in Great Britain and much larger than in the United States, shows that the burden of the taxation falls upon the people, and not upon the nobles; for, deducting the inhabitants of the towns and cities, it is plain that the great bulk of the adult males are land owners.

Among other causes mentioned by the same writer, tending to prejudice the position and augment the unpopularity of the Austrian government in Lombardy, and to accumulate burdens upon the people, are increased severities in the law of conscription, a reduction of five per cent on the value of the florin, and the recent plagues of the vine for a long course of seasons, and of the mulberry for several. What must be the real sentiments of a people so unfortunate and oppressed, it is not difficult to conjecture.

THE MORAL ATTITUDE OF THE BELLIGERENTS.

After hearing the case of France *vs.* Austria in the matter of the Italian controversy, no impartial judge or critic can fairly decide that either of the parties is altogether in the right. They do not come before the public with clean hands; and their dispute on this subject, covering a period of fifty years, reminds one of the abusive debate between the pot and the kettle as to their respective clearness of complexion. From the time when the first Napoleon invaded Italy as a liberator, and left her little better than a province of France, until lately, when Austrian influence was nearly supreme from Sardinia to the gulf of Venice, Italy has been the foot-ball of the leading states of Europe, none of which have taken a more active or spirited part in the game than France or Austria. She has been kicked and trampled upon at nearly every meeting of the great powers, from the congress of Vienna, after the fall of Napoleon I to the congress of Paris, after the close of the Crimean war. Every benefit she has received has been more than counterbalanced by some scathing wrong; every attempt to regain independence and nationality has been repulsed by foreign intervention; while at no moment during the period we have mentioned, have portions of her territory been free from the crushing and overshadowing presence of armed forces sent out by the governments at Paris and Vienna.

Against France her accusers urge, in reference to the immediate issue now pending, that she has entered into a desperate war and disturbed the peace of Europe on pretexts which, however plausible they may seem as questions of international policy, can not be justified by the moral principles which should govern nations and rulers. As a state, she had received no injury from Austria, nor had reason to apprehend any; she did not commence hostilities to redress any wrong or to secure any right of her own; and her alliance with Sardinia was only part of a well devised scheme to provoke Austria to a conflict. Europe may well distrust the motives of Louis Napoleon in entering upon a contest in which his own nation has nothing to gain except the glory and aggrandizement of conquest, especially when the pretence for the conflict is a crusade for liberty led by a monarch who fraudulently established a limited despotism upon the ruins of a republic which he had himself demolished. Laying aside questions of international law and policy, and weighing the man in the moral balance, the worst feature in his case is the part he took in the contest in the Papal states, when the citizens of Rome, following the example of France, had thrown off their grievous yoke, and established their independence. The French expedition to Rome, the siege of that city and its subsequent occupation by French troops, throw the responsibility of the oppression and misgovernment of that part of Italy at least, upon Louis Napoleon; and his warmest admirers must confess that in view of this shameful and continued interference, his claims as the partizan of Italian independence are both illogical and hypocritical. Not even Austria's invasion of Naples, in 1821, under the pretext of crushing out a threatened revolution, was a more palpable violation of the equality and independence of nations as interpreted by the international law.

If the moral attitude of France in reference to the war be anything but upright and honest, that of Austria is so perverse and crooked as to repel the sympathies of all people living under a constitutional government. In the first place, her claim to exercise rule over portions of Italy, rests not upon the right of discovery, conquest, cession, annexation, or any of the usual processes by which nations acquire territorial sovereignty, but upon certain treaties entered into by the great powers of Europe. Such treaties by no means pass a complete and unconditional fee. They are rather to be regarded as contracts for certain speeiai objects supposed to be required for the mutual good; in this case, doubtless, the protection of Venetian Lombardy from the aggressive hands of France, the peace of Italy, and the dependent peace of Europe. In this sense, it may be said that Austria took Lombardy on a deed of trust; the trust being to protect her and the peace of Europe by a wise administration of public affairs. How far she has performed this trust, we shall presently see. But there are other conditions of, or rather equitable limitations to, her title. The cession of Lombardy to Austria was only a part of the treaties of Vienna; they contained a large number of other deeds, trusts, contracts and provisions, many of which have been broken, and some of which Austria has violated. For example, the treaties of Vienna guarantied the independence of Cracow, a city of Poland; but in 1846 Austria absorbed the little republic into her own dominions, and wiped out her nationality, at one blow. The separation of Belgium and Holland, and the recognition of Louis Napoleon as emperor of the French, were both against the provisions of those treaties; and if such bargains are capable of being rendered void by repeated and continued violations, those treaties are void in equity and in fact; certainly Austria has no right to protest against their abrogation or repeal. They are, in fact, pretty well used up, or rendered obselete, by the general consent of Europe; and the real title of Austria to Lombardy is that of prescription, or adverse possession, which she must defend, as best she may, by an appeal to arms.

We have suggested on moral grounds, if not on a technical interpretation of the Vienna treaties, that Austria assumed the rule of Venetian Lombardy on the implied conditions that she would protect that province, respect the rights of her neighbors, and perpetuate the reëstablished peace of Europe. Her subsequent career has been a continued violation of those conditions. With the king of Naples she early entered into a secret treaty by which he was bound never to allow any form of government inimical or dangerous to her own, to be established in his dominions. In other words, the principles of Austrian depotism were established forever in a neighboring state, anxious and ready to fight for a constitutional government. Here was a violation of the great principle laid down by Chancellor Kent, and other publicists from the time of Grotius, that "each nation has a right to govern itself as it may think proper, and no one nation is entitled to dictate a form of government, or religion, or a course of public policy, to another." The bargain between the two monarchs was not a treaty in the true sense of the word, but a forcible dictation, by which Austria, through the threats of imported troops, compelled the Neapolitans to choose her and not their own form of government. With Parma, Modena and Tuscany, she has treaties similar in effect if not in substance, by which she can enter those duchies during a revolt or revolution, and force the dominant party or government to adopt her policy and dictation. For twenty-five out of the forty-four years which have elapsed since the treaties of Vienna, she has had military forces in some of the

Italian provinces over which she had no legal jurisdiction; she has set her heel upon freedom and public justice, crushed out, so far as she could, the nationality of Italy, and constantly jeopardized by her secret intrigues the safety of Sardinia, the only remaining constitutional government.

In this review of admitted facts in reference to the two leading belligerents, we have made no pretence of examining the principles involved in reference to the law of nations, for we doubt if there be anything in that law applicable to the case. Very many theories are put forth under the sanction of international law which can not be found in the books, and the diplomats of Europe have a fashion of covering their newly discovered principles and precedents with the mantle of Grotius, Puffendorf and Vattel in a manner which would somewhat astonish those publicists were they alive to hear them. Probably none of the parties involved in the present war have technically violated the law of nations; but the diplomatic code of Europe is a very different matter. Still different and higher in the scale, are those eternal laws of honesty, honor and good faith which should govern nations as well as individuals, and according to which, men and history will pass judgment upon the present struggle in Europe.

THE KEYS OF ITALY.

In looking back upon the campaign of 1796, the first of Napoleon Bonaparte's expeditions into Italy, one is struck with the fact that the brunt of the strife was borne on the lines of the Mincio and Adige, and that the fortresses on the latter river were the great obstacles in the progress of a military conquest whose rapidity and success had never been surpassed in the history of arms. Napoleon I, then twenty-five years old, a young bridegroom, and but recently raised to command, entered Italy late in March, 1796, with an army of about forty thousand men, which number it never exceeded during the campaign, while the forces of the allies reached fifty thousand, and were frequently re-enforced by fresh troops, or rather by fresh armies from Austria. By the 21st of April, he had fought and won the victories of Monte Notte, Millesimo and Mondovi; on the 9th of May, captured Lodi, and by the 15th of that month entered Milan. In less than two months he had made himself master of Lombardy, and brought Sardinia to terms, by compelling her to renounce the coalition, cede to France Nice, Savoy and Piedmont west of the Alps, and to grant his troops a free pass through her dominions. On the 28th of May he entered the Venetian territory, after a sharp engagement on the line of the Mincio, but it was not until January of the following year that the fall of Mantua completed the conquest of Italy. In the interim the great battles of Castiglione, Arcole and Rivoli were fought, four large armies raised by Austria to defend her possessions were destroyed, and Napoleon had several times been brought to the brink of destruction, from which he was only saved by the rapidity of his movements, and his military genius in moving with the whole force of his little army against separated bodies or wings of the enemy.

But the fact stands out clear on the record, that the fortifications of Mantua, defended by only a moderate force, were the great obstruction of the campaign, and postponed the triumph of the French for half a year. This is the more striking as they had entered the noble and strongly fortified city of Verona early in June; and at the same time occupied Legnano on the Adige, while the Austrian commander, Beaulieu, had given up Peschiera soon after the battle of Lodi. During a brief portion of the campaign, the Austrians held Legnano and Verona; but they were compelled to leave both these places, so that at the commencement and during most of the seige of Mantua, the French held three angles of the famous quadrilateral, viz., Peschiera, commanding Lake Garda and the roads to Verona; Verona, controlling the great road to the Tyrol, and with Legnano protecting and protected by the Adige, and forming with that river the great line of defence between the Alps and the Po. But with all these advantages, six months elapsed after its first investment before Mantua capitulated.

These reminiscences of the campaign of 1796 may be useful in aiding us to form conjectures — for we do not aspire to opinions — as to the probable result of the movements of the allies now concentrating their forces in and around the strategic square. It must be admitted in behalf of the first Napoleon, that he was compelled for some time to abandon active operations against Mantua by the invasion of successive troops of Austrians whom he met and overcame in the open field, and that the result of the seige was thus virtually decided.

On the other hand, the improvements of modern times have placed Mantua within three days of Vienna, whence immense masses of Austrians, swiftly gathered from all parts of the empire, may be carried to the scene of action, without the necessity of a slow and toilsome march through the mountains. The fortifications themselves have been vastly strengthened since 1796; the stern frontiers of nature now bristle with all the crafty barriers invented by modern military science. Louis Napoleon has four huge fortresses to invest, while it took his military predecessor six months to conquer one. Peschiera, which did not surrender to the Sardinians in 1848, until after a contest of nearly two months, may succumb; Verona and Legnano may fall; but Mantua, situated in the middle of a lake, surrounded by unhealthy marshes, whose miasma is pregnant with death, protected by the power of inundating the enemy, and by fortresses which seem almost impregnable, may protract the defence for months, even against the new French artillery and the skill of the military schools of Paris, developed and matured before Sebastopol. It is possible that some short and severe engagement may settle the question without the horrors of a protracted seige; but unless this should be the case, it seems highly probable that Louis Napoleon may have to knock many times at the gates of the fortresses, before he obtains the keys of Italy and permission to walk into Venice.

A BREATHING SPELL.

In the career of every man, prince or peasant, there is said to be an opportunity for wiping out the blunders of the past and commencing a new record with his fellow-men and with heaven. There is a tide in the moral world, as in the mortal life, which taken at the flood leads on to fortune; to an honest and good fortune, resulting from an acknowledgment of the mistakes of the past, expiation for mischief already committed, and a wise choice for the future. Happy is he who seizes the auspicious crisis of his fate to erase the stain upon his conscience, or the blot upon his fame, and by some noble and expiatory act convince his fellows that their condemnation was premature and ill-founded, and that he is still worthy of their respect and esteem! The heathen moralist has written that a good man struggling with misfortune is a spectacle for the admiration of the gods, but we can conceive a worthier spectacle — that of a powerful ruler, whose reputation has been damaged by an unscrupulous policy, bad faith and unprincipled ambition, seizing upon some opportune and golden moment in the flush of victory to prove by a great act of wisdom and magnanimity that the designs of his heart are neither cruel nor selfish, and to justify, whatever may have been his previous errors, his essential sincerity and honor as a prince who has a true regard for the happiness of his people, and a noble desire to obtain the approval of the world and of history.

Louis Napoleon Bonaparte needs just now but one

element of greatness; the moral confidence and faith of the nations. To judge by the external signs of success, no career in this generation has been so swift, brilliant and victorious. He has strode, as if by one step, from the condition of an impoverished exile to the empire of France, the control of European politics, and the heroism of a great military leader, conducting successfully the most splendid campaign of modern arms. But his glory can not be substantial and permanent until he proves the honesty of his aims and the sincerity of his protestations, and so gains the confidence of men. The time for the proof has come, or is near at hand. We shall soon know whether he desires the independence of Italy, or the aggrandizement of France; the liberty of an oppressed country, or the extension of his own dynasty; the peace of Europe, or the horrors and despair of a general war. He has paused at the most anxious and exciting scene in the campaign; his arms are triumphant; Austria is humbled and exhausted by Solferino and the weaknesses and dissensions of her empire; Hungary lurks near, ready to light up the revolutionary flames which may set Europe on fire; Prussia and Russia stand a little aloof, but preparing for the conflict. In this moment of suspense, which the whole civilized world shares, much depends upon the moderation, justice and honor of the emperor of the French. By fulfilling his pledges to Italy, showing himself magnanimous to Austria, respectful to the German confederacy, and attentive to the peaceful counsels of England, it is not impossible that he may guaranty the freedom of the peninsula, make an honorable peace with Austria, restore the confidence of Europe, and lead home his victorious legions crowned with the laurels of a humane and magnanimous triumph. Such a termination to his brilliant campaign would silence his enemies, endear him to Italy and the friends of constitutional government, and seat him securely on the throne of France; but the moral triumph would be brighter than the crown, and grander than the fame of military conquest. Whether the armistice ends in peace or renewed hostilities, he has now an opportunity to justify himself before the world; and as the truest and most honorable monarchs have sometimes fallen away from the path of duty, so it is possible that the — so-called — most reckless and dangerous ruler in Europe may be allured by the attractiveness of popularity and the respect of mankind, as well as by motives of state policy, to take such a judicious, moderate and disinterested, stand as will expunge from the public memory the record of his past misfortunes or crimes.

THE BASES OF PEACE.

The public is again taken by surprise. The unexpected news of the armistice is swiftly followed by the more extraordinary intelligence brought over by the North Briton, and which is altogether too brief and scanty to satisfy the eager curiosity of the public. It is certainly known, however, that the Italian campaign is over; that a treaty of peace between France and Austria has been concluded, and that the Emperor Napoleon is soon to return to Paris. Those who anticipated that he would strictly fulfil his promise of driving the Austrians beyond the Adriatic are doomed to a measure of disappointment; for instead of this wholesale and wholesome expulsion, we find a novel Napoleonic creation in the shape of an Italian confederation, which seems to embrace France, Austria and Naples, and to be under the nominal presidency of the pope! Lombardy is passed over to the king of Sardinia; conquered by the arms of the allies, it is transferred to Victor Emanuel as his share of the spoils; but under what limitations and guaranties of independence is known only to the parties immediately concerned. The negotiations which form the bases of peace for Italy beyond the Mincio are less definitely stated; but apparently Venetia will be still governed by the house of Hapsburg under this curiously mixed Italian confederation. The problem of the quadrilateral being unsolved, Venice is as much as ever under the lock and key of the Austrian fortresses. It is asserted that the pope is to be the mere nominal head of the confederacy, and that he will virtually be deprived of his temporal sovereignty. All the world will, of course, be lost in conjecture as to the causes of these wonderful and unexpected events; but until the details of the intelligence are more amply supplied, conjecture is idle. Perhaps Russia has backed down; and the third, like the first Napoleon, wishes to be crowned at Paris by the pope. And what has become of the arrangement with Kossuth?

THE IMPERIAL DECREES.

The indications of a more moderate and forbearing policy on the part of Louis Napoleon in the administration of the government of France, are generally received with the same spirit of disparagement which has greeted all his public acts since he seized the reins of imperial power. When a man's general reputation rests under a cloud, the world naturally if not logically, regards all his movements with suspicion; and it is probable that the wisest and most self-sacrificing step the emperor could take, in reference to the intricate and perplexing affairs, in which France and the other great powers of Europe are now interested, would be received with very general doubts of the honesty and purity of his purpose. Public opinion once convinced by some great act of falsehood or treachery, that a man's motives, or principles of conduct, are narrow, selfish and dishonest, is slow to forget or to forgive; and Louis Napoleon is endeavoring to strengthen the moral force of his throne, finds himself surrounded with difficulties and obstacles, which, were he the most sincere and single-heated ruler in Europe, might well weaken his zeal and discourage his hopes.

Assuming him to be a mere man of policy, governed by those principles or theories of state-craft which he deems best fitted to accomplish his purposes and to advance the interests of his dynasty, and it must still be confessed that the relaxations admitted by his recent decrees, shows a boldness and a wisdom well worthy of the keenest and most brilliant intellect in Europe. A government can not publicly acknowledge and repent of the errors of the past — but it can, without compromising its dignity or lowering its self-respect, open a new record for the future, and by a wiser and more moderate policy, teach men to forget its previous errors. This is what the recent decrees of the emperor, to a certain extent, imply; and imply in the most adroit and delicate manner. There are no longer any political prisoners in France, or any political exiles banished from France; the general amnesty, as the Greek derivation of the word indicates, declares that the empire forgets, not forgives its enemies; for forgiveness might imply its own weakness; and, as has been plausibly suggested, might be rejected by thousands who will confess to no crime. The exiles and refugees now scattered over the world, are invited to return to France, for the reasons that the past has been forgotten, and that the empire is sufficiently strong in the hearts of the people to resist the designs of its enemies. This is the meaning and logic of this decree, and also of the other, simultaneously issued, which relieves the press from the effects of previous warning, and which is accompanied by such changes in the censors' department as guaranty to publishers and the public journals, greater freedom in the discharge of its duties.

The friends of the emperor, and the well-wishers of France, now find cause for regret that the half-completed punishment and repression of Austrian intrigue and encroachment in Italy had not been carried to a point which would have further established the French emperor in the confidence of the friends of continental freedom, and of constitutional order. Had Napoleon given Italy that independence and nationality which recent events are fast teaching us she is fully competent to enjoy and use with judgment and moderation, he might have retraced his previous missteps, and secured the foundations of his empire not on a system of repressions and half measures in the direction of progress, but upon and in the hearts of the intelligent and freedom-loving men of France, and upon the good will and moral support of the constitutional states of Europe. The doubts as to his sincerity in the Italian campaign extend to the motives which have induced him to relax some of the rigors of his dynasty; and there is much plausibility in the common opinion that if he was false to Italy, he can not be true to France. At least, if he had done for Italy all that he promised, and carried out to the letter the spirit of the glowing proclamations issued at Milan, France might now be substantially a free nation. Instead of the amnesties granted to the press and political exiles, we might have a general forgetfulness of the past and of the steps by which the emperor ascended the throne, a thorough and honest popular confidence in the Napoleonic règime, and a return to those mild and lenient terms of government which can only exist when good faith and mutual respect unite the governing and the governed.

NAPOLEONIC IDEAS.

The European press is loaded down with bewildering and contradictory reports in reference to the projected settlement of the Italian question. It would be amusing to examine and compare the various statements which have been put forth, with an air of credibility, from time to time, within the last month [Oct., 1859]. Not long since, it was announced that the Zurich conference had certainly and finally closed its sessions; but at the latest advices the plenipotentiaries were busily applying themselves to the task of dining and wining with the hospitable Swiss, and this seems to be the only part of their proceedings upon which the various correspondents do not contradict each other.

Among other conditions of the Zurich settlement, it was stated that Austria was to give up to Sardinia two of the fortresses of the famous quadrilateral, besides the duchies of Parma and Modena; a proposition almost as absurd as the others which were announced almost simultaneously, namely, that a second son of King Leopold was to be sovereign of Tuscany, and that in the proposed congress at Brussels, England would be represented by Prince Albert. Asstria surrendering Peschiera and Mantua, which she was allowed to retain after the Imperial interview at Villafranca — a German prince ruling the intensely Italian Tuscans — and the powerless and much-restricted prince consort representing Great Britain in a European congress — such are some of the absurdities to which the press is driven, in the attempt to solve the most important problem of the day — the Napoleonic idea of the Italian question.

For the meat of this difficult nut lies hid in the subtle and secretive brain of the emperor of the French, at last accounts quietly enjoying the baths at Biarritz, and slowly evolving, from the complications which surround him, the idea which first induced him to set foot in Italy, and which inspires his conduct and governs his acts now as much as it did then. *There* reposes the secret which one will ask in vain from the Zurich plenipotentiaries, the busy king of Belgium, the active young Metternich, or the much-troubled cabinet of Palmerston. He who planned and conducted the Italian campaign, and probably foresaw the various movements and combinations which followed, alone holds the last link of the chain which he has forged. What is the idea for which, the *Moniteur* announces, France is the only nation in Europe which will fight? Is it the freedom of Italy, "from the Alps to the Adriatic," the alleged basis of the war, or only the glory of France, and the perpetuation and aggrandizement of the imperial dynasty?

This is the real question which underlies the whole business. The character of a man, rather than the policy of governments, is involved; the good faith and sincerity of a monarch, rather than the designs of parties and the maneuvres of diplomatic bodies. When we find out what Napoleon means to do, we shall know very nearly what has been actually effected. Not that his power is absolute; for he knows how and when to be moderate, and to mould his plans according to circumstances; but he will give the general direction and shape to the settlement, whether that may embrace the actual unity and independence of Central Italy, the restoration of the dukes, or the establishment of an Etrurian kingdom, with one of the Bonapartes at its head — the last a contingency, however, which the *Moniteur* positively denies. In the meantime, people are asking themselves, and somewhat pertinently in reference to the Italian question, whether France herself is any freer since the amnesty and the modification of the laws of the censorship; whether her people or her statesmen have any more power or influence in the government; or if the thought and intelligence of France has any wider or freer scope of utterance. They even ask each other if the evident determination of the emperor to satisfy and even gratify Austria, on almost any terms, has any connection with the acknowledged fact, that, notwithstanding the disarmament, he is now building a steel-clad fleet of war-vessels, and can lead out nearly 600,000 men under arms at a month's notice. The questioning goes still further; for all Europe is asking itself, and England throbs with anxiety at the very thought, whether the settlement of the Italian question is not the first step in the development of a secret and long-matured plan which involves the peace and security of larger and more important states in Europe.

FRENCH NAVAL ARMAMENTS.

Of the steel plated war vessels with which France is strengthening her navy, two, the liners, Castiglione and Massena, are finished, and great exertions are being made to speedily complete the Gloire and Invincible, which will carry engines of nine hundred horse power and forty rifled cannon. Two other liners, also steel clad, and of immense size, have been put on the stocks, the Magenta at Brest, and the Solferino at L'Orient. A Paris correspondent recently stated that a trial of one of these immense and almost impregnable marine monsters had proved entirely satisfactory. A shell of the largest size, projected from a short distance against the side of one of the completed vessels, did not effect the least injury. The London *Times* has stated that there are building, or under orders to be built, in the French dock yards, twenty ships of the line, ten of the very largest size, and ten of an inferior calibre. The advices by later steamers, however, throw some doubt upon this statement, and it is probable that these vessels have been mistaken for twenty large transports, capable of conveying 1,500 men each. How many of the steel plated frigates, or liners, have been ordered is uncertain; but we know of at least six, enumerated above; two of them entirely or nearly completed, and all *vaisseaux du combat*, fighting vessels, steel plated, with iron beaks or prows. Owing to the rapid operations of French science, such vessels can probably be ready for sea within eighteen months after they are ordered. It is also announced that these and various other naval preparations are being prosecuted with energy, and that

200,000 shells and 30,000 rifles have been ordered for the use of the fleet. Steam rams are in course of construction at the principal government dock yards, and also gunboats cased with iron and impervious to cannon shot; while the plan of fortifications which the emperor has adopted is being rapidly executed, and especially the defences on the coast of Normandy and between Havre and Caen.

France has always been jealous of the naval supremacy of Great Britain, but it was not until the fall of Louis Philippe and the establishment of a republic which had little in common with the elder dynasties, that she undertook to build a fleet proportionate to her military strength. The naval commission established in 1848 reported, in 1851, in favor of the construction of forty-five steam line-of-battle-ships of the first class, sixty steam-frigates, and twenty steam-transports besides troop-ships and dockyards. The money to carry this plan into effect was immediately voted. Grand and expensive as was the plan, a special report to Parliament, recently made public, shows that the estimates have been largely increased, and now embrace in all some sixty liners, eighty or ninety screw frigates, and seventy-two steam-transports, besides the iron-plated vessels. The accounts of the naval preparations in France, which we receive from time to time, show how briskly this plan is being carried into effect, and leave little doubt that it is the settled policy of France to own the largest and strongest navy in Europe.

The fact that the French fleet at this moment is nearly, if not quite, equal to that of Great Britain, and the probability that in a short time it will be one third larger, is well calculated to excite the apprehension of the only nation against which such a naval force could be suspected to have hostile designs. The leading and most thoughtful journals of England, including the *Times*, *Blackwood*, the *Saturday Review* and the *London Quarterly*, have expressed from time to time, either strong apprehensions, or strong convictions, that such a calamity is impending. Perhaps their fears are exaggerated, or are partly dissembled for the purpose of arousing the energy of the people and of stimulating the government to efforts of preparation against a contingency which is only possible. The invasion of England sooner or later by Louis Napoleon is nearly as great a cause of fright as was the first Napoleon's projected bridging of the channel in 1804-5. In such a state of public opinion, whether morbid or well grounded, it is natural that the English press should calculate closely the chances of a project which can only be attempted by a fleet. The recent *sensation* paper in the *London Quarterly*, prepared by a gentleman of great experience and high naval rank, adopted the theory that it might be possible for France to command the channel, and land 200,000 men on the English shores: and this accomplished, that nothing could hinder them from taking possession of London.

It is not our purpose to discuss at present such a theory; but a summary of the reasons presented by the English press for fearing the future supremacy of France on the sea, may perhaps be interesting at this time. In addition to the immense naval preparations now going on, and the settled policy of the government to build a great navy, points to which we have already alluded, much stress is laid upon the fact, that the French navy is almost entirely new, and is consequently made after the latest and best models. It is supposed, also, that the iron-plated vessels and gun boats will cause a complete revolution in naval warfare. If Napoleon's plan is successful, it is said that nothing but incombustible shell-proof vessels can hold their way safely on the ocean. It has been proved that the largest shell will break like glass against a plate four or five inches thick; and against an enemy so protected, the old wooden vessels would become mere hulks on the water. The French, also, excel the world in their system of naval gunnery; and they have especially made great improvements in horizontal shell-firing. The Crimean war showed that they could not be excelled in bombardments, while the Italian campaign proved their wonderful expedition in transporting men and munitions by sea. But over and above every thing else in importance, are urged the facts that since the war with Russia, scarcely a French ship has been dismantled, while the nation possesses peculiar and almost inexhaustible resources for manning the largest fleet which she can build. In both these particulars, England labors under great disadvantages; for as soon as the Russian war was over, she dismantled her line-of-battle-ships and her gun-boats, and discharged their crews; but yet has not the power fully to man the vessels now in commission.

In recounting these gigantic preparations and armaments of France, the English press confesses to other griefs, the evidences whereof are apparent. Every suspicion of French projects costs England many solid guineas. To guard against future and possible evils, her people are now heavily taxed, and the increased naval appropriations are voted almost without opposition. She only seems to fear lest the steel-cased fleet will be knocking at her doors before she is ready to receive it. The apparent necessity of constantly dipping into her purse, of increasing year by year her naval and military expenses, and of turning her eyes from the arts of peace and the gains of commerce to the possible ruin of a cruel and unprovoked war, are realities which can not be disguised, and inconveniences to which she daily submits. And whatever may be thought of the ulterior designs of France, it is certain that the heavy bill, financial timidity and dreadful suspense which these naval armaments are costing England, are as real evils as if her fears were, as we trust they are, unfounded and groundless.

THE ITALIAN LEAGUE AND THE CONGRESS.

We infer from recent events in Italy that the Emperor Napoleon intends to advance the interests of the Central states in his own way, or not at all. What those states may do, or may wish to do, seems to form no part of the imperial plan. The duchies and the legations passed through a revolution in the most clever and quiet manner conceivable, exercising wonderful self-control in moments full of temptation to the hot and revengeful Southern blood, and showing the dethroned rulers to the frontiers without violence and with respectful politeness. For six months, their provisional governments have been carried on to the satisfaction of all classes and the admiration of Europe. The old theory that Italy was not sufficiently advanced for self-government is substantially refuted; and we behold these large masses of the unexpectedly liberated maintaining moderation in the hour of triumph, and civil order under the most trying and vexatious circumstances.

One would think that by this judicious and moderate behavior, the Central states had fairly earned the right of strengthening and consolidating, in their own way, the liberty and independence which they had achieved, and of which they have shown themselves so worthy. But every wish they have expressed has been either tacitly or expressly denied. One by one, they voted with the utmost unanimity for annexation to the kingdom of Sardinia. This proposition, which involved the consolidation of nearly the whole of Northeastern and Central Italy under a limited and constitutional monarchy, seems to have been offensive to the emperor, for it was instantly quashed, on the pretence that it would disturb the preponderance of power between Northern and Southern Italy. Not being able to build up this barrier against future aggressions upon their independence, the Central states concluded to have a regency, and offered the position of regent to the prince de Carignan, a relative of the king of Sardinia. Certain weighty representations were made by the emperor to the king which induced Carignan to hold back his assent, the French press asserting that this course was taken for the purpose of preventing the interference of Naples. The suggestion that the two Sicilies would make war upon Central Italy because the latter desired a legitimate prince for a regent, is one which only an ingenious intellect could have invented. Nothing would have been less probable, as the king of Naples has as much as he can do, now that his Swiss troops have gone, to protect his own government. His weak and mercenary troops could not stand an hour before the army of Italy, but that hour would perhaps be long enough to send the throne of Bomba's son and heir tumbling about his ears. It is plain, also, that the second regent named on the part of Central Italy, Buoncompagni, will not retain his appointment with the assent of the emperor, the objection being now put upon the broad ground that any regency would interfere with the duties of the proposed European congress.

All these distinct and unanimous propositions having been, one by one, defeated by the emperor, Italy can look for a permanent reëstablishment of her independence only in the action of the European congress, unless, indeed, the king of Sardinia should take some decided position of antagonism to France. This latter contingency does not seem probable, although the king has repeatedly expressed his own willingness, if unincumbered by diplomatic relations, to annex the duchies to his kingdom. Moreover, Prince Carignan, recently speaking on behalf of the king to the deputies of Central Italy, told them "to reckon always on the king, who will support their wishes, and who will never abandon those who entrust their destinies to his loyalty." This language, although it is encouraging to Central Italy, and implies that the king will do all he can to support the league, can not be construed as a pledge that the king will give up his engagements to the emperor, nor can it be expected that the plans of France will be repudiated by Sardinia, while a French army still occupies portions of Italy.

In this state of affairs, we are willing to admit that a European congress is convenient and perhaps necessary to settle, in some way, the Italian difficulties, but its action will be beset with the most perplexing difficulties. It is not likely that Central Italy will obtain more rights and privileges than the French emperor is willing to approve, and it is evident that he would prefer a weak and artificially-constructed confederacy to a free, united and independent state, made up of consanguineous populations: We know, indeed, on the authority of his letter to Victor Emanuel, that he wishes that Tuscany should be restored to the grand duke Ferdinand, that the duchess of Parma should be called to Modena, and that the pope should be honored with the presidency of the confederation.

These conditions, when compared with the unanimous demands of the league, are hard indeed, but they may be rendered still more severe by concessions allowed, for ulterior reasons, to Austria and her supporters in the congress. And with both France and Austria, to say nothing of Naples and the Roman States, to oppose the expressed will of Italy, what has Italy to hope, except at best a humiliating compromise? What limit, indeed, will be put to the jurisdiction of the congress? Will it recognize the established condition of things, or dispose, *de novo*, of the duchies and legations, as if it had a right to ignore their present governments, fairly erected and capable of being sustained by Italian swords? Will it go behind the deliberate and often-expressed determination of the people, and issue a new title to these little but independent states? Will it protect Italy from foreign intervention, and allow her to sustain herself by her own arms, as she is willing and ready to do, or will Italy be, for the fiftieth time, the foot-ball of diplomacy and a play-thing for the great powers? These are questions apposite to the issue which the French emperor presents to Europe, and Italy has reason to tremble while she entrusts her destiny to such contingencies. She enters the congress, ignorant of the jurisdiction which may be claimed over her states, and at the mercy of powers unwilling to fully recognize the independence she has achieved. Anything less than all she asks is so much stolen from her honor and from her acquired rights as a nation, and it is difficult to conceive of any fair or just reason why Europe should interfere with her sovereignty, or deliberate upon the partition of her territory. But to the congress she must go, and even with the moral force of the English ministry and people to aid her, it is perhaps a question whether she will not be compelled to accept a government which will eventually require to be upheld and perpetuated by the intervention of a foreign force.

NICHOLAS AND RUSSIA.

A portion of the press has raised a great outcry about a little word for Russia lately spoken by the Washington *Union* [May, 1853]. An out-and-out republican it seems, can not brook a good word, however true, in favor of any system of government except his own. The American eagle ruffles his feathers in anger because the fur of the Russian bear has been gently titillated by a good natured paragraph. We heartily despise this bigotry, this *pseudo* patriotism, as false as it is uncharitable.

The fact is that not only is the government of Russia very well adapted to the condition of her people, but is really progressive and republicanizing in its nature and tendencies. Nicholas I, the emperor, is doing all he can to alleviate the condition of his subjects, and to secure the ultimate freedom of his serfs. These serfs we all know, are slaves, and regularly bought and sold as one of the appurtenances of real estate. Let us see what Nicholas has done for them.

1st. He has shortened the term of serfs who enter the army from twenty to eight years; at the end of which time they cease to be slaves and become free. By this act he annually secures the freedom of thousands of slaves.

2d. He has provided that no serf can be sold except by a transfer of the land to which he belongs. In cases where the owner of land is unable to pay up the loans of government, the crown takes possession of the land, and the serfs become crown peasants, or hereditary fiefs. In this case they are taxed annually a small sum, and the government is obliged to supply them with the strict necessities of life in cases of bad harvests or other unavoidable misfortunes.

3d. He has granted them the right to enter into contracts and to buy their own freedom — a privilege which they never enjoyed before.

4th. He has lent them money to buy their freedom of their masters, to secure which they mortgage themselves to the crown, paying annually three per cent interest, and three per cent of the capital, until they become free, and proprietors of the land to which they are attached. Whole parishes have thus acquired their liberty, and by labor and industry have attained a freedom which no spasmodic revolution could give them.

Nicholas has made these concessions voluntarily, and prompted only by the nobleness of his own nature. His people love and revere his government, as they revere the authority of a father. He is teaching them the alphabet of freedom, and under his tuition Russia is becoming a nation of freemen. This people is semi-barbarous, and stand afar off from that liberty in which we rejoice; but if the emperor and his subjects are really striving after better things, we can not do worse than to give them a cold shoulder, and a taste of that Pharisaical pity, more redolent of self-conceit than of charity.

MILTON'S CHRISTMAS HYMN.

We publish this morning, as in harmony with the true spirit of this day, that most noble and elevated of all English lyrics, John Milton's *Hymn of the Nativity.* No Anglo-Saxon can read its inspiring strains without a feeling of manly and honest exultation that he belongs to the same lineage, speaks the same language, and has been educated in the same religion, as the blind poet. But grand and comprehensive as is the song, it is not so grand and comprehensive as the great thought that comes borne on the wings of the morning, so full of the story of Bethlehem. To the mature in mind and heart, it brings the deep peace that rejoices to behold God clothed with and ennobling our common humanity — taking up his abode and choosing his lot among the poor of this world, as if to remind us of the duty we owe especially to the poor — making himself poor, as if so teach all men the lesson of a common interest and a universal brotherhood; a brotherhood that brings down the high and lifts up the lowly into the same great relationship.

The universal peace among the nations that waited upon the Messiah's birth, has always been understood as an emblem of his mission and purpose on the earth, as a kind of prophetic foreshadowing of his full and perfect reign. Perhaps the poverty of his birth has a kindred import. The multitudes of our world are always poor; and it seems fit that the Saviour of men should come home to the hearts of all by making himself one of the multitude. The rich and poor must win his favor by stooping to the spirit of poverty. It is a lesson of sublime humility to learn to respect man for his manhood, and not for the accidents of wealth, or talents, or learning. His wants and his nature constitutes his claim to the friendly aid of Christian men.

One other thought is suggested by the day and the hymn. The growing power of Christianity is changing the face of the world. The march of Christian civilization is steadily onward; it is nearer to-day than it ever was on any Christmas before, to the millions of Japan, China, and the islands of the sea. Without noise or sound of a trumpet, the great army of truth advances with the steadinesss of light. Human reason is devoting itself to human interests. Society and government begin to exercise the right of eminent paternity over the ignorant, the unfortunate, and the criminal; to manifest towards the insane, the blind, the deaf and dumb, the diseased, the poverty-stricken, and the deserted, as classes, something of the compassion which a merciful father extends to the calamities of his children. The great charitable institutions of the world are of Christian planting and Christian growth. The hero of life and peace is greater, in the world's esteem, than the hero of death. Every impulse of humanity feels the impulse of a growing hope. Our very ideas and standards of thought are growing higher and purer under the inspiration of the beneficent spirit which animates our civilization. We have outgrown the old world which made a god of its dead Cæsar, and have learned to reverence men of self-denial and a peaceful spirit. We have advanced then; we have inherited all that they possessed; and we have gathered the wisdom of all ages, before and since. But, chiefly among all its possessions, the world owes its highest and best feelings to the religion of him who this day became incarnate, and so elevated humanity above the capacity of human thought to estimate.

A THEORY OF MUSIC.

From those fabulous times when Orpheus and Amphion caused the rocks and mountains to dance in harmony with their melodious lyres, to these modern and artistic days, graced by such queens of song as Sontag and Alboni, divine music has captivated the senses and ravished the souls of men. The rudest and the most cultivated have yielded to the "witchery of sound," and acknowledged its power over the passions and its mollifying influence upon the heart. The charm for melancholy — the quickener of hope — the interpreter of love — the inspirer of devotion — the spell of harmony magnetizes the sense and elevates the spirit. The luxurious Romans provided a concert of musicians at their banquets, and the polished Greek imported female slaves to enchant him with melodious airs played upon golden-wired harps.

We read in holy writ that the harmony of the sweet psalmist drove away the evil spirit of king Saul, and that when the minstrel played, whom troubled Elisha summoned, "the hand of the Lord came upon him."

It was the sweet voice of Cleopatra — "Rare Egyptian!" which first inveigled Antony, and as Byron says in *Love's Labor Lost* —

> "When love speaks, the voice of all the gods
> Makes heaven drowsy with the harmony."

The Cremonas of Italy respond to the melancholy heart-music of her people; France awakes to arms and glory at the sound of the electric *Marseillaise;* the shrill bag-pipes of Scotland find an echo in the recesses of her mountains and the hearts of her people; the proud step of the Spanish peasant times itself more proudly with the clink of the national castinets. Even the phlegmatic Englishman, and the money-making American are moved by their national anthems, and throw their purses and their hearts at the favorite songstress. We adorn our banquets with music, which Solomon says, is "a carbuncle set in gold;" and, "as the signet of an emerald well trimmed with gold, so is the melody of music in a pleasant banquet." The brass band is the crowning grace of the triumphal procession; the harmony of the dirge completes the funeral pageant of the dead, and the holy sacrifices of the altar are offered up with the melody of the chant. In hope, desolation, love, prayer, music is the refined expression of human thought, the exquisite language of the soul.

Now music is such exquisite and universal language because it is the exquisite and universal expression of the harmony of the universe. The soul is embosomed in beauty as boundless and infinite as the benevolence of Him who breathed into man the breath of life. He has created nothing inconsistent with himself, and as

He is harmony, so are all his works. There is no discord in his system, and no inharmonious relations among his creatures. The soul instinctively rejects the idea of dissonance with itself, or with nature, and mindful of its divine original, claims a kindred with the divine harmony. It aspires to perfection, and its destiny is to pursue eternally an infinite ideal which grows with its growth, and expands as it expands. The fountain of our inner life—the life of the soul—wells up from infinite sources of harmony, and its outlets, like its sources, are infinite. The life breathed into us can not be discordant with the infinite source. The harmony which exists between that life and the life which animates all things, is complete.

Shakespeare says:

> "Such harmony is in immortal souls;
> But whilst this muddy vesture of decay
> Doth grossly close it in, we can not hear it,"

And again he speaks of—

> "——notes of sorrow, out of tune."

Yes! the universal poet knew full well that there are discords in life; that we do not always *hear* the harmony that *is* in immortal souls; that sorrow and sin seem, and only *seem*, to choke the divine melody of nature. The divine musician has left no *real* discords in his works; and as the skillful composer introduces discordant notes to enhance the effectiveness and melody of his measure, so suffering and shame and death are "notes of sorrow," only "out of tune" with the "muddy vesture of decay which doth so closely shut us in," that for the time we can not *hear* the divine concords of nature. It is music, "heavenly maid," that, descending from the skies, teaches us the true symphony of life — the solemn anthem — the sweet chant — the pealing organ — the great diapason of nature,

> "Where the breeze warbles, and the mute still air
> Is music, slumbering on her instrument,"

That opens the ear, and elevates the heart and soul to the comprehension of the harmony of nature. Truly as beautifully has Coleridge said:

> "And what if all of animated nature
> Be but organic harps, diversely framed,
> That tremble into thought as o'er them sweeps,
> Plastic and vast, one intellectual breeze,
> At once the Soul of each, and God of all."

THACKERAY AS A POET.

The following lines occur in Thackeray's best production, *Pendennis*, and they struck me when that most perfect of novels appeared as odd and exceedingly pretty. There is an elegant pertness in the measure, quite captivating and Horacian, and they have an artist-like smack peculiar to every production of this eminent *literateur*.

They were written to fit a frontispiece of an annual. A Spanish damsel is seen hastening to church with a large prayer-book, and a youth is hidden in a niche watching her.

THE CHURCH PORCH.

Although I enter not,
Yet round about the spot

Sometimes I hover,
And at the sacred gate,
With longing eyes I wait
Expectant of her.

The minster bell tolls out
Above the city's rout
And noise and humming;
They 've stopped the chiming bell,
I hear the organ's swell —
She 's coming, she 's coming!

My lady comes at last,
Timid and stepping fast,
And hastening hither,
With modest eyes downcast;
She comes — she's here — she's past —
May Heaven go with her.

Kneel undisturb'd, fair saint,
Pour out your praise or plaint
Meekly and duly.
I will not enter there,
To sully your pure prayer
With thoughts unruly.

But suffer me to pace
Round the forbidden place,
Lingering a minute,
Like outcast sprites, who wait,
And see through Heaven's gate
Angels within it.

There 's a picture of a young scapegrace catching a glimpse of Paradise! And if any one word can paint a man, *I* think the adjective *artistic* is the most apposite to Mr. William Makepeace Thackeray.

PALMER'S WHITE CAPTIVE.

In speaking briefly of this beautiful creation of American art, we do not propose to indulge in the usual conventional criticisms about surfaces and shadows, bold handling and inspired chisels. The impression which the White Captive makes upon the mind, is subjective; and she should be judged rather as a woman than as a statute. She has as little in common with the marble-limbed race of the Venuses, as a living man has with anatomical manikins. And yet we believe that the anatomy is perfect, and will stand the test of the most searching analysis.

Palmer's aim has been to give the world the highest ideal of American womanhood. To effect this, he has not blindly followed the antique models, nor restricted his genius to a close imitation of ancient art. He has sufficient original force to reproduce nature as he finds it, and the courage to mould into marble the character and the inner life, as well as the mere external forms of physical beauty. The world is tired of looking at small-headed Venuses, which belong like the de Medicis, to a voluptuous rather than to an intellectual age.

Palmer has accordingly given us the broad brow of a large brained and cultivated woman. Her head and face bespeak not only intellectual superiority, but high moral culture; her soul is the home of the domestic affections, and her features express a sweetness of temper and force of will which constitute the true feminine type of character. In the attitude and expression of the figure, we see an immense power of will; and although self-will may deform the feminine face, yet a strong will individualizes a woman, isolates the soul from degrading influences, and secures the supremacy of that conscious life which wells up from its own depths. Like a curb around a spring of fresh water, it shuts off the adjacent drainage, while it does not obstruct the pure and limpid flow. And there may be nothing obtrusive in its manifestation, for, like true strength, it may show itself tranquil and hopeful. The White Captive represents the idea of this force of character, associated with a sweetness of disposition almost suggestive of the thought of dependence. Such a combination of natural traits may not satisfy the antique conception of beauty, but in a cultivated and Christian age, which rank the graces and glories of the inner and spiritual life far above the manifestations of outward and unspiritual beauty, such an ideal must bear away the palm from the comparatively crude and unmatured conceptions of the past.

A question will doubtless be raised, whether or not Mr. Palmer has stepped beyond the legitimate province of sculpture in connecting the statue with an incident. Really, there is no incident; the figure explains itself. We behold a frontier girl bound to a tree in the forest; the fallen drapery indicates that she has been seized from her sleep, and in the startled and distressed face we can almost discern the presence of the crowd of revengeful and enraged savages who cluster around her. A scene in Western life which has often occurred, is illustrated — an episode of Indian warfare so familiar as to need little or no explanation. A thousand years hence she will tell her own story.

We have said that the expression is that of mingled sweetness and firmness; but the face tells also a tale of pain, perplexity and shame. As she stands bound and naked before her captors, we see that her fortitude may in a moment give way before the painful and humiliating dangers which surround her. But she is neither humiliated nor abashed, and she bears on her brow and in her eyes an expression of fearlessness which proves that her proud and womanly nature is as yet unconquered. This expression adds to rather than detracts from, the natural softness and sensibility of her nature, and increases the living sympathy which she attracts.

This Western girl shows in well rounded muscle and in the admirable harmony and proportion of the limbs, that robust but graceful strength which comes from free exercise in the open air. A statue, it is said, should have no moral, but the White Captive has an excellent one. She has not traversed the forest nor paddled the canoe in vain, and yet hard work has not disturbed the muscular harmony of her frame. Physically and intellectually, she is a woman of the highest culture, worthy of the age and of Christian civilization. In a word, the artist has had the skill to nurse into bloom the very flower and perfection of womanhood.

OCTOBER—1856.

Now it is October. Now the fields "with verdure clad" begin to assume the russet and sombre hues of autumn. Now the forest-leaves change color and rival in their dun but intense tints the glories of a flower-bed in June. Now the air grows clear and cold, and the sunsets more purple; now morn, her rosy steps in the Eastern clime advancing, sows the earth with *more* than orient pearl; while the rich autumnal sunset leaves behind "fertile golden islands, floating in a silver sea." O! these clear, cerulean, American skies; Italy can not rival them, nor does the artist dare reproduce them on canvas! Now, even we of the city, enjoy a season unparalleled in attraction by the glories of the east and south of Europe; an autumn six weeks in length and sometimes lasting to Christmas. Thank heaven! New York is open at the top, and the glories of these October skies and the crisp and champagney weather of early autumn are shared by all.

Now New York is again New York, and Broadway once more Broadway. Now our Southern and Western cousins, darkened forever in black broadcloth, no longer monopolize the streets, but share the honors of the highway with young New York, clad in wide-legged drabs and checks, and covered by the fall beaver at the proper angle. Now the butterflies of fashion are with us again, and we recognize the old face under the new bonnet, and admire the inimitable aplomb with which the New York girl surmounts a muddy crossing, or hails a passing stage. Now of sunshiny mornings and moonlight evenings the lines of the streets and public buildings and the towers and steeples of churches stand out in bold relief in the clear atmosphere; while upon the heated crowds emerging from the concert-room or the theatre, the blue etherial sky shines with new lustre, and "the benediction of the covering heavens falls like dew." Now the town gathers itself up for a fresh plunge into the whirl of business, excitement and pleasure; now the great tide of life flows on more briskly and the heart of the city beats with more tumultuous throbs. And now the mature in heart garner the lessons taught by the fading year, and remember that they must fall, as the leaves fall, in October.

HAIL AND FAREWELL.

As we write, at twelve o'clock, on the night of the thirty-first of December, the chimes of old Trinity are tolling the knell of the dying year. While we listen to the sweet strains, the air seems full of farewells to the happy months, and days, and hours, which now

> Follow the bier
> Of the dead, cold year,
> And like dim shadows watch by the sepulchre.

The requiem is over; the sobbing strains have ceased; there is a lull in the very pattering of the raindrops which for hours have made melancholy music on the roof. The clock strikes twelve; the death and sepulture of "the dead, cold year are complete;" and now the merry peals ring out a welcome to the new year. Hail and farewell!! We welcome the coming as we speed the parting guest, and greet and take home to our bosoms the new year, with its new cares, pleasures, duties and responsibilities!

ROMANCE AND THEOLOGY, 1851.

Discussions on mooted topics of theology excite little interest among the miscellaneous public. The age is eminently utilitarian in its aims and purposes; devoted to the attainment of practical results, it regards with indifference the abstruse and the polemical. The combats of the disputants in the theological arena are occasionally regarded with curiosity, but seldom with interest. Sometimes a polemical gladiator will make an uncommon exhibition of prowess, determination, or length of wind, and the public will favor him with an admiring and curious glance, as he drives his adversary from one position to another, harasses him with unceasing blows; and, after having overwhelemed him with logic and learning, administers the *coup de grace* with a rhetorical flourish. In fact, theological writers are invariably partizans, and their readers belong to some one school of faith; beyond their own circle, they care little for the opinions of others, and are content if they are permitted the undisturbed enjoyment of their own creed. Theological literature — if that term be allowable — appeals only to classes of men, and while a few polemical writers are universally known by reputation, none can be said to be universally read.

Of late years, however, a bastard species of literature has crept into existence, and acquired a wonderful popularity — we mean the religious novel; and by this term is not meant the romance or tale, written for the purpose of enforcing some moral or religious truth — like the tales of Miss Edgeworth — but a fiction, containing all the allurements and many of the faults of the yellow-covered species, and written for the purpose of controverting some doctrine of faith, or worship, or church organization. Lately a large number of books of this sort, more or less objectionable, have been p lished by respectable houses, and have found a re sale. They are purchased by heads of families, affording instruction and amusement for the young, are devoured by that class of sentimental readers, wh mental stomach has became so depraved as to be unable digest anything less piquant or highly seasoned. And now that, within a few days, Mr. Huntingdon has published another work of this nature, under the romantic name of Alban, and more objectionable in its details than any that has hitherto appeared, it is time that the respectable portion of the public press should give a decided opinion on the subject.

We do not urge, as an objection to this novel, that it is written by a Roman catholic, for the evident purpose of propagating the tenets of his church, nor that it attacks the doctrines of other religious associations with an unusual degree of bitterness. No man, in this country at least, can object to a fair and free discussion of religious truth, and the Romanist is at equal liberty with the Protestant, to a public exposition of his faith. But we protest, as a matter of taste, against this whole system of mingling together things so entirely incongruous; and as a matter of morality, against this work, in which the author has woven his religious opinions into a novel of the loosest description, and thus presents it to the public, professing to be what it is not. If intended as a love tale, all discussion of a religious nature is out of place, and in the worst possible taste; if intended as a defence of the Roman church, the course he has pursued in Alban, is one the most calculated to debase his subject, and bring discredit on his cause.

A scrupulous attendance upon the services of the church, and a rigid observance of its formalities, from the chief employment of the hero; and when not so engaged, he indulges his passion for indiscriminate love-making. Between these two pursuits — theology and love-making — he oscillates with varying success from the introduction to the finis.

These peculiarities form the staple from which the author has created his heroine; love and theology engross her conversation, her thoughts, and her soul. When she is not in church, she is generally making love, and her mind is alternately occupied by her lover and her church. To one of these two poles the magnet of her mind is continually attracted — rather exciting topics for a young miss just turned sixteen; but then she occasionally relieves her mind by embroidering a surplice or an altar-piece. She falls in love about the time of her baptism, and the hero makes a discovery of the same fact just after his first confession to a priest.

And the reader is left in an unhappy state of doubt, to ascertain upon which of these circumstances the denouement depends. These are the hero and the heroine, and such the tissue of this novel.

Against such a combination of incongruities, such a confusion of things divine and things temporal, such a mingling of the spiritual and the sensual, God and mammon, such a medley of religion and sensuous passion, romance and theology, we enter our solemn protest, as contrary to good taste and good morals.

MR. CHOATE'S ELOQUENCE.

At the trial of a celebrated patent case in an eastern city some years since, Mr. Choate's concluding argument, which occupied a whole day in its delivery, was heard attentively by one of the largest audiences ever crammed into the court-room. The heads, if not the whole of his speech, were written out in that wonderfully crooked chirography of his, on numerous slips of paper. When he came to the end of his last stately and electrical sentence, the spectators, affected by the fire and enthusiasm of the speaker, seized upon the manuscript, tore it into shreds and distributed it among themselves, so that there was scarcely a person who did not carry away a memento of the great Boston lawyer. This anecdote was related to the writer by one of the counsel engaged in the cause, and there can be no doubt of its authenticity.

The word *electrical* expresses perhaps better than any other, the leading characteristic of Mr. Choate's oratory. When he had reached the height and acme of his passionate declamation, one almost expected to see the sparks fly from his person as they did from his eyes, and his head grow luminous from the electrical fires which were playing about his brain. More than the vigorous strength of his logic, his wonderful mastery of the language, and the purity and classic severity of his style, did this sympathetic power, which proceeded from his nervous system, rather than from his intellect, prevail among and sweep away the emotions of his auditors. When the mysterious affinity was once established, no audience could resist him, any more than an electrical circle can resist the mysterious thrills which shoot through the nerves and cause the extremities to quiver; and the example mentioned above is but one of many which might be given to illustrate the influences which Mr. Choate exercised over men. We have seen an audience of ten thousand cultivated persons rise and cheer the magnificence of one of Mr. Everett's sentences; but the eloquence which so impresses men that it puts them for the time under the control of the speaker, makes their sympathies and emotions the mere channel of his own, and sweeps from heart to heart in a controlling current of passion, was a peculiar power with Mr. Choate, in which he had no rival among his countrymen. It is true that his oratory was at times extravagant, and perhaps inflated; but even then the severest critic could not always withstand his earnestness and fervor.

NIGHT SCENERY.

A fair morning, about 3:30, he who looks upward to the north and north-east, will see in the firmament a celestial display which no dream of sleep can realize. The clusters of the autumnal and winter stars are slowly emerging from the east. The earth, moving forward through the celestial vault, encounters new and brilliant orbs ascending in unison the canopy of heaven. Here are the Pleiades, six chaste sisters, whose "sweet influences" were sung by Job, now slowly rising towards the meridan, where they culminate at their greatest altitude from the earth. Below them we see the huge outlines of Orion, now first visible above the horizon, with his gorgeous belt pointing downwards toward the the Dog Star, which, notwithstanding the intense heat, has not yet been visible. In this latitude, the dog days, although the weather has been hot, do not belong to the serious (Sirius) family. More to the north, shine Aldebaran and Capella, two stars of the first magnitude, while the circumpolar constellations, as Cassiopeia, Andromeda and Perseus, are closely approaching the meridan. But the most captivating of all these celestial appearances in the blue ethereal, is the planet Venus, which, having just passed her superior conjunction, now presents to the earth her hemisphere fully illuminated, shining with much greater lustre than she did last July, when her brilliant crescent gilded the shades of evening. An hour later, Jupiter, dim but ruddy, appears, having apparently made within a few months, a circuit around Venus.

As one looks upon these celestial glories, grander and more attractive than terrestrial scenery even when lighted by the sun, he can not but call to mind the immortal words of Addison:

> "The spacious firmament on high,
> And all the blue ethereal sky,
> And spangled heavens, a shining frame,
> Their great Original proclaim."

THE NEW PLANET VULCAN.

The latest number of the *North British Review* contains an interesting summary of the discussions by the French astronomers on the alleged discovery of a new planet between Mercury and the Sun. M. Lescarbault, an humble but honest physician, living at Orgeres, who has studied astronomy from his earliest youth and has provided himself with rude but accurate instruments of observation, saw on the 26th of May, 1859, a black point immediately after its entrance upon the Sun's disc which it crossed in one hour and seventeen minutes. From calculations soon after made, it was estimated that the new body, which is appropriately named Vulcan, is only one seventeenth as large in mass, as Mercury, and that the time of its revolution is 19 days and 17 hours. It is never at a greater elongation, or distance from the Sun, than eight degrees.

Leverrier, the discoverer of Neptune, and the head of the National observatory, had expressed his partial belief in the theory that certain disturbances in the movements of Mercury could be accounted for by the existence of small bodies circulating between Mercury and the Sun, like the ring of such bodies as there are between Mars and Jupiter. He received, however, with doubt the news of Lescarbault's discovery, and it was was not until after a severe examination of the latter's work, papers and instruments, that he became convinced that the doctor had really made the discovery. When satisfied that an intra-Mercurial planet had actually been seen, he made the facts public, and the discoverer of Vulcan became famous. Some of the leading astronomers, hereupon took up the subject, holding opposite opinions. M. Wolf made calculations founded on the records of many black spots which had passed across the Sun since 1762, confirmed the credibility of Lescarbault's narration, and moreover expressed the opinion that the observations can only be reconciled by the admission of at least three intra-Mercurial planets.

On the other hand, M. Liais, another French astronomer, denies the whole story of Dr. Lescarbault's, both as to the observation, which he declares to be false, and as to the truth of his hypotheses. He argues the matter with great skill and force; his course of reasoning, however, being too elaborate to be properly condensed in this paragraph. It is perhaps sufficient to say, that the reviewer in the North British, after carefully stating all the facts and criticisms, does not doubt the honesty of Dr. Lescarbault, nor does he believe that he is mistaken.

ASTRONOMICAL PHENOMENA FOR 1861.

The *American Almanac* for 1861, contains a variety of astronomical and meteorological intelligence. The eclipses there recorded have already been noticed in our columns, and we find nothing especially new or original in an astronomical point of view in this issue of the Almanac except the tide table, tables of the passage by the planets of meridian (mean-time) and their declination at transit; also an article on meteorology. The other portions of this article are derived from other sources.

In reference to the tides, it is computed in this Almanac by the formula of La Place that the highest tides of 1861, according to the Washington mean-time of new or full Moon, will be those of February 23, March 26, April 24, Oct. 4 and Nov. 2. The actual rise, however, depends upon the strength and direction of the wind; so that the above estimates are very uncertain approximation for the coast of the United States.

It may be useful to sum up from other sources, intelligence in reference to this period of the astronomical year. On the 20th March the Sun enters the constellation Aries; the planes of the equator and the ecliptic become coincident; the centre of the Sun is directly opposite the centre of the Earth, and astronomical spring commences, the day and the night being equal. As the Earth advances to the East, the great stars which have adorned the North and the East during the brilliancy of winter evenings, seem advancing further to the West; Altaire, Vega and Denib appear no longer in the evening horizon, but will come again in the East; Orion with his belt, and the Pleiades with their sweet influences, seek earlier repose behind the Western horizon. There are, therefore, now portions of starless space in the celestial vault towards the East at certain periods of the night, and the glories of the firmament seem to concentrate near where the Sun sets, and in the frequent company of the Moon descending to the horizon. The great circumpolar constellations do not go below the horizon; Perseus, Andromeda, and the great Regulus, have all passed the meridian; Cassiopeia nestles close to the Little Bear, and the North Star stands on a line horizontal with the pointers of the Dipper, at midnight. It is one of the proofs of the translation of the solar system through space, that four thousand years ago, a star in Draco was the polestar, while it is ascertained that in some thirteen thousand years Vega will be the point at which the magnetic needle will be directed.

As to the planets visible, Jupiter and Saturn at about 5 P. M., rise near each other. The earth moves in a narrower orbit and with a swifter motion, which causes them to appear earlier night by night, both having passed the meridian on the 19th of February, within about an hour of each other. Venus will be the evening star after May 11th, for the rest of the year; from August 27th, Mars will be a morning star. It is said that Mercury may be seen soon after sunset about February 24, June 22, October 17, and just before sunrise about April 15, August 13, and December 2. We place little reliance on this promise; for the nearness of this interior planet to the Sun, and the obscurity of the horizon at the periods mentioned, render it almost impossible to detect him. Half a dozen sharp eyes last November strained their vision through a clear atmosphere on the horizon to see the promised stranger, and saw him not. Copernicus himself died mourning that he had never seen this swift messenger of the heavens. There will be a transit of Mercury over the Sun's disc, November 12, invisible in America, and an occultation of Mars, beginning on May 12th, at 7.30, and ending at 8.42, in the evening.

The two most recent astronomical discoveries announced are Lescarbault's (a poor French physician) planet called Vulcan, and which he saw and calculated as it passed the Sun's disc; also the fifty-seventh Asteroid between the orbits of Mars and Jupiter. It was discovered by Biek, and christened Mnemosyne. Last summer there was a little comet in the west, soon after sunset; but he carried his tail off, and left an incomplete record. Five great comets, Biela's which sweeps around the Sun in 6¾ years, D'Arrest's in 6¾, Borsen's in 5½, Winnecke's in 5, and Encke's in 3½, will reappear within the next five years.

Much might be said of meteorology and its development, through the articles of friend Meriam, and the weather reports sent to the Smithsonian Institution by the telegraph. Storms can be discovered before they come, and their path quite correctly ascertained in advance. The *American Almanac* has an excellent paper on meteorology, in which the various theories of the earth's temperature are discussed; it is written by Professor Lovering of Harvard University. If Humboldt still lived, under recent discoveries and investigation, he might solve the infinite problem of the weather.

THE SUSPENSION BRIDGE.

Passing a few days at this delightful resort for tourists from all parts of the world [August, 1859], I feel called upon to perform a duty incumbent on all conscientious travelers; namely, to correct misstatements calculated to mislead the public. A letter from this place, published a few days since in that intelligent and judicious sheet, the *New York Herald*, stated, at least, three palpable and transparent untruths.

One statement of the correspondent of the *Herald* was to the effect that many of the locomotive-drivers were so fearful of the security of the Suspension bridge that they refused to drive their engines across. Under my own eyes, some forty trains pass daily in perfect safety; and on the authority of the managers and engineers of the bridge, I state that their only difficulty with the locomotive-drivers is to keep them down to the slow time allowed by the regulations. So far from showing any anxiety, the drivers move across the bridge with the utmost *nonchalance*, knowing thoroughly, as they do, the perfect safety of the structure.

This well instructed correspondent of the *Herald* states, in the second place, that a large portion of the travelers alight at the bridge and pay 25 cents *extra*, rather than run the risk of crossing on the cars. On the authority of my own observation and that of the managers of the railways and of the bridge, I assert that not one out of one hundred passengers cross the bridge on foot; and that the pedestrian is usually a feeble-minded old woman, or a traveler who prefers to view the falls and the rapids at leisure and on foot.

This profound and industrious letter-writer for the *Herald*, and who, I am informed reliably, was not allowed to pass the Suspension bridge *gratis*, because he was a Bohemian, or a wandering newsmonger who could not authenticate himself properly — states, in the third place, that the bridge has sagged lately about twenty inches. I have stood upon the railway-track of the bridge when an engine (the most trying test) passed, and with my eye on the track, have discovered nothing that could be called a sag; the utmost was a slight vibration of the cable, which might be caused by a small pack of dogs, trotting across in step. The cable is elastic and has a natural, honest and intended spring, or elastic movement, well known to, and prophesied by the architect, so long ago as 1855. There is *no* movement from side to side; if the anchors, foundations and piers which pierce the earth to an immense distance had been disturbed $\frac{1}{16}$ of an inch, the whole structure would have fallen instantaneously. The elasticity, vibration or deflection of the cable, have always been admitted; so far back, at least, as 1855, when the whole railway track was piled up so full as it could hold, with heavy masses of stone. The elasticity now is as great as then; and it is admitted that with a load of 326 tons, the cable might deflect so much as ten inches. But when the bridge is loaded with eight cattle cars and an engine, weighing altogether 250 tons, (as much as can be put on the bridge at once), the deflection is scarcely perceptible. I have watched trains from the railway track, from the carriage and foot-paths below, and from an outside stand-point (in fact from the workman's platform under the bridge), and have never been able to discern anything like sagging, or anything except the minutest vibration; and then with my eye on the line of the track.

There were about 5,000 persons here on Wednesday last to see Blondin's performances on his rope. He ran a race across the Niagara with a boat pulled by two strong rowers; distance 700 feet; height above the surface of the river, 200 feet; time, five minutes; Blondin ahead. It *is* true that Travis shot a pistol-ball through Blondin's hat, held by the latter at arm's length; the ball was projected from a boat in the river, distant from B. 300 feet. It is *not* true that Blondin ever carried a man across in his arms. The Niagara mountebank is a permanency here; he makes about $800 at each ascension. His next will be on the 17th. The Clifton, International and Cataract are all full; and the Monteagle, with its invigorating mineral baths, draws a large concourse of visitors.

ELECTING JUDGES.

Our citizens will soon be called upon to cast their votes for the following important judicial officers: a supreme court judge, the city judge, recorder, surrogate, judge of the court of general sessions, and several justices of the police courts.

It is a generally admitted fact, that the character of judicial officers in this state, of all ranks and degrees, has deteriorated since the constitution of 1846 went into effect. The opinion of our best and most judicious lawyers and business men, as well as the unanimous voice of the respectable portion of the press, now condemn the new method of appointing judges. The whole system of an elective judiciary has proved a failure, degrading to judicial station, and poisonous to those great moral principles which underlie and support the administration of public justice. There is danger, indeed, that the whole bench will, in time, be contaminated by the corrupting political influences which to a great extent govern the municipal affairs of the city. Unprincipled and selfish men too often have the power to control and direct legislative and executive functions for their own personal benefit, or the advancement of parties; but the position of a corruptible and unscrupulous judge is infinitely more hazardous to the public, and may be perverted to uses beyond the reach of ordinary political villany. The best and most reliable members of the legal profession begin to avoid competition for judicial office. They prefer the liberal and honest rewards of their business, and that character for unspotted integrity which makes them the counselors of great moneyed institutions, and safe advisers of individuals and families. The most meritorious members of the bar in this city know and realize the dangers of running a muck race for the bench; and the bench actually suffers under the ignorance and incompetency of third or fourth class men, who in too many instances displace tried, learned and trustworthy jurists.

The practical result of the new system of judicial elections is to reward political services by a seat on the bench. Judicial candidates and judges are seen in political conventions; they take a share in the routine and discipline of party, and so become liable to be unjustly influenced, or tempted into partial judgments. The *Tribune*, and other journals of the same reckless class, personally vituperate judges whose legal decisions do not correspond with certain popular opinions, and claim that the people are better judges of the law than the courts. The political adventurer is to be petted, but the cold shoulder is turned upon the irreproachable and inflexibly honest man, whose conscience walks above the fascinations of politics, and the clamors of the rabble. With all due respect for the higher judiciary of this state, including the appellate, supreme and superior courts, we can not fail to notice that there has been a falling off in the character of the judges within the last ten years. There are now fewer of these solid, learned, discreet and honest jurists who once administered justice in this state, and who did so much towards moulding and developing those great legal principles upon which our rights and duties are founded. Such men may have been statesmen, but they never dabbled in dirty politics, or contaminated themselves by contact or rivalship with the vagabonds of the profession.

In those courts of this city, in which the great mass of criminal cases are tried and decided, local politics disturb the administration of the law and the due punishment of crime. Could all the facts of this subject be fully laid before the public; could we make known, in detail, the favors and forbearance extended to political rowdies, drunken emissaries of the pot house, emigrant robbers, dealers with thieves, the race of gamblers, panderers, and that influential but generally depraved class which elect recorders, city judges and police magistrates; could we see how justice is perverted, the truth dishonored, false swearing, subtle and mean pettifogging encouraged; could we penetrate the mysterious secrets of some of the detailed officers and wire pullers at the little court rooms, and look in upon the monstrous deceit and corruption which pervade this system, and the horrid orgies which go on under the name and authority of the law, we should draw back in horror at the spectacle. When rowdies, ruffians and criminals control the election of magistrates, it is time to resort to some better system.

LEGAL REFORM—THE NEW CODES.

Every member of society is interested not only in those great principles of law which guaranty him the undisturbed enjoyment of his civil rights, but also in the means of so applying these principles as to secure him equal and exact justice. The forms and technicalities of law are frequently of immeasurable importance to the suitor, and a mistake in choosing the proper method for obtaining his rights may entirely preclude him from legal redress. It is true, that a man going to the law generally leaves the machinery of his case to his lawyer; but it is equally true that if that machinery is defective, or slow, or in any way unreliable, sooner or later, he will suffer for it.

The forms or remedies of law under which our courts are now acting [1858] have been handed down to us from remote ages. Originally simple and precise, they have grown into a vast and complicated system. The mother country especially, groans under cumbrous and unwieldy technicalities which surround the avenues to justice and waylay the steps of the unwary suitor. The delay and injustice of the English court of chancery has made it a "by word and a hissing," and will in a few years exterminate it forever. Efforts are now being made in high quarters to reform the English courts; efforts in which Lord Brougham has not been backward, and to which Charles Dickens has dedicated his last novel.

In our country, legal reform has been commenced with spirit, and carried out with determination. In this state, great and important changes have already commenced.

The court of chancery, with all its cumbersome machinery, has been abolished, and has given place to a simple and more efficacious system. The old fashioned distinction between actions at law and suits in equity no longer exists, and there is now but one form for all civil actions. The structure of the courts has been reorganized, and the judges are not appointed for life by the executive, but elected by the people for a term of years. Last, but not least of these eventful changes, the onerous and burdensome fee bill, has been abolished, and a man can go to law without being eaten up by costs.

The seed of most of these reforms was sown by the convention held for the revision of the constitution in 1846. The new constitution authorized the legislature to appoint three commissioners to reduce into a written and systematic code the whole body of the law of the state, or so much thereof as the commissioners should deem expedient. Another section provided for the appointment of three commissioners to reform, simplify and abridge the rules, practice, forms and proceedings of all the courts of the state, and the legislature was authorized to establish tribunals of conciliation, and to reorganize the courts of the state.

These proposed changes in our judicial system were not adopted without long and able discussion. But they are adopted, and the revolution which has commenced in the practice of law is fairly due to the well directed efforts of that able convention.

The next legislature accordingly passed an act in relation to the judiciary which reorganized the courts of the state, and made numerous provisions in relation to the court of appeals, the supreme court, criminal and local courts, the terms of those courts, and the election and classification of the judges. The next year the first code was presented by the commissioners appointed for that purpose, and was adopted by the legislature. It covers about sixty closely printed pages, and makes minute provision for the jurisdiction and practice of the courts. The next year, 1849, came an amendment of one hundred pages, and 473 sections, which was swallowed by the legislature without much hesitation.

In 1850, the legislature slept in peace, and contented itself with passing about twenty distinct and separate acts in relation to the courts in different parts of the state; although it is perhaps worth while to mention the proposed criminal code (480 pages) which was not acted upon by the legislature. In 1851, the code was again remodeled and published in an interesting little pamphlet of 150 pages. In 1853, we have another new code, containing many new and important provisions, and which is now before the committee of the whole in the assembly, in the shape of a document of 360 pages.

It is in reference to this last instalment of codification that we must say a few words. In the first place it is to be noticed that the codifiers of 1853 are not content simply to reform the practice and pleadings, but have embraced in their volume a range of subjects of much greater importance. We have, for instance, a title on the enforcement of liens, a chapter on assessments, another on the proceedings of an insolvent to discharge himself from debt, together with a long title on evidence. There are also important provisions in relation to cases of insanity and habitual drunkenness.

Very summary proceedings are authorized in cases of alleged insolvency. For instance, a merchant, broker, factor, or banker, whose note has been protested for ten days, and who fails to give notice that he has a valid defence, is liable to be dragged before a court and declared an insolvent? We mention these facts to show the importance of the proposed changes, and how seriously the interests of every business man is affected by what is termed a code of civil procedure.

Another circumstance which will strike the reader, is the evident haste and carelessness with which the last code has been prepared. Accuracy and explicitness in the use of words are of the first importance in a work which purports to condense, arrange and codify the vast framework of principles by which our courts are governed. A badly constructed sentence may protract litigation for years. In this respect, the code of 1853 is a slovenly and disgraceful affair. In many cases the sense is obscure, and the grammar villainous. What under heavens do the codifiers mean by the title on the *productiveness of evidence*, unless they mean to establish a system of obstetrics, in which case the *productiveness* of evidence would naturally be associated with the *writ of deliverance*, the new name for the good old habeas corpus. And here is a batch of general provisions:

"§ 1738. Words used in this code, in the past or present tense, include the future as well as the past and present; words used in the masculine gender include the feminine and neuter; the singular number includes the plural, and the plural the singular; the word person includes a corporation as well as a natural person; writing includes printing or printed paper; oath includes affirmation or declaration," &c., &c.

The commissioners are fairly entitled to a patent for getting over grammatical difficulties. To save themselves the trouble of being accurate, they have codified grammar as well as law, and hope to make both plain to "the common understanding." Even in the assembly, which is not apt to be excessively rigid in matters of criticism, the slovenliness and verbal inaccuracies of the new code have hitherto met with almost universal condemnation.

Six years have now elapsed since codification commenced, and yet we are far from having arrived at a uniform and reliable system of practice. And there is another reason for this besides the frequent changes introduced by the commissioners, and adopted by the legislature. Nearly every section of the previous codes has received the judicial construction of the courts. Nor have these decisions always been uniform and consistent. Different judges in different judicial districts, not having an opportunity for mutual consultation, often differ widely in their decisions, and in many cases it is impossible to settle a point of practice without going to the court of appeals. In fact every disputed point of practice which affects the substantial rights of parties is uniformly carried to the court of appeals. This involves serious delay to the suitor, and as each new provision has to go through the same judicial mint before it can be properly stamped, the vexation and delay are endless.

We have made these remarks and have presented these facts in order that the public may understand the importance of the subject which is now before the legislature. We are a warm friend of judicious reform, and yet we can't help asking how many more years — how many more codes will be required to settle the practice of the New York courts? Intelligent lawyers say that there is more delay, vexation and expense now than there ever has been in the conduct of legal proceedings. Will the legislature in the short ten days which remain, be able to digest the 360 pages of the new code? Will the next legislature have the time and ability? Are there not important provisions in this proposed law which deeply concern the interests of every broker, merchant and business man in the state? Copies of the new code are scarce, hardly a single lawyer has had an opportunity of perusing it. We don't believe that there are in this city, twenty copies of a document which so nearly concerns the civil rights and privileges of every citizen.

In view of these facts, we think that this subject demands a more general and serious consideration. Legal reform is too serious a matter to be trifled with. We have waited patiently for six years, and it is now time that we had something more than mere experiments at codes which seem to dissatisfy even the codifiers. We desire a well considered, well digested code, written accurately, and in good English: And in view of the importance and necessity of the subject, we trust that the present bill will not be smuggled through the legislature, without a thorough and critical examination.

WHO SHOULD BE WITNESSES?

We have a word to say in regard to the act pending before the state legislature repealing the law allowing parties in law suits to testify as witnesses. We borrowed the reform from England, where it has received the sanction of parliament, of the judges and of the bar, bodies slow to depart from the established usages of the realm, or to adopt innovations not founded on common sense and deliberate forethought. Though in direct conflict with the rules of evidence and the theories of conducting trials, as established for centuries, the new system has been found to work admirably in the courts of Great Britain. We have the authority of several of her best jurists and her leading journals for saying, that it has shortened and simplified trials, accomplished, in some cases, the ends of justice, which could have been accomplished by no other method, and reached with directness the facts of the case, which could not have been reached except by the examination of parties the most directly informed of those facts. The opinion of our judges and lawyers is almost unanimous in opposition to the repeal, as was shown by the very respectable and numerously signed memorial recently transmitted to Albany.

The opposition to the present law is based principally upon the ground that it is said to encourage parties to suits to swear falsely. Now, we believe willful and corrupt perjury to be a very rare offence, in civil actions at least. The chances of detection are a thousand to one against the perjurer; and the party to a suit who offers himself as a witness must stand up before a jury who scrutinize him all the more closely because he is a party to the controversy. He must also submit to the rigors of a cross-examination; and it will fare hard with him if the collateral circumstances and details of his story do not harmonize with the naked facts as stated in the direct examination. It is easy to invent the skeleton of a falsehood, but it is a terribly difficult task to clothe it with flesh and blood, and make it live and move and have the being of truth. On the other hand, there is no resisting the story of an honest man, who tells it with frankness and with that minuteness of knowledge which every person is presumed to possess, with regard to his own case. In no other way can a man of integrity sometimes refute an attack upon his character, or repel the plots of conspirators.

In fact, it is the carelessness, forgetfulness and innocent (because unconscious) prejudices of third parties, acting as witnesses, which most complicate and injure the truth of a case. Let those in full possession of the facts state them; and if they willfully lie, they must have a long memory to escape detection.

We will conclude by giving one or two illustrations of the happy manner in which the present law has operated, illustrations all the more interesting to our readers, because they arose out of commercial cases.

A capitalist of this city assigned to an insurance company, at the time of its organization, a bond and mortgage for $5,000, with the understanding that he should receive in return, fifty shares of their capital stock, as soon as the company should commence business. The company took the bond and mortgage and collected the interest regularly, but never delivered any stock to the assignor. He brought suit for the value of the bond and mortgage, which was defended, the company averring that they had loaned the plaintiff $5,000 in consideration of the assignment. When the case came on for trial, the plaintiff found himself unable to establish his case. The business had been transacted hastily and with entire but misplaced confidence in the good faith of the company. At this stage of the case, the law in question was passed; the plaintiff came forward as a witness, told a perfectly straightforward story, which the defendants *did not attempt to contradict*, and so recovered a just judgment.

In a case recently tried in the supreme court (and reported in these columns), the plaintiff sued the defendant as the maker of a note for $3,000. The defence was that the note originated in a fraud practiced on the defendant, was wholly without consideration, and that the plaintiff, who was endorsee, knew these facts when he took it, and was suing for the benefit of the payee, who had fraudulently obtained the note. The burden of proof was of course on the defendant, and his own testimony was the only evidence he could furnish. He testified to conversations with the plaintiff, which proved clearly the knowledge of the plaintiff of the circumstances in which the note originated, and of its fraudulent character. The plaintiff did not dare to contradict him, could only say that he "did not recollect," and so the defendant gained his cause.

In both these cases, it will be noticed that the plain narrative of the truth teller was not contradicted. It is a daring act to invent a wholesale lie and to insist upon it before a jury. In fact, these two cases are so complete an answer to the objections of the friends of the repeal, and so fair an illustration of the principle upon which our present law is founded, that we here "rest our case."

Since the above remarks were written, the assembly has stricken the enacting clause from the bill to repeal, which probably disposes of the matter for the session.

VISITATION AND SEARCH ACCORDING TO THE LAW OF NATIONS.

The letter of Mr Cass, then minister to France, to M. Guizot in 1842 against the quintuple treaty of 1841 (which letter, in connection with an essay published in Paris about the same time "*concernant le droit de visite*," and ascribed to the same source, probably had much influence in preventing the ratification of that treaty by the French government), and Mr. Webster's letter to Lord Ashburton, Aug. 8th, 1842, (*Works*, vol. v, p. 142; vol. vi, p. 329), are familiar to the public. They have lately been extensively copied by the press, and the principles they set forth have not only been reaffirmed by the present administration, but have also met the cordial approbation of both houses of congress now in session, and of the bulk of the American people.

But it is not alone upon the authority of these distinguished statesmen, that our government is preparing to resist the right of *visiting* American vessels, now claimed by the British cruisers in the gulf. Their view is supported by a uniform course of practice on the part of our own government from the earliest period, and by the well ascertained principles of international law.

Vattel, one of the oldest of modern writers on the law of nations, discusses "the right of searching ships" exclusively under the title of *war*, nor is there a word in his voluminous treatise to justify search or visitation in time of peace.

Kent, with his usual perspicuity, lays down the principle which covers the whole subject, in the following language:

"No nation has any right of jurisdiction at sea, except it be over the persons of its own subjects, in its own vessels; and so far territorial jurisdiction may be considered as preserved, for the vessels of a nation are, in many respects, considered as *portion of its territory*, and persons on board are protected and governed by the law of the country to which the vessel belongs. This jurisdiction is confined to the ship; and no one ship has the right to prohibit the approach of another at sea, or to draw around her a line of territorial jurisdiction, within which no other is at liberty to intrude. Every vessel in time of peace, has a *right to consult its own safety and convenience, and to pursue its own course and business*, without being disturbed when it does not violate the right of others."—II Kent's *Commentaries*, p. 26.

As to the right of search, the same author says:

"It is founded upon necessity, and is strictly and exclusively a *war-right*, and *does not exist in time of peace.*"—Ib., p. 153.

The same principle is stated by all the standard writers on the law of nations, and the right of visitation and search are always spoken of in connection with each other.

The African slave trade, though prohibited by the municipal laws of most nations and declared to be piracy by the statutes of Great Britain and the United States, and since the treaty of 1841 with Great Britain, by Austria, Russia and Prussia, is not such by the general international law, and its interdiction can not be enforced by the exercise of the ordinary right of visitation and search. That right does not exist in time of peace, *independently of special compact.*—Dodson's *Admiralty Reports*, vol IV, p. 210. Wheaton's *Reports*, vol. X, p. 66. Wheaton's *International Law*, p. 186.

There can be no pretence of a special compact on the part of the United States. The right of search has never been conceded by our government. Great Britain and France, by the treaties of 1831 and 1833, conceded the mutual right of search; and the five great powers did the same in 1841; except France, which, by a special treaty with England in 1845, *substituted* a naval force on the coast of Africa for the mutual right of search. By our treaty of 1842, we also provided for a naval force of not less than eighty guns on the coast of Africa; and practically, though not expressed in the treaty, this was a substitute for the right of search conceded to England in the quintuple treaty by Austria, Russia and Prussia.

It is thus conceded (as indeed all writers on national law have held) that the right of search, unless conceded by treaty or special compact, can only be exercised in time of war. It only remains to point out the authorities upon which it has been held that visitation and search are identical.

The celebrated French publicist, Ortolan, in his work on *Diplomatie de la Mer*, has examined the whole subject elaborately, and the distinctions he draws are so precise and logical that they are worthy of being translated. He distinguishes clearly between the right of visitation and search (*droit de visite ou de recherche*), and the right of enquiry as to the flag (*droit d'enquette du pavillon*), and we translate his definitions and distinctions on this subject:

" These rights differ essentially in their scope, and in the means by which they are exercised.

The enquiry as to the flag has this object only; that of recognizing the nationality of the ship, in order to render to her, from the moment she is met on the ocean, the rights growing out of that nationality.

The object of a visit is to prove aboard of a ship, whose nationality is recognized, certain facts in relation to her cargo or in reference to some ulterior object.

The first of these rights (*enquette du pavillon*) depends upon the respect due to the nationality and independence of sovereign states; it is exercised in order that the rights belonging to that nationality may be guarantied; and also as a means of recognizing and impeaching fraudulent usurpations; *but the moment the flag is recognized*, the stranger arrests the enquiry and leaves the ship to the immunity of her flag (*a toute l'independence de son pavillon*).

The exercise of the second of these rights (*visite ou recherche*) is a *taint* upon the nationality and the independence of reciprocal states; and the offence is, that a stranger, after a recognition of nationality, thrusts himself on board a ship on the high seas, in order to satisfy himself of certain facts.

Briefly, in the one case (inquiry as to the flag), a sovereignty recognizes another; in the other case (visit or search), it invades the nationality after having recognized it."

These views are important and forcible, not only from their logical clearness, but from the fact that they come from a leading writer of a nation which has steadfastly refused to concede the right of search and visit, and with whom, as with our own countrymen, the sanctity of the national flag is a passion.

Ortolan writes in substance with Mr. Wheaton — our own celebrated publicist and expounder of international law — that the right of visitation and search does not exist except in time of war; and in that case he confines the right to ascertaining the nationality of the ship, and whether there be any contraband articles on board. See what Mr. Wheaton says on this subject:

" An attempt appears to be made to distinguish between the right of visit and the right of search. Now we have no hesitation in affirming that this distinction has no foundation whatever in the maritime law of nations, or the usage of the admiralty courts of any country. * * We repeat, if the visitation is not accompanied by search, it is an empty mockery and a wanton interruption of the navigator's voyage."—Wheaton's *Enquiry as to the Right of Visitation and Search, p.* 124.

What Great Britain has thought on the subject (until the extraordinary discovery of Lord Ashburton) may be judged from the fact that during the whole course of her negotiations on the suppression of the slave trade with the United States, from 1818 to 1824, she did not avow or pretend a right of visitation or search on the high seas in time of peace, for any purpose whatever, independent of special compact and the free concession of the powers on whose vessels the right was to be exerted.

To conclude; the whole doctrine, as established in the books and by the practice of civilized nations, is this: In time of peace you can not go behind the national flag without a special compact. Strictly speaking, indeed, there is no such thing as a *right* of search or visit in the time of peace; it is a wrong, an injury, an insult, to every one except the culprit; as much as if the unfortunate victim of a pick-pocket in a crowded thoroughfare should undertake to stop the great wayes of travel and search every passenger. If he lay his hand upon the guilty one, it is well; but woe to him if he stops or arrests the innocent traveler! No nation has a right to set itself up as *custos morum* on the high seas, or to detail its cruisers as special policemen. The claim of visit as distinguished from search is a mere sham; for once go behind the flag, and there is no end to the inquiry; for visitation (unless an idle ceremony) is followed by search, and search by seizure, and seizure by confiscation. In a word, the whole doctrine and the only safe doctrine may be summed up in a single sentence of Ortolan, the French jurist whom we have already quoted. "Every nation has the right to exercise at sea an exclusive police over its own vessels."

PROPOSED CHANGES IN THE LAW OF REAL ESTATE.

There are pending before the legislature at Albany some curious amendments to the laws relating to the collection of rent. They originate on the petition of the tenants of the old manor lands, and we understand are urged upon the attention of the representatives of the people with considerable vehemence. The anti-renters, as they are called, have resisted in every possible form the collection, and the legal consequences of the noncollection of the rents reserved by the original owners of the lands they occupy. Protracted and armed conspiracies embracing whole counties, and the most persistent and persevering litigation, carried before the highest courts of the state, having failed to secure them the exemptions they claim, they now come before the legislature asking for a series of radical changes in the law of leases or conveyances with reservations, which may injure not only the landlords of manor lands, but the rights of others interested in real estate.

There is one proposed amendment, for instance (in the copy with which we have been furnished), which will render it unsafe to transfer or assign leased property when the lease contains conditions of reëntry or forfeiture. It provides that no person can recover in an ejectment suit, by means of any condition of reëntry, or forfeiture, "unless the reversion of such estate shall have remained in the person to whom and in whose favor such condition shall have been made at the time of the making thereof." That is, no one but the original lessor can reënter the lease-hold, or eject the tenant, or forfeit the lease; the reversionary interest, or the right to reënter, can not be transferred; and as the provision is *ex post facto* in its action, an ejectment suit could not be maintained where the transfer has already taken place.

Another sweeping amendment prevents the seller of real estate from attaching any permanent conditions to the sale. The grantee can make no covenant which "shall attach to the estate conveyed, or run thereon as a burden upon subsequent grantees or owners." In other words, if the deed of transfer covenants that the grantee, his heirs and assigns, shall not erect a certain fence, or build certain boundary walls, or interfere with certain water-courses, or make certain excavations, such a covenant would be null and void so far as it affected all subsequent purchasers.

By the effect of another amendment, when property is sold on a perpetual lease, with reserved rents, and the grantee sells his interest, the grantor can not collect the reserved rents, or enforce any of the conditions of the conveyance.

It is evident that the design of these amendments is first, to break up the leases between landlords of manor lands and their tenants, to cut off every possibility of enforcing the collection of rents heretofore lawfully created or reserved, and to destroy vested rights hitherto protected by law. But this is not the only consequence involved. The effect of the amendments would be to take away *all* remedies for the collection of rents upon *existing* leases in fee, while it puts it in the power of the lessee or grantee, by transferring his interest, to cut off the grantor or lessor, from enforcing the conditions of the conveyance, or from ejecting the tenant, or from reëntering the property, in accordance with the original conditions.

We notice with surprise that the judiciary committee in the senate seem to approve these schemes, and have reported a bill which we presume embodies the substance of these amendments. The report was sent back by a vote of 14 to 14, the president of the senate giving a casting vote against the scheme. This action, however, is not necessarily final; and the assembly will be apt to be less considerate and conservative. At any rate, in these days of pro rata bills and Susquehanna railroad grants, it may be well for those interested in real estate to keep their eyes open and to watch over those vested rights which in most civilized governments are considered beyond the reach of the legislature.

THE BATTLE IN THE CITIES.

While the casuists and humanitarians are theorizing over the causes of crime, charging upon that good-natured scapegoat, society, the consequences of individual depravity, and shedding cheap tears of sympathy over the criminal, it becomes the good citizen, the energetic police-magistrate and the conscientious legislator, to inquire whether some potent and practicable barrier can not be erected against the rising tide of insolent and triumphant wickedness which threatens to overwhelm and pollute the great cities of the nation.

It may be that we have had too much of these theories; these accusations against society; these weeping sympathizers with crime; that we have unconsciously weakened the rigors of the even-handed law, which is a faint emblem of divine justice, and have enthroned in its stead a sickly and sentimental humanitarianism, as fatal to the viciously inclined as it is pernicious to the true interests of the community.

There is no dispute about the facts. In every large city there are several thousand human beings who belong to what the French aptly call "the perishing and dangerous class." Born in the back streets and dirty alleys, nursed on the milk of a drunken mother, growing up under the oaths of a profligate father, educated among street vagabonds and thieves, and graduated in the high school of first-class ruffianism, pickpockets and cracksmen; recruited continually by expelled criminals from distant cities and by adroit villains from the interior, attracted by the superior inducements presented by town life,—the criminals of the large cities form a distinct and peculiar class, having habits, customs, traditions and a language of their own,—an organized, trained and skillful band, waging a ceaseless and relentless warfare against the peace and security of society.

Now the civilized cities of Europe hunt down these organized criminals, on scientific principles, just as they hunt down rats and other vermin. They declare war against them, and they carry on the war on an effective system. They match against the dexterity and experience of professional thieves and burglars the greater dexterity and experience of policemen and detectives. The criminal magistrates are men of position and character. Their jurors are selected from reputable and responsible classes in the community. The courts of assize are held by judges of ability and special experience in the business, and neither pains nor expense is spared to bring home conviction upon the guilty. There is not much mawkish sympathy for the criminal, nor are pardons easily obtained. The machinery for detecting guilt is well contrived, and works smoothly; and the result is, that the criminals are to a great extent kept under. In Paris and London especially, the professional rascal, whatever may be his rank or condition in life, rarely escapes his just deserts; sooner or later the policeman's brawny hand will tighten on his collar; and that policeman's shadow pursues him ever, in his guilty terror, like an avenging Nemesis. In a word, the battle between the law and the criminal is fought with great odds in favor of the former; and the moral consciousness of this fact strengthens the pursuers, and unnerves the pursued.

In American cities, where, added to aboriginal vice, we have thousands of imported criminals, driven from their native country by the terrors of the law, we imitate the European system, but not very successfully. Most of our policemen are not up to their business; they do not go into the ranks for the purpose of learning a profession for life, but for obtaining a temporary support. Not many Americans will settle down to that position; their ambition prompts them to look forward to a higher career; they had rather be poor politicians than good officers. The detective force is not large enough, nor, with a few brilliant exceptions, well trained. Too many policeman like to stand well with the ward bullies; and when they begin to hob-nob with that class their efficiency is gone. They will compare neither physically, mentally, nor morally with the great bulk of English policemen. The police magistrates have not always the dignity, learning or character becoming the grave and reponsible interests over which they preside. The noble jury system has been weakened by exempting from duty the classes best fitted for that really honorable service; and their place is largely supplied by inferior men and temporary make-shifts. And lastly, our higher courts, instead of aiding the speedy administration of justice, frequently put themselves, or are put in the position of a *chevaux de frise* for the entanglement of the prosecution; so that, between the loopholes of the law and the mercies of a lenient governor, the chances of the escape of a prominent criminal are largely increased.

The result of all this may be read in the daily newspapers. In the never ending contest between the law and "the perishing and criminal class," the former is apt to come off second best. While in London and Paris the criminal is kept in wholesome fear of his enemy, the policeman, in New York, Philadelphia, Baltimore and St. Louis, the policeman is under continual terror that the criminal may get the advantage of him. At the best, the game is a drawn one, with the advantage a little on the side of the scoundrel, who swaggers accordingly. And in a game played with so much energy and skill on both sides, a trifling advantage gives the victor a moral superiority which impresses the whole community. And so the contest goes on, until we occasionally see a whole city rising and arming in its might, wresting the authority from the constituted authorities, and driving forth the dangerous class in a body. Towards this end, so mortifying to the majesty of the law, the unequal battle in the cities constantly gravitates.

THE PUBLICITY OF CRIME.

To judge from the newspapers, this people is desperately wicked. In no country is such publicity given to crime and all sorts of naughtiness. Such are the facilities for transmitting intelligence, that every great crime perpetrated, is in a day or two published all over the Union. Nearly every arrest by the police, even for trivial misdemeanors, finds its way into the newspapers. The culprit of the inland and secluded village, who goes to rest in the consciousness of fancied secrecy, awakes to find the records of his guilt scattered broadcast over the land; while the details of metropolitan depravity are read with open-mouthed wonder in the backwoods and on the distant prairies. There is no longer seclusion or secrecy for crime, it is read and known of all men. Though it flee to the uttermost parts of the earth, it is pursued and dragged to light by those bloodhounds of civilization, steam, the printing-press and the electric telegraph.

We shall not discuss the question whether or not this increased publicity given to crime is wholesome in itself, and advantageous to the ends of justice; or whether it is not more than counterbalanced by the morbid taste which it fosters in the public mind. But the picture of American life thus presented by the press, is exaggerated and distorted, and tends to mislead the stranger and the thoughtless reader. We forget that there is no telegraph to communicate, no press to chronicle the private virtues, as well as the public wickedness of the people; to record the unobtrusive charities and nameless benignities which grace and enrich social and domestic life. Those quiet and modest forms of benevolence and piety which minister to the wants of frail and suffering humanity; the patience, disinterestedness, and self-sacrifice of parents, mothers, sisters, friends; the bold physician battling with the king of terrors in the seclusion of the sick-chamber; the clergyman standing manfully by his post, without reward, endeavoring to give relief; the prayers and kind offices of strangers, the manly attributes of friendship, and the sweet voice of religion, —

these do not seek the glare of day, or the notoriety of the press; but it is in these that man's better nature and humanity triumph. The best things in life and the best side of human nature are not always reported in the newspaper; and were it not for the general although perhaps unconscious recognition of this fact, the damp sheet would be often dropped in the morning with a stifled cry of disgust—almost despair.

THOUGHTS ON THE SOCIAL SYSTEM.

The history of the old republics has taught us a truth confirmed by our own experience of practical government, that public virtue is the only foundation of a republic. Loyalty and fear, the ancient props of monarchy, have done their work, and like the uncouth armor of by-gone times, should be hung up with the insignia of heraldic pride. Virtue is henceforth to be the active principle of national and social existence, the arbiter of the destinies of men and of nations.

There is no higher theme to engage the philosophic mind, than the study of what may serve to defend national virtue and to foster its growth. And this virtue is rendered efficacious only through the social system—indeed, it is the product of the social system in the same sense, in which liberty is the product of political institutions. The social ideas and condition of a republic, then, must be based upon the wide and enduring principles of human nature.

In this view, and in relation to the national system, how important becomes the knowledge of the structure of society, of the ideas and forces that vitalize it, and give to it that animated expression which we call national virtue! We have reason to believe that the study of organic society will before long be recognized as a science, with its galaxy of savans and a literature no less dignified than that of its sisters, who in different ages have been led to the kindred thrones of wisdom. Like them, its advent is foreshadowed by a host of filmy theories, based upon partial and speculative notions, and blown into extravagant forms by the vanity of those who would rather be the *founders of a system* than the simple students of nature. Alchymy led forward chemistry; astrology preceded astronomy, and in the same way socialistic speculations will inaugurate the science of organic society, as the painted clouds announce the advent of the rising sun.

But what is meant by organic society, or an organic social system?

Society is a complex organism of ranks, or orders and relations; and these ranks or orders form a series of gradations from the lowest to the highest positions. Each gradation exercises a positive influence in the propagation of certain ideas—an influence proportional in degree to its elevation—and each is a powerful instrument in the formation of principles, opinions and character.

These ranks of social life are determined either by *external law*, as in the aristocratic societies of Europe, or by the formative power of certain ideas acting *outwardly* upon its structure and gradations. American society is subject to the power of ideas alone, and is free from the influence of external or artificial law, and thus exhibits a *natural* development of social life.

In such a state of social freedom, four predominant ideas have uniformly determined the gradations of society. These are *virtue*, *intellect*, *wealth* and *heroism*—the grand points of crystalization around which it naturally organizes itself. We shall hereafter examine the method by which these ideas govern the organization of society; and in what manner society thus organized is made to cherish and propagate the growth of these, its organic ideas.

We say, then, that society is *organic* when the estimation in which it holds certain moral, intellectual and physical qualities becomes the law of its development, and fixes the gradation of the social system. When this occurs, the influence of the social ranks gives increased force to those ideas. In such a state of society, we have nothing to do with the advantages or disadvantages of social position, except as they serve to inculcate moral and intellectual ideas. In this light alone are they worthy of philosophic consideration.

Under despotic and monarchical systems of government, where society is artificially arranged, and has its ranks and orders established by unalterable laws, empires have stood for centuries, and still continue to stand, unshaken by the corruption of popular morals, or the absence of virtue; but no such security surrounds the institutions of a republic. With the former, the stability of the law lasts while there is an arbitrary will to wield it; but with the latter, law and security rest upon national virtue, and with it, must prevail or perish.

The Roman senate, when apprehensive for the public safety, conferred dictatorial powers upon the consuls, for the protection of the state. The men and women of America are charged with this august dictatorship, and let them beware that "no harm befalls the republic." This is too grave a trust for legislators, too solemn a responsibility for the halls of legislation, and must be fulfilled within the sacred precincts of social life, under the holiest influences of religion and love.

To accomplish this high purpose, we need the aid of a more perfect system of social organization. True and lofty ideas of the purposes of life, and of those traits that impart dignity to man, must invigorate society, and become embodied in public opinion, which should always be the language of public virtue.

There is a radicalism of ideas, however, the tendency of which betokens danger to the social system — an ardent and inconsiderate desire to attain social improvement, which in its hurry and eagerness overleaps itself. There is too much boldness and self-confidence in handling matters of social interest. It is when this bold spirit attacks too violently the social relations of the nation, that superficial and empirical attempts at social reform become dangerous. It would be difficult for the wisest and the best to take the social fabric to pieces and to reconstruct it with greater elegance and completeness. The lessons of such a philosophy are the teachings of an unripe manhood, and they are taught and learned with almost superhuman rapidity. The solitary dreamer of to-day, filled with the ecstacies of a newly interpreted faith, is to-morrow the high priest of a sect. We are not surprised that Mohammedanism acquired a strong hold upon the oriental mind, deeply susceptible to the impressions of a shadowy faith; but the false prophet of the Great Salt lake has within the space of a score of years recorded his faith, and laid the foundations of an empire in the midst of an intellectual and eminently practical people.

Other forms of socialistic fanaticism multiply in our midst, culminating in the wildest and most dangerous extravagance. From what cause do these strange revelations spring? To what do they lead? They reveal a great movement of mind, subject like all powerful forces to irregularities. They spring from the tendency of the age to theoretic speculation; and although suggestive of bold and sometimes true ideals, disclose rather the weakness than the strength of its faith.

On the other hand is a strong conservative influence, from which the most hopeful expectations may be indulged. But the conservatism of social life, that is fit for this age of the world must, while it adheres to the truth of the past, be the ally of progress. It must not sit down and weep among the monuments of by-gone splendor, but must mingle in the battle as the gods of old mingled in the strife of heroes.

Social organization, in its highest and truest sense, implies the existence of fixed and definite laws, governing the phenomena of social life. It gives society a constitution, a unity, a definite individuality, the exact opposite of that chaotic, shapeless and inorganic mass which it becomes in the hands of ultra-social reformers.

We are conscious of being surrounded by an influential, moral medium, constantly applying motives and incentives to the individual mind, and giving to it activity, direction and force. This influence of mind on mind is the essence and substance of the all-pervading atmosphere of social life, and in this enlarged sense embraces all the elements of society. And the difficulty of gaining a comprehensive view of the complex and diverse movements of these social elements lies in the want of a recognition of fixed laws.

When lofty ideas of the nature and destiny of man pervade the community, it will uniformly place in the highest position those whose lives are the worthiest examples for imitation. When popular sentiment conforms to the highest reason, the good and the bad will not be reduced to a common level. The external distinctness of society will not be overturned, but will correspond exactly to individual worth. The worthiest will be elevated to the most influential ranks, and will diffuse noble sentiments and true models for individual imitation throughout the channels of society. The influence of example is heightened by the respect uniformly paid to social dignity, and would be exerted in behalf of moral and intellectual advancement.

Could we contemplate a more delightful picture than that presented by a pure society, elevating its worthiest members to positions of the highest consideration, and making public rank and station correspond to individual virtue and honor? In such a community might we not confidently expect a social system adequate to support the glory of the state and to fulfill the high destinies committed to man.

We have already remarked that when society is free from external restraints and is vitalized by the force of ideas only, three leading ideas control its relations, viz: virtue, wealth and heroism. Public sentiment attributes dignity to the representatives of these qualities, and when not observed by the fallacious lustre of arbitrary distinctions, they elevate their possessors to positions of the highest consequence and dignity. As these ideas exert a giant and reciprocal influence on the present structure of society, we will examine them somewhat in detail.

Feudality, and its effeminate offspring, chivalry, idealized physical power animated by heroic self-devotion, and heroism became the central principle of its organization. The feudal lord, the knight, the squire, the yeoman, and even the serf, were more or less inspired by the splendid idea, and the ranks of preferment — so far as opened by the iron rule of that rigorous system — became the mark of an active, militant ambition.

Commerce has uniformly tended to develop the influence of wealth as a predominant social element. Credit, the conscience of commerce, recognizes the solid qualities of industry and economic forethought as worthy of admiration, and rewards them with whatever advantages or distinctions wealth commands. And as commerce tends to centralization about certain localities favored with peculiar advantages for commercial intercourse, it is at those points, usually large commercial cities, that society is most deeply impressed by the great and often exaggerated value attributed to wealth.

Virtue and intellect have never acted with that force upon society which is due to their intrinsic excellence. That is, we have not yet reached a state of society in which these ideas have received the rank and homage which is due to them. Certain artificial and arbitrary forms represent those ideas — but in a more perfect state of society these qualities will gain an independent sovereignty, and the ranks or gradations of social life will exactly correspond to intellectual and moral merit. When the manhood of civilization begins, the extravagant fancies which have led the imaginations of men hither and thither in quest of the great *Eidolon* — whether embodied in the socialistic phalanx, or in whatever form — will be remembered only as the pranks of child-folly. In that day, those who would reform the social condition by forms and classifications, elongations and compressions, will have learned that society, like man, must be reformed from the heart outwards, and not from the surface inwards.

If the foregoing thoughts are true, it follows that true social progress must be based upon the improvement of the intellect and the heart. Whatever refines, intellectualizes, purifies social life, elevates society above the distinctions of arbitrary rank, and makes it the representative of true and noble ideas.

Books, then, for the intellect, and pure social influences for the heart — what desiderata are more indispensable to social improvement than these? — " books, women, books" — the sweet influence of a wholesome literature, and the sweeter influence of virtuous women; what can these do for society, or rather what can they not do?

The structure of society is interwoven with the influence and position of woman. Her's is the irresistible power to mould character, develop virtuous sentiments, and to enfranchise the soul from the bondage of gross and ignoble ideas. Over youth her's is the ascendant influence, and the virtues of manhood are the outgrowth of her teachings.

It is not necessary that her voice should mingle in the wrangling and clamors of the halls of legislation — that she should deal blows on the battle field — that her wits should play at thrust and parry with the loud-mouthed disputants of the forum. It is her right to be mistress of social life, without climbing to power by ignoble steps. It is her right to punish without wielding the sword and the axe, and to reward with an approbation which is better than the smile of kings. No false principle of honor, no mistaken idea of social dignity, could long out-live *that* approbation. The history of social life is the history of women.

We say then, again, "books, women, books" — these are the fountains which are to purify and invigorate society — to obliterate the arbitrary distinctions of social rank, and to make the social system a republic, open only to individual worth. We yearn for this third republic to correspond to the republic of letters, and to that political system which is our pride and boast. The trinity of republics will be complete when society shall bow to the undivided sovereignty of intellect and virtue.

MARRIAGE AND DIVORCE.

Our readers probably remember a kind of quadrangular duel which came off last summer [1852] between the *New York Observer*, Henry James, Horace Greeley, and Stephen Pearl Andrews. The *Observer* took Mr. James to task for certain alleged heresies on the subject of marriage and divorce, to which that gentleman replied in sundry caustic and able articles in the *Tribune*. Mr. Andrews appeared in the controversy as a volunteer, and succeeded in obtaining some notoriety and a good many hard blows. For failing to attract the attention of Mr. James, who was intent upon dispatching his enemy of the *Observer*, the gauntlet which he had so unceremoniously thrown into the ring, was picked up by the editor of the *Tribune*. Whereupon a brief but spirited passage at arms ensued between the two; Andrews apparently finding himself no match for the affluence of disparaging epithets showered upon him by his unscrupulous adversary soon retired from the contest. So, at least, it appeared then. But a small pamphlet, which has lately appeared, containing a republication of the controversy, indicates that Mr. Andrews was silenced, not discomfited. Said pamphlet—of which ten thousand copies have been published—complains that Mr. Andrews was unfairly treated; and contains those of his letters which were rejected by the *Tribune*.

So much for the combatants. As to the various opinions and theories advanced in the controversy, we have a word to say. The subject is important, and has already excited a large share of public attention.

The *New York Observer*, being a stiff presbyterian newspaper, advocates the orthodox and commonly received notions on the subject with considerable zeal and some ability. Horace Greeley, although a lover of Fourier and an advocate of socialism, is on this point strictly conservative, and professes to shudder at a system which is one of the cardinal tenets in the creed of his master in France. Henry James, a brilliant idealist, and a logician of no mean power, advocates a greater latitude of divorce. He contends that two persons should not be compelled to live together, "when they hold the reciprocal relation of dog and cat," and that the law should on the application of *both* parties grant a divorce, provided the state is guarantied against the charge of their offspring.

Mr. Andrews goes the whole figure, and is as radical as the most ardent lover of Fourier could desire. He regards marriage as a mummery — a mere mockery — a kind of legalized prostitution — and advocates the largest liberty which passion or caprice may ask for. He loudly and unblushingly contends for the promiscuous intercourse of the sexes on the ground that the law has no right to interfere with that individual sovereignity which allows a man to do as he pleases, provided he will take the consequences. He argues that man and woman should only be compelled to live together during the continuance of affection — which is another name for passion or caprice, and says:

"Indeed, it may be stated as the growing public sentiment of Christendom already, that the man and woman who do not love have no right, before God, to live together as man and wife, no matter how solemn the marriage service which may have been mumbled over them. This is the negative statement of a grand truth, already arrived at and becoming daily louder and more peremptory in its utterance. How long, think you, it will be before the converse, or positive side of the same truth will be affirmed, namely, that the man and woman who do love, can live together in purity without any mummery at all — that it is love that *sanctifies* — not the blessings of the church?

Such is my doctrine. Such is the horrid heresy of which I am guilty. And such, say what you will, is the eternal, inexpugnable truth of God and nature. Batter at it till your bones ache, and you can never successfully assail it. Sooner or later you must come to it, and whether it shall be sooner or later is hardly left to your option. The progress of opinion, the great growth of the world in this age, is sweeping all men, with the strength of an ocean current, to the acceptance of universal freedom — freedom to feel and act, as well as freedom to think — to the acceptance, in fine, of the sovereignty of every individual, to be exercised at his own cost. If our remaining institutions are found to be adverse to this freedom, so that bad results follow from its acceptance, then our remaining institutions are wrong, and the remedy is to be sought in still farther and more radical changes."

Mr. Andrews tells us in another part of his pamphlet that every woman has a right to choose the father of her own child, meaning that she has the right to choose as many fathers for her children as she desires. But we do not dare to make further quotations. Specious and adroit as Mr. Andrews is in the use of words, he leaves no doubt as to his real meaning; that meaning is, that no man need to restrain his passions from any sense of duty to society or fear of God. He aims to destroy the most cherished relations of life. The purity of woman, the majesty of law, the sacredness of religion, must yield to the selfishness of the individual. Fortunately such monstrous opinions can do no harm. They shock the moral sense of the most depraved; no man so wicked as to wish to live in such a pandemonium, none so utterly debased as not to shrink back from such shadows of hell. The poison contains its own antidote.

Mr. James belongs to a class which entertains little confidence in the potency of the law, but cherishes a profound faith in the goodness of humanity. He consequently contends that the unhappy relations in which many married people find themselves, are entirely curable by enlarging the grounds of divorce. He can not believe — with his notions of "the inward sweetness and humanity" of men and women — that "legal bondage secures conjugal fidelity." There is a show of truth in this; and yet we can't but believe that Mr. James would be one of the first to shudder at the practical consequences of his own theory. The fact of it is that a large majority of men are slaves, and must be kept in a state of legal bondage. They are the slaves of their own appetites and passions, and have not the moral stamina to govern themselves. Where one man does his duty because his "heart is the home of constancy and every virtuous affection," five thousand do the same thing from compulsion. It is a "base legal slavery" this compulsion, but it answers the purpose. Now our present rigid law of divorce acts on this principle. It is a kind of constant moral press to make a man behave himself in his social relations. It is founded, like all law, upon the principle of *compulsion*, and the theory of man's inability to govern himself; and history shows conclusively that a laxity of the law of divorce has ever been followed by a laxity of public morals, and the corruption of the virtue of the people. In fine, a rigid and inflexible law of divorce is a great moral necessity which is demanded by the licentiousness and caprices of human nature.

We have said enough on this subject and more than was necessary. It was our intention to give a little resumé of some of the new notions on the subject of marriage and divorce, and not to write a homily. The good old common law on this subject has remained unchanged in substance for a thousand years; always full of wisdom, and fitted exactly to the necessities and character of the Anglo-Saxon race, it is the best homily in the world, and is its own commentary.

A POOR RICH CITY.

No municipality on this continent was ever so munificently endowed as this. The grant in the Montgomery charter, of all the soil under water, on the Hudson and East rivers, extending four hundred feet out from low water mark, was of itself sufficient to endow a German principality. Our common lands, water lots, ferries, piers, wharves and markets, properly and economically husbanded from the beginning, would now furnish a revenue sufficient to support the whole city government on a liberal scale. It is not too much to say that if the grants to the city in the reign of James II and Queen Ann had been made to private persons, and managed by them with ordinary business prudence and skill, they would now yield a revenue equal to the enormous tax-levy for the current year.

Notwithstanding all that has been misapplied and squandered and leased for long terms (which amount to a perpetuity) for a nominal rent, the city has still property enough to make its management a matter of moment to tax-paying citizens. The value of its real estate is estimated by the comptroller, according to the *Corporation Manual* for 1858, at $41,625,639. Striking out from his list the property in use for public purposes, such as for the parks and by the fire, police and alms house departments, the following table shows the value of the real estate now owned by the city:

Uncommuted quit rents reserved on property, when sold, and water grants yet to be issued,	$900,000
Lots under lease, without covenant of renewal, - - - - - - -	325,000
Lots under lease, with covenants of renewal,	500,000
Real estate in Brooklyn, - - -	50,000
Common lands, - . - - - -	500,000
Sundry lots and gores, - - - - -	250,000
Markets, - - - - - - -	1,150,000
Bulkheads, wharves and piers, - -	3,400,000
Ferries, - - - - - - -	1,200,000
	$8,370,000

Here is an amount of real estate which in private hands and at the usual rates of interest, would produce an income of over half a million. How is it managed in the hands of the common council? With the exception of the ferries — which are notoriously leased for much less than their real value, several of them for thousands of dollars less than had been offered by responsible bidders — the property in the above table may be said to be almost nonproductive.

To give a general idea of the manner in which the real estate of the city is managed, we have prepared from the report of the comptroller and from other reliable sources, a little statement of the real estate account for 1857. The total revenues from it are as follows:

Markets, - - - - - -	$78,000 00
Common land rent, - - - - -	50 00
Docks and slips " - - - - -	159,799 37
Ferry " - - - - -	97,085 00
Ground " - - - - -	24,276 74
House " - - - - -	14,236 12
Water lot " - - - - -	7,600 47
Total, - - - -	$381,047 70

This is several hundred thousand dollars less than the interest of the property at the comptroller's low valuation would be at 7 per cent, but from these gross receipts, there must be fairly deducted the following expenditures connected with the real estate account:

Docks and piers, - - - - - -		$135,000
Real estate, - - - - - -		31,325
" " expenses, - - - - -		21,634
Markets, cleaning, - -	$7,000	72,000
Gas, salaries and miscellaneous, estimated, - - -	* 65,000	
Repairs and supplies, - - - - -		12,516
Fencing vacant lots, - - - - -		2,104
		$274,579

* These items are kept in general separate accounts, such as salaries, lamps and gas, which we have had no opportunity of examining; but gentlemen familiar with the subject, say that we have not overestimated them. There can be no doubt that the expenses of the market property are not much less than the gross receipts. Mayor Kingsland reported to the

Or to show the account at a glance:

Receipts on account of real estate, -	$381,047 70
Expenditures on account of real estate,	274,579 00
Net income, - - - - -	$106,468 70

This is about one and a quarter per cent interest on the comptroller's valuation; but a rigid analysis of the different heads of account would probably show that the net income of the city from these sources, taking one year with another, for the last five years, was nothing or less than nothing. For instance, the expenditures on the wharves and piers, during one year at least, were several hundred thousand dollars more than the receipts; and if such expenses as the Battery enlargement properly belong to the debit side of the account, the deficiency must always be large. But without being too curious, or going behind the official records, the fact that an estate valued by the comptroller, at $8,370,000, produced a net revenue of but little over a hundred thousand, is an exhibition of financial mismanagement as mortifying as it is disgraceful.

It may be stated, generally, that in nearly every case where the control of the city property has been in the

common council several years since, that the markets were a pecuniary loss to the city.

We have excluded from this table two items in the expenditures of 1857, viz: lands and places $23,500, and rents $29,000, because, although they in one sense belong to the real estate account, they are not connected with the productive property of the city.

hands of the common council, the profits are very much below what they would have been, were the same property managed by private persons, and that a considerable portion of the real estate of the city has been a positive bill of expense.

We have stated these well known facts, *i. e.*, the munificent endowment of the city under the old charters, the gradual waste and loss of a great part of its inheritance, and the profuse and injurious manner in which the remainder thereof has been administered, for the purpose of raising the question, whether a body like the common council is the proper custodian of the private property of the city? Whether its functions should not be municipal and political, rather than fiduciary? Whether the control of such immense pecuniary interests, — private in their character and disconnected from the ordinary and legitimate duties of government, — does not place the common council in the position of an irresponsible board of directors? And lastly, whether it would not be proper to separate the political powers of the common council from its responsibilities as the custodian of the private resources of the city?

CHARLES O'CONOR.

Mr. O'Conor may be considered at the head of the New York bar — a distinction not easily attained, and one that may well satisfy the proudest aspirations for professional advancement. As an orator, he has many superiors; and indeed his delivery, never fluent, is sometimes faulty. But Mr. O'Conor never speaks to an indifferent, or uninterested audience; — bench, bar and jury are equally attentive to every utterance that falls from his lips.

In person, he has little to excite enthusiasm or inspire zeal. His triumphs are achieved by the force of intellect alone. No one is more conscious than himself that he is incapable of investing a prejudged or unpopular cause with a self-created atmosphere of sympathy. He seldom attempts to stem the tide of popular disfavor, unless the intrinsic excellence of his cause will recommend it to favor when its facts and reasonings are fully understood. But he never declines a cause through fear, and would at any time prefer to lead the forlorn hope in a just cause than to triumph in a bad one. But when he recommends a client to apply to other counsel, it is from an intellectual conviction that an advocate is needed of a different mental constitution from his own.

If it be observed that Mr. O'Conor is generally found upon the side of a question upon which popular favor arrays itself, the credit is due rather to his sagacity in discovering the elements of success, than to his genius for creating them. But his position once taken, and his advocacy engaged, no obstacle can daunt his determined energy. He will take a storm of popular fury as indifferently as he would an April shower, and glory in a strife, the fierceness of which would appall the heart of others less circumspect than himself.

It is as a reasoner in the higher walks of legal science that Mr. O'Conor is most distinguished. His studies are of the most minute and careful character. No jurist of the day has a more thorough and intimate knowledge of the adjudications in England and his own country, although he does not possess the happy but equivocal talent of some in always having at his tongue's end a case supposed to have decided the exact point in controversy. Yet his citations of adjudicated cases are sound and veracious, and are always listened to with respect and confidence.

He is in the truest sense a thorough-bred lawyer, and has devoted himself with unremitting zeal to the matters of the profession of which he is an ornament. The loose and empirical studies of the present day will hardly supply his place at the bar.

His person is as remarkable in its endowments as his mind. Erect and slender — full of nervous energy, but cold as steel — he strikes the imagination as a frozen embodiment of his own intellect. His eye is brilliant and piercing; but as cold as the phosphorescent gleam of a winter ocean.

This coldness is not absence of native kindness, but the product of an intellect overbalancing the passional and sensitive traits. As a friend, he will be kind, but not sympathetic. He admires the beautiful, not from an inspiration of its beauty, but from an intelligent appreciation of its fitness and perfectness. If he is ever won from bachelorhood to taste the quick sympathies of love, it will be when the demands of his discriminating intellect are met by a perfect object, or when he finds the fitness and necessity of sympathy.

GREENE C. BRONSON.

Chief Justice Bronson belongs to a class whose merits and demerits usually excite a great variety of conflicting opinions. Such men never head a party nor follow a party, and thus lose the doubtful advantage of securing the partizan regard that detests or admires as fear or favor dictates. They must be regarded as individuals. They are a class only as they fall under the common head of exceptions, not as possessing common peculiarities by which the description of one is made the description of all.

Judge Bronson has a marked and vigorous stamp of character — such as can not escape notice or fail to excite respect. His mental peculiarities single him out to figure as a conspicuous object in whatever he engages, and leave him no opportunity to mingle unobserved with the unrecognized many. Whether this is an advantage or a misfortune, opinions seem to differ. Fortunately, the claim of our present subject upon our consideration is not dependent upon the settlement of this mooted point.

The withdrawal of Judge Bronson from the bench of the court of appeals to resume the active duties of the bar illustrates a peculiarity of our countrymen alike creditable to the individual and advantageous to the interests of society. It may seem strange to those who surround the idea of public station with a sort of unapproachable dignity from which one is expected to retire only to higher dignity or oblivion, that one who has enjoyed the distinction of filling the highest judicial position, should voluntarily relinquish its honors and privileges to mingle again in the turmoils of business. But those who have seen an ex-president of the United States reënter the arena of political life as a representative of congress, and cabinet officers guiding the affairs of a nation to-day, and advocating the cause of a client to-morrow — exchanging the helm of state for a well paid brief — will understand the active elements of character that bring about such transitions. Instances of this kind — unless the result of an unwise parsimony denying to public officers suitable compensation — are creditable to the spirit of our people.

The late chief justice is possessed of a mind at once acute and discerning, but prone to flow in the peculiar channels marked out by his mental idiosyncracies. He scorns the well-defined and thoroughly beaten highways on which others delight to travel in security and ease. He seldom fails to find a by-path — though sometimes so overgrown through disuse as to be almost hidden from the common eye — on which he travels with long and powerful strides, albeit, sometimes at the cost of some straining and a few scratches.

His opinions are always strong, though that strength is derived rather from the force of his own intellect than from the common approbation and consent of others. Such a mind fortifies its intrinsic strength, often at the sacrifice of that solidity of judgment which springs from the combined action of mind with mind. Its conclusions are more valuable than any aggregate of weak opinions, but even such a mind would gain stability by attention to opinions less valuable than its own.

Judge Bronson's conclusions are rapidly formed and seldom subject to revisal or qualification. To convince him against his inclination would be an enterprise too formidable for one prudent of his resources. But whatever opinion he may form, it is honestly entertained and fearlessly expressed. Whether on or off the bench, he is equally indifferent to the effect of the announcement of his conclusions, nor is he restrained by party affinities or prejudices, from arriving at the results to which the peculiarities of his mind tend.

The salient points of his mind are marked by antagonism springing from his intellectual organism rather than from his nervous constitution. His opinions are not colored by passion or prejudice, but are the acknowledged children of his brain. The point and spiciness of his writings are not the product of warmth engendered by opposition, but of a mind endowed in itself with the elements of intellectual strife without requiring opposition or an adversary to call forth its energies.

His distinction as a lawyer rests on a solid basis. There is nothing meretricious in his mode of handling subjects. He does not strike for effect, or for the sake of an attitude, but to do execution. His learning is comprehensive and profound, and is available to sustain his positions. If an authority is to be questioned, or a case doubted, it is not mutilated and misrepresented, but fairly and openly attacked. No timidity prevents him from meeting an objection, wherever it may present itself — whether in the opinion of distinguished judges or of eminent counsel.

As a speaker, he is not gifted with an impressive address. His remarks are pointed, and to the purpose; but a natural hesitancy of manner, and the want of warmth of imagination deprive him of much of the power that is due to the strength of his intellect. The rhetorical talent is perhaps more often over valued than any other intellectual gift. All mankind covet it, for it symbolizes the power of the mind — as the sceptre and the crown represent the sovereign dignity. The effect of eloquence is to move men rather than to set them thinking. But it is the business of the lawyer to convince rather than to arouse, to satisfy doubts rather than to create them. And if he is often found swerving from this end, it is when he has discovered his inability to attain it.

Judge Bronson and Charles O'Conor work with the cold-chisel, and though the anvil and sledge-hammer lawyers throw off more sparks and seem to do more execution, yet the former leave their work complete and finished, while the latter are often unable to recognize it after it has become cold.

Judge Bronson possesses many admirable traits of character. His bearing is dignified; he is courteous and affable in his address, and pleasing in his manners. There is neither affectation nor stiffness in his presence or conversation, but an easy dignity, enlivened by an agreeable pleasantry. It is rare to find these latter qualities combined with a mind of such singular power and strongly marked individuality. Judge Beardsley resembles him in many of these traits, but wants that genial flexibility of disposition, by which the latter enters into the spirit and feelings of those that surround him. Both are gentlemen in the true sense, and as such, exercise an influence that is denied to intellect, however brilliant, when allied to an uncongenial disposition.

A little more of this gentlemanly finish would be of service now-a-days, both within and without the bar, while its absence is less excusable in the lawyer than in those whose occupation does not offer the same inducements to its cultivation.

GEORGE WOOD.

It is not our purpose in these brief sketches to present a full length portrait of the prominent lawyers of the city of New York, who will fall under our notice. All that is attempted is a mere chalk sketch, done in a sort of blackboard style. Should the subjects of our sketches be recognized by any other peculiarity than their names, it will be the good fortune of the writer, for which he will be sufficiently grateful.

Had our purpose permitted so agreeable an undertaking, the rare qualities and attainments of Mr. O'Conor would have opened a broad and refreshing field, full of matter for study as well as entertainment. And the subject of the present notice would sustain the interest of a more elaborate survey than we have the leisure to bestow.

Mr. Wood belongs to the past as well as to the present. His early contemporaries were the great men whose honored names have survived their labors. His later cotemporaries are the vigorous lawyers of our own day. His calm address, his suavity and manly logic, are the product of early contests at the bar with the most distinguished men, who have impressed their strong minds upon our jurisprudence. In these stirring times of reform, he is now and then a little at fault to discover where the old landmarks have been shifted to — but in the main, takes progress in a very good natured and considerate manner.

Mr. Wood is emphatically a lawyer of the old school. He has been a hard student in his day; though he is not one of those who bring upon themselves an intellectual dyspepsia by undertaking to digest more than is wholesome at a time. He is more properly known as a jurist than an advocate, or in other words, one who looks to the law as his patron, rather than to his client as his master. Without possessing a technical mind, he has mastered the most profound and technical department of legal study, the law of real estate. In this and in public law, he is most at home, though his grasp of the broad principles of law that underlie the entire fabric of jurisprudence is sufficiently comprehensive, to mark with distinction his labors in all other departments.

As a speaker, the operations of his mind are exact and methodical. His manner is deliberate and impressive, and apt to carry conviction to the mind. His subjects are discussed in the broadest lights. His tendency is to solidification, rather than to analytic dissection, and his arguments present principles of law applied and embodied in a form so symmetrical and complete, that their genuineness is no less apparent to the common understanding than to a cultivated and acute legal mind. In this respect, Mr. Wood's best efforts are instructive models of legal discussion.

Minds possessed of this intuitive faculty of discernment have a proclivity to indolence. The ease with which they develop their subjects, in time renders protracted study irksome, and they scarcely arrive at the full maturity of their powers, before their force is impaired by relaxed effort. Mr. Wood has been a sufferer of late years from this cause, or rather, we should say, that law has been the sufferer; for such powers as Wood possesses, when exerted to their fullest force, confer rare advantages upon the profession. It is the undisputed right of those who have achieved honor and affluence sufficient to satisfy their ambition, to withdraw from the severer labors of professional life. But it is nevertheless to be regretted that a mind richly endowed and cultivated by careful study to the highest point of usefulness, should be withdrawn in the least degree from the important labor of strengthening and perfecting our system of jurisprudence.

Mr. Wood is still in practice, but it must be a good fee and a good case that will tempt him to take down and buckle on his sturdy old armor. He will hardly lay claim to that indefatigable industry that followed a

Story and a Kent to the close of life, and which still animates the veteran octogenarian of the bar, Chief Justice Jones.

We have observed that as a real estate lawyer, Mr. Wood deserves the distinction he has attained. This most important branch of legal study, which has laid the foundation of almost every great legal reputation, is not pursued at the present day with the avidity its importance deserves. The consequences of this neglect will be felt a quarter of a century hence.

Mr. Wood is one of those lawyers of the old school, who look upon the doctrines of the common law as venerable old castles still strong for shelter and defence. He will discuss a *remainder* or a *use*, with as pleasant a gusto as a wild fowl cooked to a turn. And would as little expect to see a *remainder* without a *particular estate* to sustain it, as a pyramid without a base.

Mr Wood is no less remarkable for the raciness of a vein of pleasantry and quiet humor running through his mental composition, than for the grave and demure expression that gives it its point and delicacy. His great efforts, as well as his lighter and familiar conversations are touched with this happy peculiarity. Those who have listened to him while addressing a solemn bench of judges, upon some otherwise dry topic of discussion, often find themselves shaking with a sensation of inward satisfaction, quite inconsistent with the demure aspect of the speaker.

In this respect he is the opposite of Mr. O'Conor. The one possesses the happy faculty of constructing, by an elaborate and careful process, a ludicrous solecism, that can be remembered and repeated, and laughed over, again and again; while the other invests the objects of his humor with an unobtrusive and quiet absurdity, that can be felt by all, but scarcely repeated or described.

Mr. Wood is cordial and communicative with his equals, affable and social with his inferiors; and on the whole, such a character as one likes to know and converse with. His distinction is never fortified by reserve or affectation; nor is it the less secure for this reason. Whether you see him in conversation, or in consultation, quietly and benignly twirling his snowy hair with his finger, or erect and dignified, uttering the manly creations of his intellect, in a case of magnitude, you feel secure in the belief that you have no common man before you.

One peculiarity of Mr. Wood ought not to be omitted. He is conscientious in regard to his fees; believing that the interests of his profession, and of morality in general, are concerned in correcting the habitual looseness that prevails in regard to the moral obligation of paying one's lawyer. And though a moderate man himself, who would be shocked by the value that some men place upon their labors, he never fails to set a good example, by relieving his clients with the greatest convenient despatch of that uncomfortable feeling that results from the consciousness of having withheld from meritorious services their just reward.

We close this sketch by saying that we have the greatest respect for Mr. Wood, and though we hardly hope for such a result, yet for the advantage and credit of the law, we would desire that his ripe experience might create for itself a permanent monument amidst the juridical literature of our country.

DANIEL LORD.

In selecting the subjects of these sketches, two considerations have influenced the writer. First, that none but thorough-bred lawyers should thus be presented to the public; and second, that those subjects should be so well known that the portraits may be readily and generally recognized. Exclusion from this series does not therefore imply the absence of ability or reputation, but merely that the two do not happen to be conjoined to such an extent as to serve for illustration of those traits of legal character that it is our purpose to sketch. We endeavor to present examples for imitation, rather than objects for admiration. We have accordingly selected men so widely known as to have become a sort of public property, and whose acknowledged reputation can not suffer from the effects of the scrutiny that is necessary to discriminate excellencies from faults.

Daniel Lord enjoys a reputation rarely achieved at the metropolitan bar. He has been eminently successful. And that success is the more deserved as it has not been filched from the accidents of fortune, but is the result of severe labor and study. There are reputations that start upwards from the earth, blaze meteor-like across the heavens, and expire. There are those that from the cradle to the grave, seem to be held aloft by an invisible power — like fixed stars. There are those, too, that rise from the earth, like the pyramids, firm, lofty and enduring — but the work of industry inspired by ambition. Of the first sort, many may be seen at any time when the atmosphere is clear and free form storms and clouds. Of the second, a Bacon and a Webster are brilliant illustrations, while a Blackstone and a Story are fitting examples of the latter class.

Mr. Lord belongs appropriately to the class last described. His mental qualities fit him for success in his profession. The basis of his intellectual character is a strict conservatism that disinclines and unfits him for theoretic speculation. Unlike certain modern lawyers of the Young America school, his principles of law are derived from the solid experience of the past, rather than from the transitory relations of the present, or illusive prognostications of the future. If this conservatism is at times a little too unyielding, it must be remembered that the office of the lawyer is to reproduce the wisdom of the past in its relations to the rights of individual and social man. That while those fiery spirits that drag the car of progress are blinded by the dust and excitement they create, he must stand like a wary pilot, guiding and watching the sacred vehicle, lest it swerve from the broad highway, and comes to run among incalculable dangers.

Mr. Lord has acquired a thorough and accurate knowledge of the history of legal adjudications. He is guided less by intuitive perceptions of right than by scientific knowledge of the law. He has accordingly attained his chief excellence in that department of the law which relates to the rights and obligations of individuals, in contradistinction to the law as it affects the relation of communities of men and states. Thus while as a commercial, maritime and real estate lawyer, he has attained undoubted superiority at the New York bar, as a constitutional lawyer he is excelled by others. In the former department of law, the circumstances under which legal principles are applied are less variable than in the latter; for with all the changes that have been wrought upon society by its increased power of production and locomotion, the rights and obligations of individuals have undergone comparatively little change, since the earliest code of law was promulgated. On the other hand, public law as propounded in the United States has no type in the codes and institutions of the ancient world, and is indebted to such men as Chief Justice Marshall and Alexander Hamilton for its stability.

Mr. Lord is a close and severe reasoner. His arguments are clear and forcible, and abound in nice discriminations. He does not possess that expansive power that rises to eloquence, nor has he made the graces of oratory his peculiar study. But as a speaker, he commands attention and respect. He is uniformly respectful to the bench, and courteous towards an opponent. He avoids collision rather than seeks it. If strongly attacked on debatable ground, he shifts his position to the vantage ground with an adroitness that disarms an incautious adversary. With more of the combative element he might at times give greater force to his positions; but he avoids at least the foible of those who through desire to display their valor in combat, invite attack by assuming questionable ground.

Mr. Lord is a diligent and laborious student. His preparation is always thorough. Though enjoying affluence, his industry is unremitting. He has found leisure to cultivate a taste for literary and artistic subjects, as his conversation exhibits. His manners are affable, and his familiar conversation enlivened by a pleasant flow of genial good feeling.

His mental character suits him for a judicial position. It would be an acquisition to the courts of our state, to elevate to the bench a lawyer whose learning exceeds his ingenuity, and who would be less inclined to follow the fancies of his own imagination than the deliberate judgments of his learned predecessors. Unfortunately, the public do not justly appreciate the value of this quality, and is prone to fix its hopes upon enthusiastic idols, whose stores of theory are like to outlive the exhaustion of their learning. Should the elevation of men of this stamp prove to be the fruit of the present elective system, our noble profession will be bowed to the dust in shame.

WILLIAM CURTIS NOYES.

Mr. Noyes may be regarded as the representative of a class of lawyers far from numerous, but of great influence at the bar. They seldom figure in newspaper paragraphs. Their cases rarely display that exuberant morbid anatomy of passion and folly which the buzzard-like nose of the public snuffs up from afar. Their public efforts are not served up in laboriously reported cross-examinations, portraying zealous and astute counsel wading through an unwholesome puddle of filthy particulars, and scrutinizing, with painful nicety, every loathsome detail.

They move in a different sphere and breathe a purer atmosphere. Without the vanity of desiring to see their portraits hung up with those of knaves and felons, they have sufficient ambition to rise above the common walks of their profession. To this class is committed the conservation of that honorable character which the profession of the law ought always to exhibit.

It will readily be inferred that Mr. Noyes is more solicitous of an honorable than of a conspicuous position. In this respect, his wishes are abundantly realized. With talents fitting him to shine in those brilliant contests that attract the public attention, he has chosen the graver and more honorable fields for the arena of his labors and his triumphs.

The subjects of our previous sketches were taken from those who have reached the fullest development of their intellectual powers, and have attained the zenith of their distinction. They can hope for little more than to leave untarnished the honorable names achieved by their industry and ability. Mr. Noyes is yet upon the thrifty side of middle age. He has only begun to pluck the fruit of his ripened powers, and the golden autumn with its mellow, sun-brown fruit, is to him a distant and a pleasant prospect.

His mental characteristics combine opposite peculiarities seldom so happily harmonized. Naturally of quick insight, rapid in his conclusions, swift to parry a blow and follow it with a thrust, he has acquired a steady hand and a clear and cool judgment. Gifted with vivacity and impressibility, the active forces of a brilliant and energetic mind, his study has been to curb their vehemence and render them subservient to a steady and well considered purpose.

Few men, whose composure does not arise from stolidity, preserve under all circumstances a more even temper. The thrusts and annoying sallies of an adversary glance from the smooth surface of his composed temper and bound harmlessly in the air; but not so with the keen shafts that are returned with a sure aim and a gentlemanly grace. They have a knack of searching out the most vulnerable part. Mr. Noyes aims to accomplish by directness what many prominent lawyers seem to think can only be obtained by blustering and circumlocution. If he have occasion to force the truth from an unwilling witness, he dissects it out in a clean and handsome manner, without leaving his subject a hacked and bruised object of pity.

A false popular idea of that which constitutes the most brilliant quality of a jury lawyer, has beguiled many a lawyer of splendid promise from the legitimate fruits of his profession, to seek for a mere will-o'-the-wisp reputation. To reduce a tremulous and distracted witness to the last extremity of torture is very generally thought a clever performance, and highly creditable to a lawyer. It is supposed to indicate almost as much power as those withering strokes of thinly disguised impudence which sometimes cause a judge to change color or to bite his lips. The public accept these as legitimate, and throw up their hats, while the elated gladiator rubs his hands with glee, and meditates still more murderous onsets.

Such examples are degrading to the bar. They level the dignity of the bench to a mean obsequiousness, and display a pitiful selfishness that would sink every object of respect to the office of a mere stepping-stone to an ambition satisfied with popular applause. We have nothing to do in these sketches with this class, except as they furnish contrasts. But for the sake of their speedy extinction we can not but express a hope that opportunities for recrimination, if not for extenuation, may be less often found in the unguarded expressions of counsel who value their reputations.

In contrast to the class we have just described, true lawyers, like the subject of this sketch, stand in bold and agreeable relief. Though the full recognition of their ability may not arrive so early in life, it is sure to reward their efforts. Like a meridian sun, it stands above the high-noon of life, and sinks in a glowing west. Although those lawyers whose policy is kept always in sight get credit for great shrewdness, the public, in the end, find out by results that it is with the lawyer as with mankind in general,—that those who seem to do the least are generally doing the most.

Mr. Noyes is thorough in his studies and laborious in his preparations. His method is orderly and exact, enabling him to classify and elaborate the most voluminous accumulations of facts. This quality has been advantageously displayed in a series of litigations of the most important and widely extended character in which he has been engaged for several years. Had his attention been less absorbed by cases of this character, and bestowed upon a more diversified class of subjects, he would have attracted towards himself much of the attention that has been bestowed upon other leading counsel. But he has gained in solid reputation what is more desirable than the *eclat* that attends those who move constantly under the public eye, and are cheered on by popular applause.

He possesses qualities fitting him for success either as a jury-lawyer, or in the purer and less exciting discussions of legal principles that are removed from public observation. In the former sphere a different order of talent and acquirement is needed than the latter requires. Instances, however, occur in which both fields of action seem equally open to the same gifted mind. To possess this versatility of talent, to have the faculty of seizing by quick intuition the points of advantage that arise in the rapidly shifting panorama of a jury-trial, and at the same time to be capable of devoting assiduous and unwearying study to the vast and diversified learning of the law, is the highest ideal of the lawyer.

Mr. Noyes, although enjoying the fruits of a lucrative practice, looks to the future as the field in which there are yet many conquests to achieve. Though he has performed an amount of labor that many would consider a just fulfillment of the doom of toil laid on man, he is unexhausted in his intellectual and physical powers.

His period of activity and usefulness is likely to survive many of his professional brethren who are wasting away with rust and mildew.

JAMES T. BRADY.

It was not the design of the writer of these sketches to exhaust either his readers or his subjects; but from time to time, as the occasion served, to present little pictures of those striking characters that appear most luminous in the firmament of the legal profession.

The subject of the present notice escaped from the incubative state of his non-age with something of meteoric suddenness and brilliancy. Possessing one of those minds that ripen early he stepped upon the stage of action with the air of a man who had something to do, and was going directly about it. The world — we mean the metropolitan world — was pleased with his manliness, and soon learned to respect his good sense, as well as to admire his humorous eccentricities. There was something bold and striking in the outlines of his head, a breadth and fullness of development that might have done for a Jupiter. Here was the promise of intellectual strength and manly force. Beneath his bold brow were not the fierce eyes of a Webster or a Calhoun, shot through with pride and passion, but a pair of eyes strong, gentle, inviting friendship and confidence. As your eye traveled down along the lines that give the fullest expression to the social traits, it observed a waviness of outline suggestive of an humorous inclination. Here was the epitome of the man intellectually strong, gentle and humorous.

His rapid rise at the bar fulfilled the promise of his intellectual gifts. At an age when young men are generally borne down by the *prestige* of the accomplished reputations that surround them, he was admitted with scarcely the formality of an introduction to divide the honors of professional championship with the achievements which had cost years of labor and study.

Mr. Brady neither desired nor stood in need of the extrinsic aids of influence or patronage. His independent and self-reliant individualism bore him erect, spurning the aids and props to which the weak and dependent nervously cling. He displayed traits that commended him to that discriminating aristocracy—the public—and the public adopted him. This proneness of the public to adopt the children of promise is a striking trait in our national character. It has its periodical ebullition of hero-worship, and is at times fickle and indiscriminating; but to its praise it may be said, that it is spontaneous and in the main unselfish. It has dragged unpedigreed genius from the garret, and has crowned it again and again. It does not ask for the indorsement of my lord this, or the right honorable sir that, but delights in seeing with its own eyes, and rewarding with its own hands.

The success that early rewarded the exertions of our subject were not wholly due to the gifts with which nature endowed him. He was from the first diligent as a student, and laborious as a man of business. He compressed into the first early years of his professional career the labor that many reserve for a later period of life. With a mind quick and suggestive, he applied himself diligently to the learning of the law. His studies were characteristic of the qualities of his intellect.

He does not belong to that class of minds that exhibit the power of analytic reasoning in creating a substratum of philosophical opinion. The normal condition of such minds is the absence of an intuitive faculty of discriminating intellectual ideas. They owe all they attain to acquisition, little to intuition. Observation supplies them with certain axiomatic truths that are laid, as the great foundation timbers, upon the bare surface of their unsuggestive natures. Upon these they build with induction and analysis, until the structure, rising high and imposing, is baptized with the name of philosophy.

Mr. Brady, by an intuitive faculty of discriminating the true from the false, rapidly appropriates the ideas that assimilate to his native perceptions of truth. His method of acquisition is direct and assimilative, rather than methodical and scientific. The tendency of such a mind is to desultory reading. Possessing unity in its -own system of thought, and independent of the external helps that a habit of logical analysis furnishes to minds less liberally endowed, it avoids the tedious path of the progressive ratiocination, and walks freely hither and thither, culling the fruits of thought or flowers of fancy, as it happened to be attracted. From this order of mind, the great geniuses have arisen.

But mountains sometimes rise higher than eagles fly, and the patient builders often outstrip by their industry their more gifted but indolent competitors — in the same way that the turtle outran the hare in the race. Those who acquire readily are strongly tempted to seek for little more than that which serves their present necessities. For them a stirring, sleepless ambition is the only salvation.

Mr. Brady possesses too much ambition to be content with inferiority to those about him, and too little to exert himself after he has fairly passed his competitors. He would rather be a palace among cottages, than a pyramid in the desert. All that he needs to develop his mental powers, still vigorous with youth, to their fullest capacity of exercise, is to fight by the side of some rugged old chief like our lamented Webster, whose blows crush like an avalanche.

As an orator Mr. Brady possesses the faculty of pleasing his audience while he addresses their convictions and their sympathies. A rich fund of humor enlivens his speeches and establishes a hold upon his audiences, enabling him to give the fullest expression to his opinions, however distasteful they may be to those he addresses. Had he more of the artistic feeling that clothes its images in the elegant grace of refined wit, he would be a more finished orator. But as an effective speaker few excel him. Clear and vigorous in his reasonings, copious in apt illustration, and zealous rather to establish his cause than to display his rich endowments, there bursts through the warmth of the advocate the genial kindliness of a generous nature.

Mr. Brady possesses the respect of the entire bar. His social qualities attract to his friendship all who are brought into contact with him. His conversation is enlivened by the gayest humor, and is without reserve or ostentation. That may be said of him which is true of but few, that neither hatred nor jealousy grow in his pathway to distinction.

SAMUEL JONES.

There is no nobler spectacle, or more impressive lesson, than a bright and vigorous intellect, invigorating the wasting energies of a life yielding to the inexorable doom of mortality. When we are reminded that the temple of the spirit is perishable, we know that that mysterious essence, the "genius of the place," is immortal.

Such reflections are awakened in those who observe Chief Justice Jones contending daily at the bar with the zeal and the power of an advocate in the prime of life, though bearing the weight of more than four score years. He has outlived his generation, and is the only living representative of the learning and ability that characterized the New York bar, at the close of the last century.

His infancy was cotemporaneous with the infancy of the legal system of our state. These two have grown up together; but the one has grown strong and healthful, with the promise of centuries upon its brow, while the other is bowed, though unbroken, and counts the days to that rest which shall be forever,. Chief Justice

Jones is identified with the history of the law in our state. His life has been one of uninterrupted activity. The distinguished names that we are accustomed to respect, as the lights of the New York bar in its earlier days, were numbered among his familiar acquaintances. He has filled several important judicial stations in our higher courts, and at the close of life, has returned to the bar, where he is now engaged in an active and successful practice.

It is not our purpose to dwell upon his services or the incidents of his life, but to sketch, briefly, those essential characteristics that have developed the eventful history of his labors. But so deeply interwoven with the present is the past, and so intimately is the history of a distinguished man blended with the picture of the inner form of his life, that we have not forborne to yield to those pleasant allurements that invest the recollections of the past.

Chief Justice Jones stands alone at the bar as the historic representative of former times. Time has laid its hand heavily upon all of him except his intellect and invincible spirit. As you observe him enter the court room with a feeble step and bowed form, and seat himself in the circle of the hot-blooded and vigilant advocates, with an oppressive air of langour and abstraction, you see but little promise of his power. Presently you observe him rise and you listen attentively to catch his feeble and almost inaudible accents, but are not long held in painful suspense. His eye soon brightens, his form becomes erect, his gestures animated and often violent, his voice rises like the winds when they are stirred, and rings out clear and startling tones. His passionate nature and his discerning intellect are now in full play, swaying his feeble body to and fro like a reed in a tempest, until you tremble lest the unsubdued power of his nature should snap the last string of life.

The sluggish current you thus observed a moment since, has become a rapid torrent, pouring down a wild and rocky bed. When thus roused, nothing escapes his keen vision or eludes his vigilance. If an adversary assumes a false position or involves himself in a contradiction, the storm of denunciation falls upon him with no measured violence. It is a fine sight to see this venerable old lawyer aroused and kindled with the zeal and ardor of youth; standing amidst the records of his youth that look down upon him from urn and animated bust, and mournful epitaph — shaming the cold marble that perpetuates the memory of his early companions; himself the most eloquent monument of the past.

Chief Justice Jones is, by nature, an advocate. Antagonism is necessary to call out his power. His mental operations, when cold are sluggish — his efforts prolix, labored and unsatisfactory; but when fully aroused, his positions are clear and his illustrations forcible. There are many who would be willing to cross quills with the old warrior, who would dread to encounter him in the open arena. This quality fits him to shine at the bar, rather than for distinction upon the bench. That patient assiduity that holds the even balances of justice and calmly and attentively gathers every argument, and weighs all considerations fully and dispassionately, is not a part of his mental composition.

This is no detraction from the honor or fame of our subject. The office of the advocate is no less honorable than that of the judge, nor are his qualifications less admirable, though different from those that form the best judicial character.

Chief Justice Jones is remarkable for his industry in the investigation and preparation of his cases. His labors, at his advanced age, are arduous and unremitting. Whatever may be required of him, whether the preparation of an argument, or an opinion, no amount of labor is too much for him to bestow. His written opinions are long and carefully prepared and rewritten, and the process of elaboration is seldom completed while the paper remains in his possession. This degree of application is the more remarkable in one who has always found leisure to bestow on social enjoyments and often enlivens convivial gatherings by his presence.

As a lawyer, Chief Justice Jones is studious and discriminating. Few men have studied more carefully the whole body of our jurisprudence, or have more completely at command that learning which is the indispensable accomplishment of the lawyer. From this storehouse of learning and experience, he rarely fails to draw forth material to sustain whatever position he may be called upon to assert. And by the aid of subtle reasoning and an emphatic and convincing manner, his positions, always formidable, are often forced upon an unwilling court.

The class of business in which Chief Justice Jones is now employed is of the most weighty and responsible character. There are few cases of great magnitude argued at the bar in this city in which he does not take a leading part; and few practising lawyers who would not deem his industry and power, as valuable acquisitions as his profound learning and enlarged experience.

Such instances are an instructive lesson to that class who look forward to retirement from professional labor, and a life of easy and indulgent affluence, as the goal of their ambition. It may serve to check a tendency that has already slacked the vigor of more than one highly gifted and accomplished lawyer, and has deprived the law of many of its most valuable supports.

DEATH OF JUDGE JONES.

This distinguished jurist died August 10, 1853, at Cold Spring, L. I., in his 84th year. For several months his health had been feeble, and his friends entertained little hope of his ultimate recovery. Until his last sickness, however, he seemed to have been unaffected by the weight of advancing years, and neither his body nor his mind lost their wonted strength and elasticity. He was daily in court, and distinguished himself, as ever, by the skill and indomitable perseverance with which he conducted his cases. In fact, no young lawyer in his first aspirations for professional distinction could try or argue a cause with more zest, spirit or ambition to succeed, than did Judge Jones, in his 84th year.

His professional labors and experiences run back for half a century; he belonged to the *ancien regime*, and lived long enough to see two generations of lawyers grow up around him; among whom he could recognize scarcely one whom he knew in his youth.

Judge Jones has occupied successively the highest judicial offices in the state. In 1826 he was appointed chancellor by Gov. Clinton, an office which he held for two years, when he became chief justice of the superior court. After presiding in that distinguished court for twenty years, he was elected to the bench of the supreme court; and under the provisions of the constitution of 1846, he was a member of the court of appeals for nearly two years.

The qualities of his mind, and his peculiarities as an advocate, were lately fully discussed in an article in the *Mirror*, which formed one of the series of the *Sketches of the New York Bar*, and we subjoin one or two extracts:

His infancy was cotemporaneous with the infancy of the legal system of our state. These two have grown up together; but the one has grown strong and healthful, with the promise of centuries upon its brow, while the other is bowed though unbroken, and counts the days to that rest which shall be forever. Chief Justice Jones is identified with the history of the law in our state. His life has been one of uninterrupted activity. The distinguished names that we are accustomed to respect, as the lights of the New York bar in its earlier days, were numbered among his familiar acquaintances. He has filled several important stations in our highest courts, and at the close of life has returned to the bar, where he is now engaged in an active and successful practice.

He stands alone at the bar as the historic representative of former times. Time has laid its hand heavily upon all of him except his intellect and invincible spirit. As you observe him enter the court room with a feeble step and bowed form, and seat himself in the circle of the hot-blooded and vigilant advocates, with an oppressive air of languor and abstraction, you see but little promise of his power. Presently you observe him rise, and you listen attentively to catch his feeble and almost inaudible accents. But are not long held in painful suspense. His eye soon brightens, his form becomes erect, his gestures animated and often violent, his voice rises like the winds when they are stirred, and rings out clear and startling tones. His passionate nature and his discerning intellect are now in full play, swaying his feeble body to and fro like a reed in a tempest, until you tremble lest the unsubdued power of his nature should snap the last string of life.

The sluggish current you thus observed a moment since, has become a rapid torrent, pouring down a wild and rocky bed. When thus roused, nothing escapes his keen vision or eludes his vigilance. If an adversary assumes a false position or involves himself in a contradiction, the storm of denunciation falls upon him with no measured violence. It is a fine sight to see this venerable old lawyer aroused and kindled with the zeal and ardor of youth; standing amidst the records of his youth that look down upon him from urn and animated bust, and mournful epitaph — shaming the cold marble, that perpetuates the memory of his early companions; himself the most eloquent monument of the past. * * * *

As a lawyer, Chief Justice Jones, is studious and discriminating. Few men have studied more carefully the whole body of our jurisprudence, or have more completely at command that learning which is the indispensable accomplishment of the lawyer. From this storehouse of learning and experience, he rarely fails to draw forth material to sustain whatever position he may be called upon to assert. And by the aid of subtle reasoning and an emphatic and convincing manner, his positions, always formidable, are often forced upon an unwilling court. * * * *

Chief Justice Jones is remarkable for his industry in the investigation and preparation of his cases. His labors, at his advanced age, are arduous and unremitting. Whatever may be required of him, whether the preparation of an argument, or an opinion, no amount of labor is too much for him to bestow. His written opinions are long and carefully prepared, and rewritten, and the process of elaboration is seldom completed while the paper remains in his possession. This degree of application is the more remarkable in one who has always found leisure to bestow on social enjoyments, and often enlivens convivial gatherings by his presence.

The intelligence of his death yesterday was received with profound grief, for he was both loved and reverenced by his professional brethren. A meeting of the bar was immediately called, at which Judge Duer presided, assisted by Justices Paine and Daly. A committee of ten was appointed for the purpose of adopting proper measures to express the regard of the bar "for the memory of their late associate;" and after a few pertinent remarks by Mr. Hiram Ketchum and others, the following resolutions were adopted:

Therefore, Resolved, That the bar of the city of New York have received with deep sensations and profound regret the melancholy intelligence of the decease of the late Samuel Jones. That they deplore the loss of his extensive learning, his great abilities, his indefatigable industry, his elevated integrity. That by his decease the community have sustained the loss of an accomplished jurist, whose life has conferred honor upon his native state, and whose eminent public services were acknowledged by the confidence and esteem of the whole people.

Resolved, That the bar of the city of New York will testify their regret for his loss by attending his funeral in a body, and by wearing the usual badge of mourning for thirty days.

Resolved, That a committee of ten be appointed by the president to adopt such measures as may be deemed best adapted to express the regard of the bar of New York for the memory of our late associate.

Resolved, That a copy of the preamble and these resolutions be signed by the officers of this meeting and communicated to the family of the deceased, and also that they be presented to the general terms of the supreme court and the superior court of the city of New York at their next sessions, and published in all of the city papers.

DEATH OF DR. T. R. BECK.

In the death of Dr. Theodric Romeyn Beck, our city has lost one of its most valuable and estimable citizens. A long life devoted to the pursuit of the liberal arts, science, literature and education has closed. After an illness of many months duration he expired yesterday morning in the sixty-fifth year of his age, at the residence of his son-in-law, Mayor Parmelee, in this city. His demise long expected, is a public calamity. Our city has lost in him not only a *savant* most thoroughly accomplished in many departments of science, but an old and honored instructor of its young, who held for thirty years the paternal relation of teacher for hosts of our citizens, and whose death has thus severed one of the most intimate and tender relations of life.

Dr. Beck comes of a family which has contributed largely to the advancement of human knowledge. His grandfather, Rev. Derick Beck was a distinguished scholar of his day, and a professor of theology in the school of the Reformed Dutch church. Of his four brothers, two died at an early age, one a lawyer of great promise, at St. Louis, and the other was adjutant general of the state under De Witt Clinton. Dr. John B. Beck, the oldest of the surviving brothers, was an author and professor of materia medica in the College of Physicians and Surgeons of New York. He died in 1851. Lewis C., the remaining brother, held the chair of chemistry at Rutgers college, and subsequently at the medical institution in our own city. He was also the author of a popular and valuable elementary text book on chemistry.

T. Romeyn Beck was born in Schenectady, August 11th, 1791, acquired the rudiments of his education at the grammar school of that city, and graduated at Union college in 1807. He studied the profession of medicine in this city, and subsequently in New York, where he received his degree in 1811, and wrote an inaugural thesis on the subject of insanity, of extraordinay merit, and which excited considerable attention at the time. Two years afterwards, he was appointed one of the counsellors of the Society for the promotion of agricultural arts and manufactures, and delivered an annual address before that honorable association. Soon after his graduation, he returned to this city and commenced the practice of his profession. In 1815, he was chosen professor of the institutes of medicine and lecturer on medical jurisprudence in the College of physicians and surgeons in the western district of New York, a post he held for several years. In 1817, he became principal of the Albany academy, and occupied that responsible and laborious position until 1848, when he resigned. In 1823, he issued his celebrated work on Medical Jurisprudence. In 1829 he was elected president of the Medical society of the state of New York, and during his continuance in that office, read several valuable and original addresses, which are preserved in the transactions of the society. From 1841 he was the secretary of the board of regents of the University of the state of New York, and *ex officio* secretary of the trustees of the State library. For the last fifteen years of his life he was one of the managers of the State lunatic asylum, and for the last ten has contributed largely to his favorite study as contributor to, and editor of, the *American Journal of Insanity*. From 1843 to 1854, he was also professor of materia medica in the Albany medical college, and delivered regular lectures to his classes during the terms.

The most important work accomplished in his useful and eventful life, was the publication of his *Medical Jurisprudence*. The authorship of this treatise has given Dr. Beck a world-wide reputation, and placed his name in that distinguished galaxy of noted men who have added to the stock of human knowledge. A most barren and unexplored branch of science grew up under his hands to symmetrical proportions. The work is in two large octavo volumes, of two thousand pages, and may be found in the library of nearly every lawyer and medical man in the country. It has passed through five American, one German and four English editions. The testimony of Europeans as to its excellence and superiority is most flattering and decisive, and has done much to attract the attention of the old world to scientific research in the United States.

As secretary of the board of regents, Dr. Beck's labors have been onerous and unremitting. The compilation and preparation for the press of the yearly volumes of the regents' report, which furnish the most elaborate statements in reference to the condition of our academies and colleges — was done under his supervision. To our state library he has been a firm and judicious friend. The arrangement of that excellent collection of books — one of the most perfect and complete in the country — has been his work. In the selection and purchase of books Dr. Beck had no rival, with the exception perhaps of Dr. Cogswell of the Astor library. His memory was seldom at fault in reference to old editions and rare or curious publications, while his judgment was so excellent and discriminating that the legislature had the most perfect confidence in his opinions.

But it was as principal of the Albany academy that Dr. Beck is most thoroughly known to our citizens. From 1817 to 1848 — a period of thirty years — he has had charge of that then famous institution. Scarcely a young or middle aged man has grown up in our city without coming as a pupil under his vigilant eye. To them his admirable system of his instruction, as well as his peculiarities of character are well know. If a strict disciplinarian, he was inflexibly just. If sometime irascible — for he had many provocations — he was ever faithful and single-hearted. His impulses were genial and kindly, and his overtures of good will, if quaint and off-hand, were thoroughly honest. Boys, who have a sure-eyed intuition of human character, loved his simplicity, his truth, his magnanimity. He never bore malice and never lost an opportunity of doing his old pupils a kindness. In all the relations of life, he was high minded, honorable and generous, and he thoroughly detested every species of meanness. Great as is the reputation he leaves behind, and wide as is the gap his lamented death will make in the fields of literature and science, his best monument will be the affectionate memory of his old pupils, and a most grateful and touching epitaph is written already in the hearts of the young and middle aged men of Albany.

We can not better conclude this brief sketch than by applying to Dr. Beck, the beautiful words, with which, twenty years ago, he concluded a eulogium delivered before the Albany institute on Simeon De Witt, one of New York's most distinguished sons: "Happy, if when our account is made up we shall be found, each in his appropriate sphere, like our honored fellow member, to have done some service to the state. Then, whether in the morning of life, or at its fervid, bustling noon-day, or in the declining hour, we depart, our memories will be cherished and our names implore the passing tribute of a sigh."

THE ONE SHADOW.

In the horoscope of this free and hopeful land, one baneful influence only portends and threatens. One shadow obscures the glass as we look out upon the golden tinted perspective of the future; one cloud, such as the old prophet saw coming up from the sea—not larger than a man's hand—rises up from the placid waters of the past. As it rises, it gathers force, darkens and mutters, spreading itself a dusky shadow over thirty-one happy and united states; a fearful menace of the coming storm.

The shadow of the future, the cloud on the horizon is the ill-starred policy of localism.

If, in the course of Divine Providence, this Union is ever to be severed and this country destroyed—which

Heaven forbid—it will be by state prejudices; by local ideas.

We are beyond the reach of external attack. War might decimate our people, but it would unite the survivors into a gallant and irresistible phalanx. A foreign invasion might ravage our coasts; a hostile fleet might burn our seaports; the enemy might advance into the very heart of the country; but all this could not tear us asunder. It would link the confederacy together by stronger ties. North and South, state by state; South Carolina, standing hand in hand with Massachusetts, would rally around a common cause, and march out in solid columns against a common foe.

If our prosperity is ever darkened, it will be by the shadow of our own perverseness. The attack will come from within; not from without the citadel. The insidious blow will be struck by parricides. It will come in the questionable shape of sectional opinions, geographical prejudice, local ideas. The unholy enterprise will be fostered—it is fostered already—by politicians, who make it a special business to legislate for a part of, not the whole country; men who neither honor the Union, nor respect the fundamental law. The work will be consummated by legislators, who, as they thrive by localism, make it their special business to think and speak and decree localisms; wretches who stand ready to sacrifice their country on the altar of their inordinate ambition, and to seek for power among the very ruins of the republic.

The shadow grows. Local agitations seem to be gaining power. Already in the North, a large party has grown up which does not have, and does not claim to have, any connection with the South. Already in the South, there is a class of men—not very large, nor truly representing the southern people—who are ready to ruin if they can not rule; to dissolve the Union if they can not extend the area of slavery. We care not whence the malign influence comes—from the North, or from the South, from Seward or from Douglas, from abolitionists or from the slave propagandists—it is to be denounced, cursed, crushed out, as the seed of discord, disunion and destruction.

We want a renovation of public sentiment on this subject, a revival of a more patriotic spirit, a deeper devotion for the common cause and our common country. How insignificant are all localisms compared with the safety and perpetuity of the Union. How paltry and mean is the shadow compared with the glorious light shed by the consolidated states. Above all, if we would not be destroyed by localisms, we should have a stronger nationality. We have our private opinions, state prejudices, local ideas; but over all, submerging all, *drowning* all, should be that great sentiment, that always and nevertheless, we are all *Americans.** "It is as Americans that we are known, the world over. Who asks you what state you are from, in Europe or in Africa or in Asia? Is he an American? Does he belong to the United States? Does that flag protect him? Does he rests under the eagle and the stars and stripes? If he does, all else is subordinate and of little concern."

* Daniel Webster.

THE ALBANY EXPRESS

Of Saturday [1856] contains the valedictory of its late editor, from which we copy his closing words. Edwards is an editor after our own heart, and we hope soon to welcome him back into the ranks of a profession he is so well qualified to dignify and adorn.—*N. Y. Ev. Mirror.*

No pecuniary recompense, however, is worthy of being compared, in the eyes of an earnest editor, with the regard and esteem of his readers. The drudgery and toil of the conductor of a daily journal would be bitter beyond endurance unless it were sweetened by some touch of mutual sympathy, and enlivened by occasional flashes of mutual appreciation and good will.

Nor am I ungrateful to the persons employed with me in the publication of the *Express*, whose kind and patient coöperation has been of the utmost service to me in the discharge of my labors. It is pleasant, also, to remember that though I have had occasion to cross weapons with my professional brothers of the city press, my personal relations with so many of them have been of the most pleasant and cordial character, and that I have participated with some of them not only in the amenities of the craft, but in the social enjoyments of life.

I will still further lay open these fond but natural expressions to the just charge of egotism by adding, as I do most conscientiously, that in the discharge of my duties to the public I have never consciously published an untruth, turned my back upon a friend, or been wilfully ungenerous or unforgiving towards an opponent, and that though in the retrospect I could point out several occasions on which, if I had been more supple, I should have gained a temporary advantage, I find on the whole no reason to regret my attachment to my own principles or my obedience to my own impulses and convictions of duty.

CARLTON EDWARDS.

CPSIA information can be obtained
at www.ICGtesting.com
Printed in the USA
LVHW110934160522
718424LV00014B/231

9 783375 000875